CW01626528

S[illegible]K OF CA[illegible]RIES

EDITOR: FRANKLIN K. MATHIEWS

ZINC READ

Published by
This edition copyright © 2024 by Zinc Read
Design and setting By Zinc Read
Email- zincread@gmail.com
ISBN-978-93-6124-742-2

This is being sold on the condition that it cannot be used commercially or in any other form without the written prior permission of the publisher. They cannot be republished or sold or rented. And it cannot be operated among readers in bookbinding or any other form. All these conditions will also apply to the buyer of the book. All rights of copyright are reserved in this context. The contents of this edition have been taken from material available in the public domain. The View's and characters expressed in the books are of the author and his/her imagination and do not represent the views of publisher.

CONTENTS

I.—SILVERHORNS[1]

By Henry van Dyke

THE railway station of Bathurst, New Brunswick, did not look particularly merry at two o'clock of a late September morning. There was an easterly haze driving in from the Baie des Chaleurs and the darkness was so saturated with chilly moisture that an honest downpour of rain would have been a relief. Two or three depressed and somnolent travelers yawned in the waiting room, which smelled horribly of smoky lamps. The telegraph instrument in the ticket office clicked spasmodically for a minute, and then relapsed into a gloomy silence. The imperturbable station master was tipped back against the wall in a wooden armchair, with his feet on the table, and his mind sunk in an old Christmas number of the *Cowboy Magazine.* The express agent, in the baggage-room, was going over his last week's waybills and accounts by the light of a lantern, trying to locate an error, and sighing profanely to himself as he failed to find it. A wooden trunk tied with rope, a couple of dingy canvas bags, a long box marked "Fresh Fish! Rush!" and two large leather portmanteaus with brass fittings were piled on the luggage truck at the far end of the platform; and beside the door of the waiting room, sheltered by the overhanging eaves, was a neat traveling bag, with a gun case and a rod case leaning against the wall. The wet rails glittered dimly northward and southward away into the night. A few blurred lights glimmered from the village across the bridge.

Dudley Hemenway had observed all these features of the landscape with silent dissatisfaction, as he smoked steadily up and down the platform, waiting for the Maritime Express. It is usually irritating to arrive at the station on time for a train on the Intercolonial Railway. The arrangement is seldom mutual; and sometimes yesterday's train does not come along until to-morrow afternoon. Moreover, Hemenway was inwardly discontented with the fact that he was coming out of the woods instead of going in. "Coming out" always made him a little unhappy, whether his expedition had been successful or not. He did not like the thought that it was all over; and he had the very bad habit, at such times, of looking ahead and computing the slowly lessening number of chances that were left to him.

"Sixty odd years—I may get to be that old and keep my shooting sight," he said to himself. "That would give me a couple of dozen more camping trips. It's a short allowance. I wonder if any of them will be more lucky than this one. This makes the seventh year I've tried to get a moose; and the odd trick has gone against me every time."

He tossed away the end of his cigar, which made a little trail of sparks as it rolled along the sopping platform, and turned to look in through the window of the ticket office. Something in the agent's attitude of literary absorption aggravated him. He went round to the door and opened it.

"Don't you know or care when this train is coming?"

"Nope," said the man placidly.

"Well, when? What's the matter with her? When is she due?"

"Doo twenty minits ago," said the man. "Forty minits late down to Moocastle. Git here quatter to three, ef nothin' more happens."

"But what has happened? What's wrong with the beastly old road, anyhow?"

"Freight car skipped the track," said the man, "up to Charlo. Everythin' hung up an' kinder goin' slow till they git the line clear. Dunno nothin' more."

With this conclusive statement the agent seemed to disclaim all responsibility for the future of impatient travelers, and dropped his mind back into the magazine again. Hemenway lit another cigar and went into the baggage room to smoke with the expressman. It was nearly three o'clock when they heard the far-off shriek of the whistle sounding up from the south; then, after an interval, the puffing of the engine on the upgrade; then the faint ringing of the rails, the increasing clatter of the train, and the blazing headlight of the locomotive swept slowly through the darkness, past the platform. The engineer was leaning on one arm, with his head out of the cab window, and Hemenway nodded as he passed and hurried into the ticket office, where the ticktack of a conversation by telegraph was soon under way. The black porter of the Pullman car was looking out from the vestibule, and when he saw Hemenway his sleepy face broadened into a grin reminiscent of many generous tips.

"Howdy, Mr. Hennigray," he cried; "glad to see yo' ag'in, sah! I got yo' section all right, sah! Lemme take yo' things, sah! Train gwine to stop hy'eh fo' some time yet, I reckon."

"Well, Charles," said Hemenway, "you take my things and put them in the car. Careful with that gun now! The Lord only knows how much time this train's going to lose. I'm going ahead to see the engineer."

Angus McLeod was a grizzle-bearded Scotchman who had run a locomotive on the Intercolonial ever since the road was cut through the woods from New Brunswick to Quebec. Every one who traveled often on that line knew him, and all who knew him well enough to get below his rough crust, liked him for his big heart.

"Hallo, McLeod," said Hemenway as he came up through the darkness, "is that you?"

"It's nane else," answered the engineer as he stepped down from his cab and shook hands warmly. "Hoo are ye, Dud, an' whaur hae ye been murderin' the innocent beasties noo? Hae ye kilt yer moose yet? Ye've been chasin' him these mony years."

"Not much murdering," replied Hemenway. "I had a queer trip this time—away up the Nepisiguit, with old McDonald. You know him, don't you?"

"Fine do I ken Rob McDonald, an' a guid mon he is. Hoo was it that ye couldna slaughter stacks o' moose wi' him to help ye? Did ye see nane at all?"

"Plenty, and one with the biggest horns in the world! But that's a long story, and there's no time to tell it now."

"Time to burrn, Dud, nae fear o' it! 'Twill be an hour afore the line's clear to Charlo an' they lat us oot o' this. Come awa' up into the cab, mon, an' tell us yer tale. 'Tis couthy an' warm in the cab, an' I'm willin' to leesten to yer bluidy advaintures."

So the two men clambered up into the engineer's seat. Hemenway gave McLeod his longest and strongest cigar, and filled his own briar-wood pipe. The rain was now pattering gently on the roof of the cab. The engine hissed and sizzled patiently in the darkness. The fragrant smoke curled steadily from the glowing tip of the cigar; but the pipe went out half a dozen times while Hemenway was telling the story of Silverhorns.

"We went up the river to the big rock, just below Indian Falls. There we made our main camp, intending to hunt on Forty-two Mile Brook. There's quite a snarl of ponds and bogs at the head of it, and some burned hills over to the west, and it's very good moose country.

"But some other party had been there before us, and we saw nothing on the ponds, except two cow moose and a calf. Coming out the next morning we got a fine deer on the old wood road—a beautiful head. But I have plenty of deer heads already."

"Bonny creature!" said McLeod. "An' what did ye do wi' it, when ye had murdered it?"

"Ate it, of course. I gave the head to Billy Boucher, the cook. He said he could get ten dollars for it. The next evening we went to one of the ponds again, and Injun Pete tried to 'call' a moose for me. But it was no good. McDonald was disgusted with Pete's calling; said it sounded like the bray of a wild ass of the wilderness. So the next day we gave up calling and traveled the woods over toward the burned hills.

"In the afternoon McDonald found an enormous moose-track; he thought it looked like a bull's track, though he wasn't quite positive. But then, you know, a Scotchman never likes to commit himself, except about theology or politics."

"Humph!" grunted McLeod in the darkness, showing that the strike had counted.

"Well, we went on, following that track through the woods, for an hour or two. It was a terrible country, I tell you: tamarack swamps, and spruce thickets, and windfalls, and all kinds of misery. Presently we came out on a bare rock on the burned hillside, and there, across a ravine, we could see the animal lying down, just below the trunk of a big dead spruce that had fallen. The beast's head and neck were hidden by some bushes, but the fore shoulder and side were in clear view, about two hundred and fifty yards away. McDonald seemed to be inclined to think that it was a bull and that I ought to shoot. So I shot, and knocked splinters out of the spruce log. We could see them fly. The animal got up quickly, and looked at us for a moment, shaking her long ears; then the huge unmitigated cow vamoosed into the brush. McDonald remarked that it was 'a varra fortunate shot, almaist providaintial!' And so it was; for if it had gone six inches lower, and the news gotten out at Bathurst, it would have cost me a fine of two hundred dollars."

"Ye did weel, Dud," puffed McLeod; "varra weel indeed—for the coo!"

"After that," continued Hemenway, "of course my nerve was a little shaken, and we went back to the main camp on the river, to rest over Sunday. That was all right, wasn't it, Mac!"

"Aye!" replied McLeod, who was a strict member of the Presbyterian church at Moncton. "That was surely a varra safe thing to do. Even a hunter, I'm thinkin', wouldna like to be breakin' twa commandments in the ane day—the foorth and the saxth!"

"Perhaps not. It's enough to break one, as you do once a fortnight when you run your train into Rivière du Loup Sunday morning. How's that, you old Calvinist?"

"Dudley, ma son," said the engineer, "dinna airgue a point that ye canna understond. There's guid an' suffeecient reasons for the train. But ye'll ne'er be claimin' that moose huntin' is a wark o' necessity or maircy?"

"No, no, of course not; but then, you see, barring Sundays, we felt that it was necessary to do all we could to get a moose, just for the sake of our reputations. Billy, the cook, was particularly strong about it. He said that an old woman in Bathurst, a kind of fortune teller, had told him that he was going to have 'la bonne chance' on this trip. He wanted to try his own mouth at 'calling.' He had never really done it before. But he had been practicing all winter in imitation of a tame cow moose that Johnny Moreau had, and he thought he could make the sound 'b'en bon.' So he got the birch-bark horn and gave us a sample of his skill. McDonald told me privately that it was 'nae sa bad; a deal better than Pete's feckless bellow.' We agreed to leave the Indian to keep the camp (after locking up the whisky flask in my bag), and take Billy with us on Monday to 'call' at Hogan's Pond.

"It's a small bit of water, about three quarters of a mile long and four hundred yards across, and four miles back from the river. There is no trail to it, but a blazed line runs part of the way, and for the rest you follow up the little brook that runs out of the pond. We stuck up our shelter in a hollow on the brook, half a mile below the pond, so that the smoke of our fire would not drift over the hunting ground, and waited till five o'clock in the afternoon. Then we went up to the pond, and took our position in a clump of birch trees on the edge of the open meadow that runs round the east shore. Just at dark Billy began to call, and it was beautiful. You know how it goes. Three short grunts, and then a long ooooo-aaaa-ooooh, winding up with another grunt! It sounded lonelier than a love-sick hippopotamus on the house top. It rolled and echoed over the hills as if it would wake the dead.

"There was a fine moon shining, nearly full, and a few clouds floating by. Billy called, and called, and called again. The air grew colder and colder; light frost on the meadow grass; our teeth were chattering, fingers numb.

"Then we heard a bull give a short bawl, away off to the southward. Presently we could hear his horns knock against the trees, far up on the hill. McDonald whispered, 'He's comin',' and Billy gave another call.

"But it was another bull that answered, back of the north end of the pond, and pretty soon we could hear him rapping along through the woods. Then everything was still. 'Call agen,' says McDonald, and Billy called again.

"This time the bawl came from another bull, on top of the western hill, straight across the pond. It seemed to start up the other two bulls, and we could hear all three of them thrashing along, as fast as they could come, towards the pond. 'Call agen, a wee one,' says McDonald, trembling with joy. And Billy called a little seducing call, with two grunts at the end.

"Well, sir, at that, a cow and a calf came rushing down through the brush not two hundred yards away from us, and the three bulls went splash into the water, one at the south end, one at the north end, and one on the west shore. 'Land,' whispers McDonald, 'it's a meenadgerie!'"

"Dud," said the engineer, getting down to open the furnace door a crack, "this is mair than murder ye're comin' at; it's a buitchery—or else it's juist a pack o' lees."

"I give you my word," said Hemenway, "it's all true as the catechism. But let me go on. The cow and the calf only stayed in the water a few minutes, and then ran back through the woods. But the three bulls went sloshing around in the pond as if they were looking for something. We could hear them, but we could not see any of them, for the sky had clouded up, and they kept far away from us. Billy tried another short call, but they did not come any nearer. McDonald whispered that he thought the one in the south end might be the biggest, and he might be feeding, and the two others might be young bulls, and they might be keeping away because they were afraid of the big one. This seemed reasonable; and I said that I was going to crawl around the meadow to the south end. 'Keep near a tree,' says Mac; and I started.

"There was a deep trail, worn by animals, through the high grass; and in this I crept along on my hands and knees. It was very wet and muddy. My boots were full of cold water. After ten minutes I came to a little point running out into the pond, and one young birch growing on it. Under this I crawled, and rising up on my knees looked over the top of the grass and bushes.

"There, in a shallow bay, standing knee-deep in the water, and rooting up the lily stems with his long, pendulous nose, was the biggest and blackest bull moose in the world. As he pulled the roots from the mud and tossed up his dripping head I could see his horns—four and a half feet across, if they were an inch, and the palms shining like tea trays in the moonlight. I tell you, old Silverhorns was the most beautiful monster I ever saw.

"But he was too far away to shoot by that dim light, so I left my birch tree and crawled along toward the edge of the bay. A breath of wind must have blown across me to him, for he lifted his head, sniffed, grunted, came out of the water, and began to trot slowly along the trail which led past me. I knelt on one knee and tried to take aim. A black cloud came over the moon. I couldn't see either of the sights on the gun. But when the bull came opposite to me, about fifty yards off, I blazed away at a venture.

"He reared straight up on his hind legs—it looked as if he rose fifty feet in the air—wheeled, and went walloping along the trail, around the south end of the pond. In a minute he was lost in the woods. Good-by, Silverhorns!"

"Ye tell it weel," said McLeod, reaching out for a fresh cigar. "Fegs! Ah doot Sir Walter himsel' couldna impruve upon it. An, sae thot's the way ye didna murder puir Seelverhorrns? It's a tale I'm joyfu' to be hearin'."

"Wait a bit," Hemenway answered. "That's not the end, by a long shot. There's worse to follow. The next morning we returned to the pond at day-break, for McDonald thought I might have wounded the moose. We searched the bushes and the woods where he went out very carefully, looking for drops of blood on his trail."

"Bluid!" groaned the engineer. "Hech, mon, wouldna that come nigh to mak' ye greet, to find the beast's red bluid splashed over the leaves, and think o' him staggerin' on thro' the forest, drippin' the heart oot o' him wi' every step?"

"But we didn't find any blood, you old sentimentalist. That shot in the dark was a clear miss. We followed the trail by broken bushes and footprints, for half a mile, and then came back to the pond and turned to go down through the edge of the woods to the camp.

"It was just after sunrise. I was walking a few yards ahead, McDonald next, and Billy last. Suddenly he looked around to the left, gave a low whistle and dropped to the ground, pointing northward. Away at the head of the pond, beyond the glitter of the sun on the water, the big blackness of Silverhorns' head and body was pushing through the bushes, dripping with dew.

"Each of us flopped down behind the nearest shrub as if we had been playing squat tag. Billy had the birch-bark horn with him, and he gave a low, short call. Silverhorns heard it, turned, and came parading slowly down the western shore, now on the sand beach, now splashing through the shallow water. We could see every motion and hear every sound. He marched along as if he owned the earth, swinging his huge head from side to side and grunting at each step.

"You see, we were just in the edge of the woods, strung along the south end of the pond, Billy nearest the west shore, where the moose was walking, McDonald next, and I last, perhaps fifteen yards farther to the east. It was a fool arrangement, but we had no time to think about it. McDonald whispered that I should wait until the moose came close to us and stopped.

"So I waited. I could see him swagger along the sand and step out around the fallen logs. The nearer he came the bigger his horns looked; each palm was like an enormous silver fish fork with twenty prongs. Then he went out of my sight for a minute as he passed around a little bay in the southwest corner, getting nearer and nearer to Billy. But I could still hear his steps distinctly—slosh, slosh, slosh—thud, thud, thud (the grunting had stopped)—closer came the sound, until it was directly behind the dense green branches of a fallen balsam tree, not twenty feet away from Billy. Then suddenly the noise ceased. I could hear my own heart pounding at my ribs, but nothing else. And of Silverhorns not hair nor hide was visible. It looked as if he must be a Boojum, and had the power to 'softly and silently vanish away.'

"Billy and Mac were beckoning to me fiercely and pointing to the green balsam top. I gripped my rifle and started to creep toward them. A little twig, about as thick as the tip of a fishing rod, cracked under my knee. There was a terrible crash behind the balsam, a plunging through the underbrush and a rattling among the branches, a lumbering gallop up the hill through the forest, and Silverhorns was gone into the invisible.

"He had stopped behind the tree because he smelled the grease on Billy's boots. As he stood there, hesitating, Billy and Mac could see his shoulder and his side through a gap in the branches—a dead-easy shot. But so far as I was concerned, he might as well have been in Alaska. I told you that the way we had placed ourselves was a fool arrangement. But McDonald would not say anything about it, except to express his conviction that it was not predestinated we should get that moose."

"Ah dinna ken ould Rob had sae much theology aboot him," commented McLeod. "But noo I'm thinkin' ye went back to yer main camp, an' lat puir Seelverhorrns live oot his life?"

"Not much, did we! For now we knew that he wasn't badly frightened by the adventure of the night before, and that we might get another chance at him. In the afternoon it began to rain; and it poured for forty-eight hours. We covered in our shelter before a smoky fire, and lived on short rations of crackers and dried prunes—it was a hungry time."

"But wasna there slathers o' food at the main camp? Ony fule wad ken enough to gae doon to the river an' tak' a guid fill-up."

"But that wasn't what we wanted. It was Silverhorns. Billy and I made McDonald stay, and Thursday afternoon, when the clouds broke away, we went back to the pond to have a last try at turning our luck.

"This time we took our positions with great care, among some small spruces on a joint that ran out from the southern meadow. I was farthest to the west; McDonald (who had also brought his gun) was next; Billy, with the horn, was farthest away from the point where he thought the moose would come out. So Billy began to call, very beautifully. The long echoes went bellowing over the hills. The afternoon was still and the setting sun shone through a light mist, like a ball of red gold.

"Fifteen minutes after sundown Silverhorns gave a loud bawl from the western ridge and came crashing down the hill. He cleared the bushes two or three hundred yards to our left with a leap, rushed into the pond, and came wading around the south shore toward us. The bank here was rather high, perhaps four feet above the water, and the mud below it was deep, so that the moose sank in to his knees. I give you my word, as he came along there was nothing visible to Mac and me except his ears and his horns. Everything else was hidden below the bank.

"There were we behind our little spruce trees. And there was Silverhorns, standing still now, right in front of us. And all that Mac and I could see were those big ears and those magnificent antlers, appearing and disappearing as he lifted and lowered his head. It was a fearful situation. And there was Billy, with his birch-bark hooter, forty yards below us—he could see the moose perfectly.

"I looked at Mac, and he looked at me. He whispered something about predestination. Then Billy lifted his horn and made ready to give a little soft grunt, to see if the moose wouldn't move along a bit, just to oblige us. But as Billy drew in his breath, one of those fool flies that are always blundering around a man's face flew straight down his throat. Instead of a call he burst out with a furious, strangling fit of coughing. The moose gave a snort, and a wild leap in the water, and galloped away under the bank, the way he had come. Mac and I both fired at his vanishing ears and horns, but of course——"

"All Aboooard!" The conductor's shout rang along the platform.

"Line's clear," exclaimed McLeod, rising. "Noo we'll be off! Wull ye stay here wi' me, or gang awa' back to yer bed?"

"Here," answered Hemenway, not budging from his place on the bench.

The bell clanged, and the powerful machine puffed out on its flaring way through the night. Faster and faster came the big explosive breaths, until they blended in a long steady roar, and the train was sweeping northward at forty miles an hour. The clouds had broken; the night had grown colder; the gibbous moon gleamed over the vast and solitary landscape. It was a different thing to Hemenway, riding in the cab of the locomotive, from an ordinary journey in the passenger car or an unconscious ride in the sleeper. Here he was on the crest of motion, at the forefront of speed, and the quivering engine with the long train behind it seemed like a living creature leaping along the track. It responded to the labor of the fireman and the touch of the engineer almost as if it could think and feel. Its pace quickened without a jar; its great eye pierced the silvery space of moonlight with a shaft of blazing yellow; the rails sang before it and trembled behind it; it was an obedient and joyful monster, conquering distance and devouring darkness.

On the wide level barrens beyond the Tête-á-Gouche River the locomotive reached its best speed, purring like a huge cat and running smoothly. McLeod leaned back on his bench with a satisfied air.

"She's doin' fine, the nicht," said he. "Ah'm thinkin', whiles, o' yer auld Seelverhorrns. Whaur is he noo? Awa' up on Higan' Pond, gallantin' around i' the licht o' the mune wi' a lady moose, an' the gladness juist bubblin' in his hairt. Ye're no sorry that he's leevin' yet, are ye, Dud?"

"Well," answered Hemenway slowly, between the puffs of his pipe, "I can't say I'm sorry that he's alive and happy, though I'm not glad that I lost him. But he did his best, the old rogue; he played a good game, and he deserved to win. Where he is now nobody can tell. He was traveling like a streak of lightning when I last saw him. By this time he may be——"

"What's yon?" cried McLeod, springing up. Far ahead, in the narrow apex of the converging rails stood a black form, motionless, mysterious. McLeod grasped the whistle cord. The black form loomed higher in the moonlight and was clearly silhouetted against the horizon—a big moose standing across the track. They could see his grotesque head, his shadowy horns, high, sloping shoulders. The engineer pulled the cord. The whistle shrieked loud and long.

The moose turned and faced the sound. The glare of the headlight fascinated, challenged, angered him. There he stood defiant, front feet planted wide apart, head lowered, gazing steadily at the unknown enemy that was rushing toward him. He was the monarch of the wilderness. There was nothing in the world that he feared, except those strange-smelling little beasts on two legs who crept around through the woods and shot fire out of sticks. This was surely not one of those treacherous animals, but some strange new creature that dared to shriek at him and try to drive him out of its way. He would not move. He would try his strength against this big yellow-eyed beast.

"Losh!" cried McLeod; "he's gaun' to fecht us!" and he dropped the cord, grabbed the levers, and threw the steam off and the brakes on hard. The heavy train slid groaning and jarring along the track. The moose never stirred. The fire smoldered in his small narrow eyes. His black crest was bristling. As the engine bore down upon him, not a rod away, he reared high in the air, his antlers flashing in the blaze, and struck full at the headlight with his immense fore feet. There was a shattering of glass, a crash, a heavy shock, and the train slid on through the darkness, lit only by the moon.

Thirty or forty yards beyond, the momentum was exhausted and the engine came to a stop. Hemenway and McLeod clambered down and ran back, with the other trainmen and a few of the passengers. The moose was lying in the ditch beside the track, stone dead and frightfully shattered. But the great head and the vast spreading antlers were intact.

"Seelverhorrns, sure enough!" said McLeod, bending over him. "He was crossin' frae the Nepisiguit to the Jacquet; but he didna get across. Weel, Dud, are ye glad? Ye hae kilt yer first moose!"

"Yes," said Hemenway, "it's my first moose. But it's your first moose, too. And I think it's our last. Ye gods, what a fighter!"

II.—THE WILD-HORSE HUNTER[2]

By Zane Grey

I

Three wild-horse hunters made camp one night beside a little stream in the Sevier Valley, five hundred miles, as a crow flies, from Bostil's Ford.

These hunters had a poor outfit, excepting, of course, their horses. They were young men, rangy in build, lean and hard from life in the saddle, bronzed like Indians, still-faced, and keen-eyed. Two of them appeared to be tired out, and lagged at the campfire duties. When the meager meal was prepared they sat, cross-legged, before a ragged tarpaulin, eating and drinking in silence.

The sky in the west was rosy, slowly darkening. The valley floor billowed away, ridged and cut, growing gray and purple and dark. Walls of stone, pink with the last rays of the setting sun, inclosed the valley, stretching away toward a long, low, black mountain range.

The place was wild, beautiful, open, with something nameless that made the desert different from any other country. It was, perhaps, a loneliness of vast stretches of valley and stone, clear to the eye, even after sunset. That black mountain range, which looked close enough to ride to before dark, was a hundred miles distant.

The shades of night fell swiftly, and it was dark by the time the hunters finished the meal. Then the camp fire had burned low. One of the three dragged branches of dead cedars and replenished the fire. Quickly it flared up, with the white flame and crackle characteristic of dry cedar. The night wind had risen, moaning through the gnarled, stunted cedars near by, and it blew the fragrant wood smoke into the faces of the two hunters, who seemed too tired to move.

"I reckon a pipe would help me make up my mind," said one.

"Wal, Bill," replied the other, dryly, "your mind's made up, else you'd not say smoke."

"Why?"

"Because there ain't three pipefuls of thet precious tobacco left."

"Thet's one apiece, then. . . . Lin, come an' smoke the last pipe with us."

The tallest of the three, he who had brought the firewood, stood in the bright light of the blaze. He looked the born rider, light, lithe, powerful.

"Sure, I'll smoke," he replied.

Then, presently, he accepted the pipe tendered him, and, sitting down beside the fire, he composed himself to the enjoyment which his companions evidently considered worthy of a decision they had reached.

"So this smokin' means you both want to turn back?" queried Lin, his sharp gaze glancing darkly bright in the glow of the fire.

"Yep, we'll turn back. An', Gee! the relief I feel!" replied one.

"We've been long comin' to it, Lin, an' thet was for your sake," replied the other.

Lin slowly pulled at his pipe and blew out the smoke as if reluctant to part with it. "Let's go on," he said, quietly.

"No. I've had all I want of chasin' thet wild stallion," returned Bill, shortly.

The other spread wide his hands and bent an expostulating look upon the one called Lin. "We're two hundred miles out," he said. "There's only a little flour left in the bag. No coffee! Only a little salt! All the hosses except your big Nagger are played out. We're already in strange country. An' you know what we've heerd of this an' all to the south. It's all cañons, an' somewheres down there is thet awful cañon none of our people ever seen. But we've heerd of it. An awful cut-up country."

He finished with a conviction that no one could say a word against the common sense of his argument. Lin was silent, as if impressed.

Bill raised a strong, lean, brown hand in a forcible gesture. "We can't ketch Wildfire!"

That seemed to him, evidently, a more convincing argument than his comrade's.

"Bill is sure right, if I'm wrong, which I ain't," went on the other. "Lin, we've trailed thet wild stallion for six weeks. Thet's the longest chase he ever had. He's left his old range. He's cut out his band, an' left them, one by one. We've tried every trick we know on him. An' he's too smart for us. There's a hoss! Why, Lin, we're all but gone to the dogs chasin' Wildfire. An' now I'm done, an' I'm glad of it."

There was another short silence, which presently Bill opened his lips to break.

"Lin, it makes me sick to quit. I ain't denyin' thet for a long time I've had hopes of ketchin' Wildfire. He's the grandest hoss I ever laid eyes on. I reckon no man, onless he was an Arab, ever seen as good a one. But now thet's neither here nor there. . . . We've got to hit the back trail."

"Boys, I reckon I'll stick to Wildfire's tracks," said Lin, in the same quiet tone.

Bill swore at him, and the other hunter grew excited and concerned.

"Lin Slone, are you gone plumb crazy over thet red hoss?"

"I—reckon," replied Slone. The working of his throat as he swallowed could be plainly seen by his companions.

Bill looked at his ally as if to confirm some sudden understanding between them. They took Slone's attitude gravely and they wagged their heads doubtfully. . . . It was significant of the nature of riders that they accepted his attitude and had consideration for his feelings. For them the situation subtly changed. For weeks they had been three wild-horse wranglers on a hard chase after a valuable stallion. They had failed to get even close to him. They had gone to the limit of their endurance and of the outfit, and it was time to turn back. But Slone had conceived that strange and rare longing for a horse—a passion understood, if not shared, by all riders. And they knew that he would catch Wildfire or die in the attempt. From that moment their attitude toward Slone changed as subtly as had come the knowledge of his feeling. The gravity and gloom left their faces. It seemed they might have regretted what they had said about the futility of catching Wildfire. They did not want Slone to see or feel the hopelessness of his task.

"I tell you, Lin," said Bill, "your hoss Nagger's as good as when we started."

"Aw, he's better," vouchsafed the other rider. "Nagger needed to lose some weight. Lin, have you got an extra set of shoes for him?"

"No full set. Only three left," replied Lin, soberly.

"Wal, thet's enough. You can keep Nagger shod. An' *mebbe* thet red stallion will get sore feet an' go lame. Then you'd stand a chance."

"But Wildfire keeps travelin' the valleys—the soft ground," said Slone.

"No matter. He's leavin' the country, an' he's bound to strike sandstone sooner or later. Then, by gosh! mebbe he'll wear off them hoofs."

"Say, can't he ring bells offen the rocks?" exclaimed Bill.

"Boys, do you think he's leavin' the country?" inquired Slone, anxiously.

"Sure he is," replied Bill. "He ain't the first stallion I've chased off the Sevier range. An' I know. It's a stallion thet makes for new country, when you push him hard."

"Yep, Lin, he's sure leavin'," added the other comrade. "Why, he's traveled a bee line for days! I'll bet he's seen us many a time. Wildfire's about as smart as any man. He was born wild, an' his dam was born wild, an' there you have it. The wildest of all wild creatures—a wild stallion, with the intelligence of a man! A grand hoss, Lin, but one thet has killed stallions all over the Sevier range. A wild stallion thet's a killer! I never liked him for thet. Could he be broke?"

"I'll break him," said Lin Slone, grimly. "It's gettin' him thet's the job. I've got patience to break a hoss. But patience can't catch a streak of lightnin'."

"Nope; you're right," replied Bill. "If you have some luck you'll get him—mebbe. If he wears out his feet, or if you crowd him into a narrow cañon, or run him into a bad place where he can't get by you. Thet might happen. An' then, with Nagger, you stand a chance. Did you ever tire thet hoss?"

"Not yet."

"An' how fur did you ever run him without a break? Why, when we ketched thet sorrel last year I rode Nagger myself—thirty miles, most at a hard gallop. An' he never turned a hair!"

"I've beat thet," replied Lin. "He could run hard fifty miles—mebbe more. Honestly, I never seen him tired yet. If only he was fast!"

"Wal, Nagger ain't so slow, come to think of thet," replied Bill, with a grunt. "He's good enough for you not to want another hoss."

"Lin, you're goin' to wear out Wildfire, an' then trap him somehow—is thet the plan?" asked the other comrade.

"I haven't any plan. I'll just trail him, like a cougar trails a deer."

"Lin, if Wildfire gives you the slip he'll have to fly. You've got the best eyes for tracks of any wrangler in Utah."

Slone accepted the compliment with a fleeting, doubtful smile on his dark face. He did not reply, and no more was said by his comrades. They rolled with backs to the fire. Slone put on more wood, for the keen wind was cold and cutting; and then he lay down, his head on his saddle, with a goatskin under him and a saddle blanket over him.

All three were soon asleep. The wind whipped the sand and ashes and smoke over the sleepers. Coyotes barked from near in darkness, and from the valley ridge came the faint mourn of a hunting wolf. The desert night grew darker and colder.

The Stewart brothers were wild-horse hunters for the sake of trades and occasional sales. But Lin Slone never traded nor sold a horse he had captured. The excitement of the game, and the lure of the desert, and the love of a horse were what kept him at the profitless work. His type was rare in the uplands.

These were the early days of the settlement of Utah, and only a few of the hardiest and most adventurous pioneers had penetrated the desert in the southern part of that vast upland. And with them came some of that wild breed of riders to which Slone and the Stewarts belonged. Horses were really more important and necessary than men; and this singular fact gave these lonely riders a calling.

Before the Spaniards came there were no horses in the West. Those explorers left or lost horses all over the southwest. Many of them were Arabian horses of purest blood. American explorers and travelers, at the outset of the nineteenth century, encountered countless droves of wild horses all over the plains. Across the Grand Cañon, however, wild horses were comparatively few in number in the early days; and these had probably come in by way of California.

The Stewarts and Slone had no established mode of catching wild horses. The game had not developed fast enough for that. Every chase of horse or drove was different; and once in many attempts they met with success.

A favorite method originated by the Stewarts was to find a water hole frequented by the band of horses or the stallion wanted, and to build round this hole a corral with an opening for the horses to get in. Then the hunters would watch the trap at night, and if the horses went in to drink, a gate was closed across the opening.

Another method of the Stewarts was to trail a coveted horse up on a mesa or highland, places which seldom had more than one trail of ascent and descent, and there block the escape, and cut lines of cedars, into which the quarry was run till captured. Still another method, discovered by accident, was to shoot a horse lightly in the neck and sting him. This last, called creasing, was seldom successful, and for that matter in any method ten times as many horses were killed as captured.

Lin Slone helped the Stewarts in their own way, but he had no especial liking for their tricks. Perhaps a few remarkable captures of remarkable horses had spoiled Slone. He was always trying what the brothers claimed to be impossible. He was a fearless rider, but he had the fault of saving his mount, and to kill a wild horse was a tragedy for him. He would much rather have hunted alone, and he had been alone on the trail of the stallion Wildfire when the Stewarts had joined him.

Lin Slone awoke next morning and rolled out of his blanket at his usual early hour. But he was not early enough to say good-by to the Stewarts. They were gone.

The fact surprised him and somehow relieved him. They had left him more than his share of the outfit, and perhaps that was why they had slipped off before dawn. They knew him well enough to know that he would not have accepted it. Besides, perhaps they felt a little humiliation at abandoning a chase which he chose to keep up. Anyway, they were gone, apparently without breakfast.

The morning was clear, cool, with the air dark like that before a storm, and in the east, over the steely wall of stone, shone a redness growing brighter.

Slone looked away to the west, down the trail taken by his comrades, but he saw nothing moving against that cedar-dotted waste.

"Good-by," he said, and he spoke as if he was saying good-by to more than comrades.

"I reckon I won't see Sevier Village soon again—an' maybe never," he soliloquized.

There was no one to regret him, unless it was old Mother Hall, who had been kind to him on those rare occasions when he got out of the wilderness. Still, it was with regret that he gazed away across the red valley to the west. Slone had no home. His father and mother had been lost in the massacre of a wagon train by Indians, and he had been one of the few saved and brought to Salt Lake. That had happened when he was ten years old. His life thereafter had been hard, and but for his sturdy Texas training he might not have survived. The last five years he had been a horse hunter in the wild uplands of Nevada and Utah.

Slone turned his attention to the pack of supplies. The Stewarts had divided the flour and the parched corn equally, and unless he was greatly mistaken they had left him most of the coffee and all of the salt.

"Now I hold that decent of Bill an' Abe," said Slone, regretfully. "But I could have got along without it better 'n they could."

Then he swiftly set about kindling a fire and getting a meal. In the midst of his task a sudden ruddy brightness fell around him. Lin Slone paused in his work to look up.

The sun had risen over the eastern wall.

"Ah!" he said, and drew a deep breath.

The cold, steely, darkling sweep of desert had been transformed. It was now a world of red earth and gold rocks and purple sage, with everywhere the endless straggling green cedars. A breeze whipped in, making the fire roar softly. The sun felt warm on his cheek. And at the moment he heard the whistle of his horse.

"Good old Nagger!" he said. "I shore won't have to track you this mornin'."

Presently he went off into the cedars to find Nagger and the mustang that he used to carry a pack. Nagger was grazing in a little open patch among the trees, but the pack horse was missing. Slone seemed to know in what direction to go to find the trail, for he came upon it very soon. The pack horse wore hobbles, but he belonged to the class that could cover a great deal of ground when hobbled. Slone did not expect the horse to go far, considering that the grass thereabouts was good. But in a wild-horse country it was not safe to give any horse a chance. The call of his wild brethren was irresistible. Slone, however, found the mustang standing quietly in a clump of cedars, and, removing the hobbles, he mounted and rode back to camp. Nagger caught sight of him and came at his call.

This horse Nagger appeared as unique in his class as Slone was rare among riders. Nagger seemed of several colors, though black predominated. His coat was shaggy, almost woolly, like that of a sheep. He was huge, raw-boned, knotty, long of body and long of leg, with the head of a war charger. His build did not suggest speed. There appeared to be something slow and ponderous about him, similar to an elephant, with the same suggestion of power and endurance.

Slone discarded the pack saddle and bags. The latter were almost empty. He roped the tarpaulin on the back of the mustang, and, making a small bundle of his few supplies, he tied that to the tarpaulin. His blanket he used for a saddle blanket on Nagger. Of the utensils left by the Stewarts he chose a couple of small iron pans, with long handles. The rest he left. In his saddle bags he had a few extra horseshoes, some nails, bullets for his rifle, and a knife with a heavy blade.

"Not a rich outfit for a far country," he mused. Slone did not talk very much, and when he did he addressed Nagger and himself simultaneously. Evidently he expected a long chase, one from which he would not return, and light as his outfit was it would grow too heavy.

Then he mounted and rode down the gradual slope, facing the valley and the black, bold, flat mountain to the southeast. Some few hundred yards from camp he halted Nagger and bent over in the saddle to scrutinize the ground.

The clean-cut track of a horse showed in the bare, hard sand. The hoof marks were large, almost oval, perfect in shape, and manifestly they were beautiful to Lin Slone. He gazed at them for a long time, and then he looked across the dotted red valley up to the vast ridgy steppes, toward the black plateau and beyond. It was the look that an Indian gives to a strange country. Then Slone slipped off the saddle and knelt to scrutinize the horse tracks. A little sand had blown into the depressions, and some of it was wet and some of it was dry. He took his time about examining it, and he even tried gently blowing other sand into the tracks, to compare that with what was already there. Finally he stood up and addressed Nagger.

"Reckon we won't have to argue with Abe an' Bill this mornin'," he said, with satisfaction. "Wildfire made that track yesterday, before sunup."

Thereupon Slone remounted and put Nagger to a trot. The pack horse followed with an alacrity that showed he had no desire for loneliness.

As straight as a bee line Wildfire had left a trail down into the floor of the valley. He had not stopped to graze, and he had not looked for water. Slone had hoped to find a water hole in one of the deep washes in the red earth, but if there had been any water there Wildfire would have scented it. He had not had a drink for three days that Slone knew of. And Nagger had not drunk for forty hours. Slone had a canvas water bag hanging over the pommel, but it was a habit of his to deny himself, as far as possible, till his horse could drink also. Like an Indian, Slone ate and drank but little.

It took four hours of steady trotting to reach the middle and bottom of that wide, flat valley. A network of washes cut up the whole center of it, and they were all as dry as bleached bone. To cross these Slone had only to keep Wildfire's trail. And it was proof of Nagger's quality that he did not have to veer from the stallion's course.

It was hot down in the lowland. The heat struck up, reflected from the sand. But it was a March sun, and no more than pleasant to Slone. The wind rose, however, and blew dust and sand in the faces of horse and rider. Except lizards Slone did not see any living things.

Miles of low greasewood and sparse yellow sage led to the first almost imperceptible rise of the valley floor on that side. The distant cedars beckoned to Slone. He was not patient, because he was on the trail of Wildfire; but, nevertheless, the hours seemed short.

Slone had no past to think about, and the future held nothing except a horse, and so his thoughts revolved the possibilities connected with this chase of Wildfire. The chase was hopeless in such country as he was traversing, and if Wildfire chose to roam around valleys like this one Slone would fail utterly. But the stallion had long ago left his band of horses, and then, one by one his favorite consorts, and now he was alone, headed with unerring instinct for wild, untrammeled ranges. He had been used to the pure, cold water and the succulent grass of the cold desert uplands. Assuredly he would not tarry in such barren lands as these.

For Slone an ever-present and growing fascination lay in Wildfire's clear, sharply defined tracks. It was as if every hoof mark told him something. Once, far up the interminable ascent, he found on a ridge top tracks showing where Wildfire had halted and turned.

"Ha, Nagger!" cried Slone, exultingly. "Look there! He's begun facin' about. He's wonderin' if we're still after him. He's worried. . . . But we'll keep out of sight—a day behind."

When Slone reached the cedars the sun was low down in the west. He looked back across the fifty miles of valley to the colored cliffs and walls. He seemed to be above them now, and the cool air, with tang of cedar and juniper, strengthened the impression that he had climbed high.

A mile or more ahead of him rose a gray cliff with breaks in it and a line of dark cedars or piñons on the level rims. He believed these breaks to be the mouths of cañons, and so it turned out. Wildfire's trail led into the mouth of a narrow cañon with very steep and high walls. Nagger snorted his perception of water, and the mustang whistled. Wildfire's tracks led to a point under the wall where a spring gushed forth. There were mountain lion and deer tracks also, as well as those of smaller game.

Slone made camp here. The mustang was tired. But Nagger, upon taking a long drink, rolled in the grass as if he had just begun the trip. After eating, Slone took his rifle and went out to look for deer. But there appeared to be none at hand. He came across many lion tracks, and saw, with apprehension, where one had taken Wildfire's trail. Wildfire had grazed up the cañon, keeping on and on, and he was likely to go miles in a night. Slone reflected that as small as were his own chances of getting Wildfire, they were still better than those of a mountain lion. Wildfire was the most cunning of all animals—a wild stallion; his speed and endurance were incomparable; his scent as keen as those animals that relied wholly upon scent to warn them of danger; and as for sight, it was Slone's belief that no hoofed creature, except the mountain sheep used to high altitudes, could see as far as a wild horse.

It bothered Slone a little that he was getting into a lion country. Nagger showed nervousness, something unusual for him. Slone tied both horses with long halters and stationed them on patches of thick grass. Then he put a cedar stump on the fire and went to sleep. Upon awakening and going to the spring he was somewhat chagrined to see that deer had come down to drink early. Evidently they were numerous. A lion country was always a deer country, for the lions followed the deer.

Slone was packed and saddled and on his way before the sun reddened the cañon wall. He walked the horses. From time to time he saw signs of Wildfire's consistent progress. The cañon narrowed and the walls grew lower and the grass increased. There was a decided ascent all the time. Slone could find no evidence that the cañon had ever been traveled by hunters or Indians. The day was pleasant and warm and still. Every once in a while a little breath of wind would bring a fragrance of cedar and piñon, and a sweet hint of pine and sage. At every turn he looked ahead, expecting to see the green of pine and the gray of sage. Toward the middle of the afternoon, coming to a place where Wildfire had taken to a trot, he put Nagger to that gait, and by sundown had worked up to where the cañon was only a shallow ravine. And finally it turned once more, to lose itself in a level where straggling pines stood high above the cedars, and great, dark-green silver spruces stood above the pines. And here were patches of sage, fresh and pungent, and long reaches of bleached grass. It was the edge of a forest. Wildfire's trail went on. Slone came at length to a group of pines, and here he found the remains of a camp fire, and some flint arrow-heads. Indians had been in there, probably having come from the opposite direction to Slone's. This encouraged him, for where Indians could hunt so could he. Soon he was entering a forest where cedars and piñons and pines began to grow thickly. Presently he came upon a faintly defined trail, just a dim, dark line even to an experienced eye. But it was a trail, and Wildfire had taken it.

Slone halted for the night. The air was cold. And the dampness of it gave him an idea there were snow banks somewhere not far distant. The dew was already heavy on the grass. He hobbled the horses and put a bell on Nagger. A bell might frighten lions that had never heard one. Then he built a fire and cooked his meal.

It had been long since he had camped high up among the pines. The sough of the wind pleased him, like music. There had begun to be prospects of pleasant experience along with the toil of chasing Wildfire. He was entering new and strange and beautiful country. How far might the chase take him? He did not care. He was not sleepy, but even if he had been it developed that he must wait till the coyotes ceased their barking round his camp fire. They came so close that he saw their gray shadows in the gloom. But presently they wearied of yelping at him and went away. After that the silence, broken only by the wind as it roared and lulled, seemed beautiful to Slone. He lost completely that sense of vague regret which had remained with him, and he forgot the Stewarts. And suddenly he felt absolutely free, alone, with nothing behind to remember, with wild, thrilling, nameless life before him. Just then the long mourn of a timber wolf wailed in with the wind. Seldom had he heard the cry of one of those night wanderers. There was nothing like it—no sound like it to fix in the lone camper's heart the great solitude and the wild.

II

In the early morning when all was gray and the big, dark pines were shadowy specters, Slone was awakened by the cold. His hands were so numb that he had difficulty starting a fire. He stood over the blaze, warming them. The air was nipping, clear and thin, and sweet with frosty fragrance.

Daylight came while he was in the midst of his morning meal. A white frost covered the ground and crackled under his feet as he went out to bring in the horses. He saw fresh deer tracks. Then he went back to camp for his rifle. Keeping a sharp lookout for game, he continued his search for the horses.

The forest was open and parklike. There were no fallen trees or evidences of fire. Presently he came to a wide glade in the midst of which Nagger and the pack mustang were grazing with a herd of deer. The size of the latter amazed Slone. The deer he had hunted back on the Sevier range were much smaller than these. Evidently these were mule deer, closely allied to the elk. They were so tame they stood facing him curiously, with long ears erect. It was sheer murder to kill a deer standing and watching like that, but Slone was out of meat and hungry and facing a long, hard trip. He shot a buck, which leaped spasmodically away, trying to follow the herd, and fell at the edge of the glade. Slone cut out a haunch, and then, catching the horses, he returned to camp, where he packed and saddled, and at once rode out on the dim trail.

The wilderness of the country he was entering was evident in the fact that as he passed the glade where he had shot the deer a few minutes before, there were coyotes quarreling over the carcass.

Slone could see ahead and on each side several hundred yards, and presently he ascertained that the forest floor was not so level as he had supposed. He had entered a valley or was traversing a wide, gently sloping pass. He went through thickets of juniper, and had to go around clumps of quaking asp. The pines grew larger and farther apart. Cedars and piñons had been left behind, and he had met with no silver spruces after leaving camp. Probably that point was the height of a divide. There were banks of snow in some of the hollows on the north side. Evidently the snow had very recently melted, and it was evident also that the depth of snow through here had been fully ten feet, judging from the mutilation of the juniper trees where the deer, standing on the hard, frozen crust, had browsed upon the branches.

The quiet of the forest thrilled Slone. And the only movement was the occasional gray flash of a deer or coyote across a glade. No birds of any species crossed Slone's sight. He came, presently, upon a lion track in the trail, made probably a day before. Slone grew curious about it, seeing how it held, as he was holding, to Wildfire's tracks. After a mile or so he made sure the lion had been trailing the stallion, and for a second he felt a cold contraction of his heart. Already he loved Wildfire, and by virtue of all this toil of travel considered the wild horse his property.

"No lion could ever get close to Wildfire," he soliloquized, with a short laugh. Of that he was absolutely certain.

The sun rose, melting the frost, and a breath of warm air, laden with the scent of pine, moved heavily under the huge, yellow trees. Slone passed a point where the remains of an old camp fire and a pile of deer antlers were further proof that Indians visited this plateau to hunt. From this camp broader, more deeply defined trails led away to the south and east. Slone kept to the east trail, in which Wildfire's tracks and those of the lion showed clearly. It was about the middle of the forenoon when the tracks of the stallion and lion left the trail to lead up a little draw where grass grew thick. Slone followed, reading the signs of Wildfire's progress, and the action of his pursuer, as well as if he had seen them. Here the stallion had plowed into a snow bank, eating a hole two feet deep; then he had grazed around a little; then on and on; there his splendid tracks were deep in the soft earth. Slone knew what to expect when the track of the lion veered from those of the horse, and he followed the lion tracks. The ground was soft from the late melting of snow, and Nagger sunk deep. The lion left a plain track. Here he stole steadily along; there he left many tracks at a point where he might have halted to make sure of his scent. He was circling on the trail of the stallion, with cunning intent of ambush. The end of this slow, careful stalk of the lion, as told in his tracks, came upon the edge of a knoll where he had crouched to watch and wait. From this perch he had made a magnificent spring—Slone estimating it to be forty feet—but he had missed the stallion. There were Wildfire's tracks again, slow and short, and then deep and sharp where in the impetus of fright he had sprung out of reach. A second leap of the lion, and then lessening bounds, and finally an abrupt turn from Wildfire's trail told the futility of that stalk. Slone made certain that Wildfire was so keen that as he grazed along he had kept to open ground.

Wildfire had run for a mile, then slowed down to a trot, and he had circled to get back to the trail he had left. Slone believed the horse was just so intelligent. At any rate, Wildfire struck the trail again, and turned at right angles to follow it.

Here the forest floor appeared perfectly level. Patches of snow became frequent, and larger as Slone went on. At length the patches closed up, and soon extended as far as he could see. It was soft, affording difficult travel. Slone crossed hundreds of deer tracks, and the trail he was on evidently became a deer runway.

Presently, far down one of the aisles between the great pines Slone saw what appeared to be a yellow cliff, far away. It puzzled him. And as he went on he received the impression that the forest dropped out of sight ahead. Then the trees grew thicker, obstructing his view. Presently the trail became soggy and he had to help his horse. The mustang floundered in the soft snow and earth. Cedars and piñons appeared again, making travel still more laborious.

All at once there came to Slone a strange consciousness of light and wind and space and void. On the instant his horse halted with a snort. Slone quickly looked up. Had he come to the end of the world? An abyss, a cañon, yawned beneath him, beyond all comparison in its greatness. His keen eye, educated to desert distance and dimension swept down and across, taking in the tremendous truth, before it staggered his comprehension. But a second sweeping glance, slower, becoming intoxicated with what it beheld, saw gigantic cliff steppes and yellow slopes dotted with cedars, leading down to clefts filled with purple smoke, and these led on and on to a ragged red world of rock, bare, shining, bold, uplifted in mesa, dome, peak, and crag, clear and strange in the morning light, still and sleeping like death.

This, then, was the great cañon, which had seemed like a hunter's fable rather than truth. Slone's sight dimmed, blurring the spectacle, and he found that his eyes had filled with tears. He wiped them away and looked again and again, until he was confounded by the vastness and grandeur and the vague sadness of the scene. Nothing he had ever looked at had affected him like this cañon, although the Stewarts had tried to prepare him for it.

It was the horse hunter's passion that reminded him of his pursuit. The deer trail led down through a break in the wall. Only a few rods of it could be seen. This trail was passable, even though choked with snow. But the depth beyond this wall seemed to fascinate Slone and hold him back, used as he was to desert trails. Then the clean mark of Wildfire's hoof brought back the old thrill.

"This place fits you, Wildfire," muttered Slone, dismounting.

He started down, leading Nagger. The mustang followed. Slone kept to the wall side of the trail, fearing the horses might slip. The snow held firmly at first and Slone had no trouble. The gap in the rim rock widened to a slope thickly grown over with cedars and piñons and manzanita. This growth made the descent more laborious, yet afforded means at least for Slone to go down with less danger. There was no stopping. Once started, the horses had to keep on. Slone saw the impossibility of ever climbing out while that snow was there. The trail zigzagged down and down. Very soon the yellow wall hung tremendously over him, straight up. The snow became thinner and softer. The horses began to slip. They slid on their haunches. Fortunately the slope grew less steep, and Slone could see below where it reached out to comparatively level ground. Still, a mishap might yet occur. Slone kept as close to Nagger as possible, helping him whenever he could do it. The mustang slipped, rolled over, and then slipped past Slone, went down the slope to bring up in a cedar. Slone worked down to him and extricated him. Then the huge Nagger began to slide. Snow and loose rock slid with him, and so did Slone. The little avalanche stopped of its own accord, and then Slone dragged Nagger on down and down, presently to come to the end of the steep descent. Slone looked up to see that he had made short work of a thousand-foot slope. Here cedars and piñons grew thickly enough to make a forest. The snow thinned out to patches, and then failed. But the going remained bad for a while as the horses sank deep in a soft red earth. This eventually grew more solid and finally dry. Slone worked out of the cedars to what appeared a grassy plateau inclosed by the great green and white slope with its yellow wall overhanging, and distant mesas and cliffs. Here his view was restricted. He was down on the first bench of the great cañon. And there was the deer trail, a well-worn path keeping to the edge of the slope. Slone came to a deep cut in the earth, and the trail headed it, where it began at the last descent of the slope. It was the source of a cañon. He could look down to see the bare, worn rock, and a hundred yards from where he stood the earth was washed from its rims and it began to show depth and something of that ragged outline which told of violence of flood. The trail headed many cañons like this, all running down across this bench, disappearing, dropping invisibly. The trail swung to the left under the great slope, and then presently it climbed to a higher bench. Here were brush and grass and huge patches of sage, so pungent that it stung Slone's nostrils. Then he went down again, this time to come to a clear brook lined by willows. Here the horses drank long and Slone refreshed himself. The sun had grown hot. There was fragrance of flowers he could not see and a low murmur of a waterfall that was likewise invisible. For most of the time his view was shut off, but occasionally he reached a point where through some break he saw towers gleaming red in the sun. A strange place, a place of silence, and smoky veils in the distance. Time passed swiftly. Toward the waning of the afternoon he began to climb what appeared to be a saddle of land, connecting the cañon wall on the left with a great plateau, gold-rimmed and pine-fringed, rising more and more in his way as he advanced. At sunset Slone was more shut in than for several hours. He could tell the time was sunset by the golden light on the cliff wall again overhanging him. The slope was gradual up to this pass to the saddle, and upon coming to a spring and the first pine trees, he decided to halt for camp. The mustang was almost exhausted.

Thereupon he hobbled the horses in the luxuriant grass round the spring, and then unrolled his pack. Once as dusk came stealing down, while he was eating his meal, Nagger whistled in fright. Slone saw a gray, pantherish form gliding away into the shadows. He took a quick shot at it, but missed.

"It's a lion country, all right," he said. And then he set about building a big fire on the other side of the grassy plot, so as to have the horses between fires. He cut all the venison into thin strips, and spent an hour roasting them. Then he lay down to rest, and he said: "Wonder where Wildfire is to-night? Am I closer to him? Where's he headin' for?"

The night was warm and still. It was black near the huge cliff, and overhead velvety blue, with stars of white fire. It seemed to him that he had become more thoughtful and observing of the aspects of his wild environment, and he felt a welcome consciousness of loneliness. Then sleep came to him and the night seemed short. In the gray dawn he arose refreshed.

The horses were restive. Nagger snorted a welcome. Evidently they had passed an uneasy night. Slone found lion tracks at the spring and in sandy places. Presently he was on his way up to the notch between the great wall and the plateau. A growth of thick scrub oak made travel difficult. It had not appeared far up to that saddle, but it was far. There were straggling pine trees and huge rocks that obstructed his gaze. But once up he saw that the saddle was only a narrow ridge, curved to slope up on both sides.

Straight before Slone and under him opened the cañon, blazing and glorious along the peaks and ramparts, where the rising sun struck, misty and smoky and shadowy down in those mysterious depths.

It took an effort not to keep on gazing. But Slone turned to the grim business of his pursuit. The trail he saw leading down had been made by Indians. It was used probably once a year by them; and also by wild animals, and it was exceedingly steep and rough. Wildfire had paced to and fro along the narrow ridge of that saddle, making many tracks, before he had headed down again. Slone imagined that the great stallion had been daunted by the tremendous chasm, but had finally faced it, meaning to put this obstacle between him and his pursuers. It never occurred to Slone to attribute less intelligence to Wildfire than that. So, dismounting, Slone took Nagger's bridle and started down. The mustang with the pack was reluctant. He snorted and whistled and pawed the earth. But he would not be left alone, so he followed.

The trail led down under cedars that fringed a precipice. Slone was aware of this without looking. He attended only to the trail and to his horse. Only an Indian could have picked out that course, and it was cruel to put a horse to it. But Nagger was powerful, sure-footed, and he would go anywhere that Slone led him. Gradually Slone worked down and away from the bulging rim wall. It was hard, rough work, and risky because it could not be accomplished slowly. Brush and rocks, loose shale and weathered slope, long, dusty inclines of yellow earth, and jumbles of stone—these made bad going for miles of slow, zigzag trail down out of the cedars. Then the trail entered what appeared to be a ravine.

That ravine became a cañon. At its head it was a dry wash, full of gravel and rocks. It began to cut deep into the bowels of the earth. It shut out sight of the surrounding walls and peaks. Water appeared from under a cliff and, augmented by other springs, became a brook. Hot, dry, and barren at its beginning, this cleft became cool and shady and luxuriant with grass and flowers and amber moss with silver blossoms. The rocks had changed color from yellow to deep red. Four hours of turning and twisting, endlessly down and down, over bowlders and banks and every conceivable roughness of earth and rock, finished the pack mustang; and Slone mercifully left him in a long reach of cañon where grass and water never failed. In this place Slone halted for the noon hour, letting Nagger have his fill of the rich grazing. Nagger's three days in grassy upland, despite the continuous travel by day, had improved him. He looked fat, and Slone had not yet caught the horse resting. Nagger was iron to endure. Here Slone left all the outfit except what was on his saddle, and the sack containing the few pounds of meat and supplies, and the two utensils. This sack he tied on the back of his saddle, and resumed his journey.

Presently he came to a place where Wildfire had doubled on his trail and had turned up a side cañon. The climb out was hard on Slone, if not on Nagger. Once up, Slone found himself upon a wide, barren plateau of glaring red rock and clumps of greasewood and cactus. The plateau was miles wide, shut in by great walls and mesas of colored rock. The afternoon sun beat down fiercely. A blast of wind, as if from a furnace, swept across the plateau, and it was laden with red dust. Slone walked here, where he could have ridden. And he made several miles of up-and-down progress over this rough plateau. The great walls of the opposite side of the cañon loomed appreciably closer. What, Slone wondered, was at the bottom of this rent in the earth? The great desert river was down there, of course, but he knew nothing of it. Would that turn back Wildfire? Slone thought grimly how he had always claimed Nagger to be part fish and part bird. Wildfire was not going to escape.

By and by only isolated mescal plants with long, yellow-plumed spears broke the bare monotony of the plateau. And Slone passed from red sand and gravel to a red, soft shale, and from that to hard, red rock. Here Wildfire's tracks were lost, the first time in seven weeks. But Slone had his direction down that plateau with the cleavage lines of cañons to right and left. At times Slone found a vestige of the old Indian trail, and this made him doubly sure of being right. He did not need to have Wildfire's tracks. He let Nagger pick the way, and the horse made no mistake in finding the line of least resistance. But that grew harder and harder. This bare rock, like a file, would soon wear Wildfire's hoofs thin. And Slone rejoiced. Perhaps somewhere down in this awful chasm he and Nagger would have if out with the stallion. Slone began to look far ahead, beginning to believe that he might see Wildfire. Twice he had seen Wildfire, but only at a distance. Then he had resembled a running streak of fire, whence his name, which Slone had given him.

This bare region of rock began to be cut up into gullies. It was necessary to head them or to climb in and out. Miles of travel really meant little progress straight ahead. But Slone kept on. He was hot and Nagger was hot, and that made hard work easier. Sometimes on the wind came a low thunder. Was it a storm or an avalanche slipping or falling water? He could not tell. The sound was significant and haunting.

Of one thing he was sure—that he could not have found his back trail. But he divined he was never to retrace his steps on this journey. The stretch of broken plateau before him grew wilder and bolder of outline, darker in color, weirder in aspect and progress across it grew slower, more dangerous. There were many places Nagger should not have been put to—where a slip meant a broken leg. But Slone could not turn back. And something besides an indomitable spirit kept him going. Again the sound resembling thunder assailed his ears, louder this time. The plateau appeared to be ending in a series of great capes or promontories. Slone feared he would soon come out upon a promontory from which he might see the impossibility of further travel. He felt relieved down in the gullies, where he could not see far. He climbed out of one, presently, from which there extended a narrow ledge with a slant too perilous for any horse. He stepped out upon that with far less confidence than Nagger. To the right was a bulge of low wall, and a few feet to the left a dark precipice. The trail here was faintly outlined, and it was six inches wide and slanting as well. It seemed endless to Slone, that ledge. He looked only down at his feet and listened to Nagger's steps. The big horse trod carefully, but naturally, and he did not slip. That ledge extended in a long curve, turning slowly away from the precipice, and ascending a little at the further end. Slone drew a deep breath of relief when he led Nagger up on level rock.

Suddenly a strange yet familiar sound halted Slone, as if he had been struck. The wild, shrill, high-pitched, piercing whistle of a stallion! Nagger neighed a blast in reply and pounded the rock with his iron-shod hoofs. With a thrill Slone looked ahead.

There, some few hundred yards distant, on a promontory, stood a red horse.

"It's Wildfire!" breathed Slone, tensely.

He could not believe his sight. He imagined he was dreaming. But as Nagger stamped and snorted defiance Slone looked with fixed and keen gaze, and knew that beautiful picture was no lie.

Wildfire was as red as fire. His long mane, wild in the wind, was like a whipping, black-streaked flame. Silhouetted there against that cañon background he seemed gigantic, a demon horse, ready to plunge into fiery depths. He was looking back over his shoulder, his head very high, and every line of him was instinct with wildness. Again he sent out that shrill, air-splitting whistle. Slone understood it to be a clarion call to Nagger. If Nagger had been alone Wildfire would have killed him. The red stallion was a killer of horses. All over the Utah ranges he had left the trail of a murderer. Nagger understood this, too, for he whistled back in rage and terror. It took an iron arm to hold him. Then Wildfire plunged, apparently down, and vanished from Slone's sight.

Slone hurried onward, to be blocked by a huge crack in the rocky plateau. This he had to head. And then another and like obstacle checked his haste to reach that promontory. He was forced to go more slowly. Wildfire had been close only as to sight. And this was the great cañon that dwarfed distance and magnified proximity. Climbing down and up, toiling on, he at last learned patience. He had seen Wildfire at close range. That was enough. So he plodded on, once more returning to careful regard of Nagger. It took an hour of work to reach the point where Wildfire had disappeared.

A promontory indeed it was, overhanging a valley a thousand feet below. A white torrent of a stream wound through it. There were lines of green cottonwoods following the winding course. Then Slone saw Wildfire slowly crossing the flat toward the stream. He had gone down that cliff, which to Slone looked perpendicular.

Wildfire appeared to be walking lame. Slone, making sure of this, suffered a pang. Then, when the significance of such lameness dawned upon him he whooped his wild joy and waved his hat. The red stallion must have heard, for he looked up. Then he went on again and waded into the stream, where he drank long. When he started to cross, the swift current drove him back in several places. The water wreathed white around him. But evidently it was not deep, and finally he crossed. From the other side he looked up again at Nagger and Slone, and, going on, he soon was out of sight in the cottonwoods.

"How to get down!" muttered Slone.

There was a break in the cliff wall, a bare stone slant where horses had gone down and come up. That was enough for Slone to know. He would have attempted the descent if he were sure no other horse but Wildfire had ever gone down there. But Slone's hair began to rise stiff on his head. A horse like Wildfire, and mountain sheep and Indian ponies, were all very different from Nagger. The chances were against Nagger.

"Come on, old boy. If I can do it, you can," he said.

Slone had never seen a trail as perilous as this. He was afraid for his horse. A slip there meant death. The way Nagger trembled in every muscle showed his feelings. But he never flinched. He would follow Slone anywhere, providing Slone rode him or led him. And here, as riding was impossible, Slone went before. If the horse slipped there would be a double tragedy, for Nagger would knock his master off the cliff. Slone set his teeth and stepped down. He did not let Nagger see his fear. He was taking the greatest risk he had ever run.

The break in the wall led to a ledge, and the ledge dropped from step to step, and these had bare, slippery slants between. Nagger was splendid on a bad trail. He had methods peculiar to his huge build and great weight. He crashed down over the stone steps, both front hoofs at once. The slants he slid down on his haunches with his forelegs stiff and the iron shoes scraping. He snorted and heaved and grew wet with sweat. He tossed his head at some of the places. But he never hesitated and it was impossible for him to go slowly. Whenever Slone came to corrugated stretches in the trail he felt grateful. But these were few. The rock was like smooth red iron. Slone had never seen such hard rock. It took him long to realize that it was marble. His heart seemed a tense, painful knot in his breast, as if it could not beat, holding back in the strained suspense. But Nagger never jerked on the bridle. He never faltered. Many times he slipped, often with both front feet, but never with all four feet. So he did not fall. And the red wall began to loom above Sloan. Then suddenly he seemed brought to a point where it was impossible to descend. It was a round bulge, slanting fearfully, with only a few rough surfaces to hold a foot. Wildfire had left a broad, clear-swept mark at that place, and red hairs on some of the sharp points. He had slid down. Below was an offset that fortunately prevented further sliding. Slone started to walk down this place, but when Nagger began to slide Slone had to let go the bridle and jump. Both he and the horse landed safely. Luck was with them. And they went on, down and down, to reach the base of the great wall, scraped and exhausted, wet with sweat, but unhurt. As Slone gazed upward he felt the impossibility of believing what he knew to be true. He hugged and petted the horse. Then he led on to the roaring stream.

It was green water white with foam. Slone waded in and found the water cool and shallow and very swift. He had to hold to Nagger to keep from being swept downstream. They crossed in safety. There in the sand showed Wildfire's tracks. And here were signs of another Indian camp, half a year old.

The shade of the cotton woods was pleasant. Slone found this valley oppressively hot. There was no wind and the sand blistered his feet through his boots. Wildfire held to the Indian trail that had guided him down into this wilderness of worn rock. And that trail crossed the stream at every turn of the twisting, narrow valley. Slone enjoyed getting into the water. He hung his gun over the pommel and let the water roll him. A dozen times he and Nagger forded the rushing torrent. Then they came to a boxlike closing of the valley to cañon walls, and here the trail evidently followed the stream bed. There was no other way. Slone waded in, and stumbled, rolled, and floated ahead of the sturdy horse. Nagger was wet to his breast, but he did not fall. This gulch seemed full of a hollow rushing roar. It opened out into a wide valley. And Wildfire's tracks took to the left side and began to climb the slope.

Here the traveling was good, considering what had been passed. Once up out of the valley floor Slone saw Wildfire far ahead, high on the slope. He did not appear to be limping, but he was not going fast. Slone watched as he climbed. What and where would be the end of this chase?

Sometimes Wildfire was plain in his sight for a moment, but usually he was hidden by rocks. The slope was one great talus, a jumble of weathered rock, fallen from what appeared a mountain of red and yellow wall. Here the heat of the sun fell upon him like fire. The rocks were so hot Slone could not touch them with bare hand. The close of the afternoon was approaching, and this slope was interminably long. Still, it was not steep, and the trail was good.

At last from the height of slope Wildfire appeared, looking back and down. Then he was gone. Slone plodded upward. Long before he reached that summit he heard the dull rumble of the river. It grew to be a roar, yet it seemed distant. Would the great desert river stop Wildfire in his flight? Slone doubted it. He surmounted the ridge, to find the cañon opening in a tremendous gap, and to see down, far down, a glittering, sun-blasted slope merging into a deep, black gulch where a red river swept and chafed and roared.

Somehow the river was what he had expected to see. A force that had cut and ground this cañon could have been nothing but a river like that. The trail led down, and Slone had no doubt that it crossed the river and led up out of the cañon. He wanted to stay there and gaze endlessly and listen. At length he began the descent. As he proceeded it seemed that the roar of the river lessened. He could not understand why this was so. It took half an hour to reach the last level, a ghastly, black, and iron-ribbed cañon bed, with the river splitting it. He had not had a glimpse of Wildfire on this side of the divide, but he found his tracks, and they led down off the last level, through a notch in the black bank of marble to a sand bar and the river.

Wildfire had walked straight off the sand into the water. Slone studied the river and shore. The water ran slow, heavily, in sluggish eddies. From far up the cañon came the roar of a rapid, and from below the roar of another, heavier and closer. The river appeared tremendous, in ways Slone felt rather than realized, yet it was not swift. Studying the black, rough wall of rock above him, he saw marks where the river had been sixty feet higher than where he stood on the sand. It was low, then. How lucky for him that he had gotten there before flood season! He believed Wildfire had crossed easily, and he knew Nagger could make it. Then he piled and tied his supplies and weapons high on the saddle, to keep them dry, and looked for a place to take to the water.

Wildfire had sunk deep before reaching the edge. Manifestly he had lunged the last few feet. Slone found a better place, and waded in, urging Nagger. The big horse plunged, almost going under, and began to swim. Slone kept upstream beside him. He found, presently, that the water was thick and made him tired, so it was necessary to grasp a stirrup and be towed. The river appeared only a few hundred feet wide, but probably it was wider than it looked. Nagger labored heavily near the opposite shore; still, he landed safely upon a rocky bank. There were patches of sand in which Wildfire's tracks showed so fresh that the water had not yet dried out of them.

Slone rested his horse before attempting to climb out of that split in the rock. However, Wildfire had found an easy ascent. On this side of the cañon the bare rock did not predominate. A clear trail led up a dusty, gravelly slope, upon which scant greasewood and cactus appeared. Half an hour's climbing brought Slone to where he could see that he was entering a vast valley, sloping up and narrowing to a notch in the dark cliffs, above which towered the great red wall and about that the slopes of cedar and the yellow rim rock.

And scarcely a mile distant, bright in the westering sunlight, shone the red stallion, moving slowly.

Slone pressed on steadily. Just before dark he came to an ideal spot to camp. The valley had closed up, so that the lofty walls cast shadows that met. A clump of cottonwoods surrounding a spring, abundance of rich grass, willows and flowers lining the banks, formed an oasis in the bare valley. Slone was tired out from the day of ceaseless toil down and up, and he could scarcely keep his eyes open. But he tried to stay awake. The dead silence of the valley, the dry fragrance, the dreaming walls, the advent of night low down, when up on the ramparts the last red rays of the sun lingered, the strange loneliness—these were sweet and comforting to him.

And that night's sleep was as a moment. He opened his eyes to see the crags and towers and peaks and domes, and the lofty walls of that vast, broken chaos of cañons across the river. They were now emerging from the misty gray of dawn, growing pink and lilac and purple under the rising sun.

He arose and set about his few tasks, which, being soon finished, allowed him an early start.

Wildfire had grazed along no more than a mile in the lead. Slone looked eagerly up the narrowing cañon, but he was not rewarded by a sight of the stallion. As he progressed up a gradually ascending trail he became aware of the fact that the notch he had long looked up to was where the great red walls closed in and almost met. And the trail zigzagged up this narrow vent, so steep that only a few steps could be taken without rest. Slone toiled up for an hour—an age—till he was wet, burning, choked, with a great weight on his chest. Yet still he was only halfway up that awful break between the walls. Sometimes he could have tossed a stone down upon a part of the trail, only a few rods below, yet many, many weary steps of actual toil. As he got farther up the notch widened. What had been scarcely visible from the valley below was now colossal in actual dimensions. The trail was like a twisted mile of thread between two bulging mountain walls leaning their ledges and fronts over this tilted pass.

Slone rested often. Nagger appreciated this and heaved gratefully at every halt. In this monotonous toil Slone forgot the zest of his pursuit. And when Nagger suddenly snorted in fright Slone was not prepared for what he saw.

Above him ran a low, red wall, around which evidently the trail led. At the curve, which was a promontory, scarcely a hundred feet in an air line above him, he saw something red moving, bobbing, coming out into view. It was a horse.

Wildfire—no farther away than the length of three lassos!

There he stood looking down. He fulfilled all of Slone's dreams. Only he was bigger. But he was so magnificently proportioned that he did not seem heavy. His coat was shaggy and red. It was not glossy. The color was what made him shine. His mane was like a crest, mounting, then falling low. Slone had never seen so much muscle on a horse. Yet his outline was graceful, beautiful. The head was indeed that of the wildest of all wild creatures—a stallion born wild—and it was beautiful, savage, splendid, everything but noble. Slone thought that if a horse could express hate, surely Wildfire did then. It was certain that he did express curiosity and fury.

Slone shook a gantleted fist at the stallion, as if the horse were human. That was a natural action for a rider of his kind. Wildfire turned away, showed bright against the dark background, and then disappeared.

III

That was the last Slone saw of Wildfire for three days.

It took all of this day to climb out of the cañon. The second was a slow march of thirty miles into a scrub cedar and piñon forest, through which the great red and yellow walls of the cañon could be seen. That night Slone found a water hole in a rocky pocket and a little grass for Nagger. The third day's travel consisted of forty miles or more through level pine forest, dry and odorous, but lacking the freshness and beauty of the forest on the north side of the cañon. On this south side a strange feature was that all the water, when there was any, ran away from the rim. Slone camped this night at a muddy pond in the woods, where Wildfire's tracks showed plainly.

On the following day Slone rode out of the forest into a country of scanty cedars, bleached and stunted, and out of this to the edge of a plateau, from which the shimmering desert flung its vast and desolate distances, forbidding and menacing. This was not the desert upland country of Utah, but a naked and bony world of colored rock and sand—a painted desert of heat and wind and flying sand and waterless wastes and barren ranges. But it did not daunt Slone. For far down on the bare, billowing ridges moved a red speck, at a snail's pace, a slowly moving dot of color which was Wildfire.

On open ground like this, Nagger, carrying two hundred and fifty pounds, showed his wonderful quality. He did not mind the heat nor the sand nor the glare nor the distance nor his burden. He did not tire. He was an engine of tremendous power.

Slone gained upon Wildfire, and toward evening of that day he reached to within half a mile of the stallion. And he chose to keep that far behind. That night he camped where there was dry grass, but no water.

Next day he followed Wildfire down and down, over the endless swell of rolling red ridges, bare of all but bleached white grass and meager greasewood, always descending in the face of that painted desert of bold and ragged steppes. Slone made fifty miles that day, and gained the valley bed, where a slender stream ran thin and spread over a wide sandy bottom. It was salty water, but it was welcome to both man and beast.

The following day he crossed, and the tracks of Wildfire were still wet on the sand bars. The stallion was slowing down. Slone saw him, limping along, not far in advance. There was a ten-mile stretch of level ground, blown hard as rock, from which the sustenance had been bleached, for not a spear of grass grew there. And following that was a tortuous passage through a weird region of clay dunes, blue and violet and heliotrope and lavender, all worn smooth by rain and wind. Wildfire favored the soft ground now. He had deviated from his straight course. And he was partial to washes and dips in the earth where water might have lodged. And he was not now scornful of a green-scummed water hole with its white margin of alkali. That night Slone made camp with Wildfire in plain sight. The stallion stopped when his pursuers stopped. And he began to graze on the same stretch with Nagger. How strange this seemed to Slone!

Here at this camp was evidence of Indians. Wildfire had swung round to the north in his course. Like any pursued wild animal, he had begun to circle. And he had pointed his nose toward the Utah he had left.

Next morning Wildfire was not in sight, but he had left his tracks in the sand. Slone trailed him with Nagger at a trot. Toward the head of this sandy flat Slone came upon old cornfields, and a broken dam where the water had been stored, and well-defined trails leading away to the right. Somewhere over there in the desert lived Indians. At this point Wildfire abandoned the trail he had followed for many days and cut out more to the north. It took all the morning hours to climb three great steppes and benches that led up to the summit of a mesa, vast in extent. It turned out to be a sandy waste. The wind rose and everywhere were moving sheets of sand, and in the distance circular yellow dust devils, rising high like water spouts, and back down in the sun-scorched valley a sandstorm moved along majestically, burying the desert in its yellow pall.

Then two more days of sand and another day of a slowly rising ground growing from bare to gray and gray to green, and then to the purple of sage and cedar—these three grinding days were toiled out with only one water hole.

And Wildfire was lame and in distress and Nagger was growing gaunt and showing strain; and Slone, haggard and black and worn, plodded miles and miles on foot to save his horse.

Slone felt that it would be futile to put the chase to a test of speed. Nagger could never head that stallion. Slone meant to go on and on, always pushing Wildfire, keeping him tired, wearied, and worrying him, till a section of the country was reached where he could drive Wildfire into some kind of a natural trap. The pursuit seemed endless. Wildfire kept to open country where he could not be surprised.

There came a morning when Slone climbed to a cedared plateau that rose for a whole day's travel, and then split into a labyrinthine maze of cañons. There were trees, grass, water. It was a high country, cool and wild, like the uplands he had left. For days he camped on Wildfire's trail, always relentlessly driving him, always watching for the trap he hoped to find. And the red stallion spent much of this time of flight in looking backward. Whenever Slone came in sight of him he had his head over his shoulder, watching. And on the soft ground of these cañons he had begun to recover from his lameness. But this did not worry Slone. Sooner or later Wildfire would go down into a high-walled wash, from which there would be no outlet; or he would wander into a box cañon; or he would climb out on a mesa with no place to descend, unless he passed Slone; or he would get cornered on a soft, steep slope where his hoofs would sink deep and make him slow. The nature of the desert had changed. Slone had entered a wonderful region, the like of which he had not seen—a high plateau criss-crossed in every direction by narrow cañons with red walls a thousand feet high.

And one of the strange turning cañons opened into a vast valley of monuments.

The plateau had weathered and washed away, leaving huge sections of stone walls, all standing isolated, different in size and shape, but all clean-cut, bold, with straight lines. They stood up everywhere, monumental, towering, many-colored, lending a singular and beautiful aspect to the great green and gray valley, billowing away to the north, where dim, broken battlements mounted to the clouds.

The only living thing in Slone's sight was Wildfire. He shone red down on the green slope.

Slone's heart swelled. This was the setting for that grand horse—a perfect wild range. But also it seemed the last place where there might be any chance to trap the stallion. Still that did not alter Slone's purpose, though it lost to him the joy of former hopes. He rode down the slope, out upon the billowing floor of the valley. Wildfire looked back to see his pursuers, and then the solemn stillness broke to a wild, piercing whistle.

Day after day, camping where night found him, Slone followed the stallion, never losing sight of him till darkness had fallen. The valley was immense and the monuments miles apart. But they always seemed close together and near him. The air magnified everything. Slone lost track of time. The strange, solemn, lonely days and the silent, lonely nights, and the endless pursuit, and the wild, weird valley—these completed the work of years on Slone and he became satisfied, unthinking, almost savage.

The toil and privation had worn him down and he was like iron. His garments hung in tatters; his boots were ripped and soleless. Long since his flour had been used up, and all his supplies except the salt. He lived on the meat of rabbits, but they were scarce, and the time came when there were none. Some days he did not eat. Hunger did not make him suffer. He killed a desert bird now and then, and once a wildcat crossing the valley. Eventually he felt his strength diminishing, and then he took to digging out the pack rats and cooking them. But these, too, were scarce. At length starvation faced Slone. But he knew he would not starve. Many times he had been within rifle shot of Wildfire. And the grim, forbidding thought grew upon him that he must kill the stallion. The thought seemed involuntary, but his mind rejected it. Nevertheless, he knew that if he could not catch the stallion he would kill him. That had been the end of many a desperate rider's pursuit of a coveted horse.

While Slone kept on his merciless pursuit, never letting Wildfire rest by day, time went on just as relentlessly. Spring gave way to early summer. The hot sun bleached the grass; water holes failed out in the valley, and water could be found only in the cañons; and the dry winds began to blow the sand. It was a sandy valley, green and gray only at a distance, and out toward the north there were no monuments, and the slow heave of sand lifted toward the dim walls.

Wildfire worked away from this open valley, back to the south end, where the great monuments loomed, and still farther back, where they grew closer, till at length some of them were joined by weathered ridges to the walls of the surrounding plateau. For all that Slone could see, Wildfire was in perfect condition. But Nagger was not the horse he had been. Slone realized that in one way or another the pursuit was narrowing down to the end.

He found a water hole at the head of a wash in a split in the walls, and here he let Nagger rest and graze one whole day—the first day for a long time that he had not kept the red stallion in sight. That day was marked by the good fortune of killing a rabbit, and while eating it his gloomy, fixed mind admitted that he was starving. He dreaded the next sunrise. But he could not hold it back. There, behind the dark monuments, standing sentinel-like, the sky lightened and reddened and burnt into gold and pink, till out of the golden glare the sun rose glorious. And Slone, facing the league-long shadows of the monuments, rode out again into the silent, solemn day, on his hopeless quest.

For a change Wildfire had climbed high up a slope of talus, through a narrow pass, rounded over with drifting sand. And Slone gazed down into a huge amphitheater full of monuments, like all that strange country. A basin three miles across lay beneath him. Walls and weathered slants of rock and steep slopes of reddish-yellow sand inclosed this oval depression. The floor was white, and it seemed to move gently or radiate with heat waves. Studying it, Slone made out that the motion was caused by wind in long bleached grass. He had crossed small areas of this grass in different parts of the region.

Wildfire's tracks led down into this basin, and presently Slone, by straining his eyes, made out the red spot that was the stallion.

"He's lookin' to quit the country," soliloquized Slone, as he surveyed the scene.

With keen, slow gaze Slone studied the lay of wall and slope, and when he had circled the huge depression he made sure that Wildfire could not get out except by the narrow pass through which he had gone in. Slone sat astride Nagger in the mouth of this pass—a wash a few yards wide, walled by broken, rough rock on one side and an insurmountable slope on the other.

"If this hole was only little, now," sighed Slone, as he gazed at the sweeping, shimmering oval floor, "I might have a chance. But down there—we couldn't get near him."

There was no water in that dry bowl. Slone reflected on the uselessness of keeping Wildfire down there, because Nagger could not go without water as long as Wildfire. For the first time Slone hesitated. It seemed merciless to Nagger to drive him down into this hot, windy hole. The wind blew from the west, and it swooped up the slope, hot, with the odor of dry, dead grass.

But that hot wind stirred Slone with an idea, and suddenly he was tense, excited, glowing, yet grim and hard.

"Wildfire, I'll make you run with your namesake in that high grass," called Slone. The speech was full of bitter failure, of regret, of the hardness of a rider who could not give up the horse to freedom.

Slone meant to ride down there and fire the long grass. In that wind there would indeed be wildfire to race with the red stallion. It would perhaps mean his death; at least it would chase him out of that hole, where to follow him would be useless.

"I'd make you hump now to get away if I could get behind you," muttered Slone. He saw that if he could fire the grass on the other side the wind of flame would drive Wildfire straight toward him. The slopes and walls narrowed up to the pass, but high grass grew to within a few rods of where Slone stood. But it seemed impossible to get behind Wildfire.

"At night—then—I could get round him," said Slone, thinking hard and narrowing his gaze to scan the circle of wall and slope. "Why not? . . . No wind at night. That grass would burn slow till mornin'—till the wind came up—an' it's been west for days."

Suddenly Slone began to pound the patient Nagger and to cry out to him in wild exultance.

"Old horse, we've got him! We've got him! We'll put a rope on him before this time to-morrow!"

Slone yielded to his strange, wild joy, but it did not last long, soon succeeding to sober, keen thought. He rode down into the bowl a mile, making absolutely certain that Wildfire could not climb out on that side. The far end, beyond the monuments, was a sheer wall of rock. Then he crossed to the left side. Here the sandy slope was almost too steep for even him to go up. And there was grass that would burn. He returned to the pass assured that Wildfire had at last fallen into a trap the like Slone had never dreamed of. The great horse was doomed to run into living flame or the whirling noose of a lasso.

Then Slone reflected. Nagger had that very morning had his fill of good water—the first really satisfying drink for days. If he was rested that day, on the morrow he would be fit for the grueling work possibly in store for him. Slone unsaddled the horse and turned him loose, and with a snort he made down the gentle slope for the grass. Then Slone carried his saddle to a shady spot afforded by a slab of rock and a dwarf cedar, and here he composed himself to rest and watch and think and wait.

Wildfire was plainly in sight no more than two miles away. Gradually he was grazing along toward the monuments and the far end of the great basin. Slone believed, because the place was so large, that Wildfire thought there was a way out on the other side or over the slopes or through the walls. Never before had the farsighted stallion made a mistake. Slone suddenly felt the keen, stabbing fear of an outlet somewhere. But it left him quickly. He had studied those slopes and walls. Wildfire could not get out, except by the pass he had entered, unless he could fly.

Slone lay in the shade, his head propped on his saddle, and while gazing down into the shimmering hollow he began to plan. He calculated that he must be able to carry fire swiftly across the far end of the basin, so that he would not be absent long from the mouth of the pass. Fire was always a difficult matter, since he must depend only on flint and steel. He decided to wait till dark, build a fire with dead cedar sticks, and carry a bundle of them with burning ends. He felt assured that the wind caused by riding would keep them burning. After he had lighted the grass all he had to do was to hurry back to his station and there await developments.

The day passed slowly, and it was hot. The heat-waves rose in dark, wavering lines and veils from the valley. The wind blew almost a gale. Thin, curling sheets of sand blew up over the crests of the slopes, and the sound it made was a soft, silken rustling, very low. The sky was a steely blue above and copper close over the distant walls.

That afternoon, toward the close, Slone ate the last of the meat. At sunset the wind died away and the air cooled. There was a strip of red along the wall of rock and on the tips of the monuments, and it lingered there for long, a strange, bright crown. Nagger was not far away, but Wildfire had disappeared, probably behind one of the monuments.

When twilight fell Slone went down after Nagger and, returning with him, put on bridle and saddle. Then he began to search for suitable sticks of wood. Farther back in the pass he found stunted dead cedars, and from these secured enough for his purpose. He kindled a fire and burned the ends of the sticks into red embers. Making a bundle of these, he put them under his arm, the dull, glowing ends backward, and then mounted his horse.

It was just about dark when he faced down into the valley. When he reached level ground he kept to the edge of the left slope and put Nagger to a good trot. The grass and brush were scant here, and the color of the sand was light, so he had no difficulty in traveling. From time to time his horse went through grass, and its dry, crackling rustle, showing how it would burn, was music to Slone. Gradually the monuments began to loom up, bold and black against the blue sky, with stars seemingly hanging close over them. Slone had calculated that the basin was smaller than it really was, in both length and breadth. This worried him. Wildfire might see or hear or scent him, and make a break back to the pass and thus escape. Slone was glad when the huge, dark monuments were indistinguishable from the black, frowning wall. He had to go slower here, because of the darkness. But at last he reached the slow rise of jumbled rock that evidently marked the extent of weathering on that side. Here he turned to the right and rode out into the valley. The floor was level and thickly overgrown with long, dead grass and dead greasewood, as dry as tinder. It was easy to account for the dryness; neither snow nor rain had visited that valley for many months. Slone whipped one of the sticks in the wind and soon had the smouldering end red and showering sparks. Then he dropped the stick in the grass, with curious intent and a strange feeling of regret.

Instantly the grass blazed with a little sputtering roar. Nagger snorted. "Wildfire!" exclaimed Slone. That word was a favorite one with riders, and now Slone used it both to call out his menace to the stallion and to express his feeling for that blaze, already running wild.

Without looking back, Slone rode across the valley, dropping a glowing stick every quarter of a mile. When he reached the other side there were a dozen fires behind him, burning slowly, with white smoke rising lazily. Then he loped Nagger along the side back to the sandy ascent, and on up to the mouth of the pass. There he searched for tracks. Wildfire had not gone out, and Slone experienced relief and exultation. He took up a position in the middle of the narrowest part of the pass, and there, with Nagger ready for anything, he once more composed himself to watch and wait.

Far across the darkness of the valley, low down, twelve lines of fire, widely separated, crept toward one another. They appeared thin and slow, with only an occasional leaping flame. And some of the black spaces must have been monuments, blotting out the creeping snail lines of red. Slone watched, strangely fascinated.

"What do you think of that?" he said, aloud, and he meant his query for Wildfire.

As he watched the lines perceptibly lengthened and brightened and pale shadows of smoke began to appear. Over at the left of the valley the two brightest fires, the first he had started, crept closer and closer together. They seemed long in covering distance. But not a breath of wind stirred, and besides they really might move swiftly, without looking so to Slone. When the two lines met a sudden and larger blaze rose.

"Ah!" said the rider, and then he watched the other lines creeping together. How slowly fire moved, he thought. The red stallion would have every chance to run between those lines, if he dared. But a wild horse fears nothing like fire. This one would not run the gantlet of flames. Nevertheless Slone felt more and more relieved as the lines closed. The hours of the night dragged past until at length one long, continuous line of fire spread level across the valley, its bright, red line broken only where the monuments of stone were silhouetted against it.

The darkness of the valley changed. The light of the moon changed. The radiance of the stars changed. Either the line of fire was finding denser fuel to consume or it was growing appreciably closer, for the flames began to grow, to leap, and to flare.

Slone strained his ears for the thud of hoofs on sand.

The time seemed endless in its futility of results, but fleeting after it had passed; and he could tell how the hours fled by the ever-recurring need to replenish the little fire he kept burning in the pass.

A broad belt of valley grew bright in the light, and behind it loomed the monuments, weird and dark, with columns of yellow and white smoke wreathing them.

Suddenly Slone's sensitive ear vibrated to a thrilling sound. He leaned down to place his ear to the sand. Rapid, rhythmic beat of hoofs made him leap to his feet, reaching for his lasso with right hand and a gun with his left.

Nagger lifted his head, sniffed the air, and snorted. Slone peered into the black belt of gloom that lay below him. It would be hard to see a horse there, unless he got high enough to be silhouetted against that line of fire now flaring to the sky. But he heard the beat of hoofs, swift, sharp, louder—louder. The night shadows were deceptive. That wonderful light confused him, made the place unreal. Was he dreaming? Or had the long chase and his privations unhinged his mind? He reached for Nagger. No! The big black was real, alive, quivering, pounding the sand. He scented an enemy.

Once more Slone peered down into the void or what seemed a void. But it, too, had changed, lightened. The whole valley was brightening. Great palls of curling smoke rose white and yellow, to turn back as the monuments met their crests, and then to roll upward, blotting out the stars. It was such a light as he had never seen, except in dreams. Pale moonlight and dimmed starlight and wan dawn all vague and strange and shadowy under the wild and vivid light of burning grass.

In the pale path before Slone, that fanlike slope of sand which opened down into the valley, appeared a swiftly moving black object, like a fleeing phantom. It was a phantom horse. Slone felt that his eyes, deceived by his mind, saw racing images. Many a wild chase he had lived in dreams on some far desert. But what was that beating in his ears—sharp, swift, even, rhythmic? Never had his ears played him false.

Never had he heard things in his dreams. That running object was a horse and he was coming like the wind. Slone felt something grip his heart. All the time and endurance and pain and thirst and suspense and longing and hopelessness—the agony of the whole endless chase—closed tight on his heart in that instant.

The running horse halted just in the belt of light cast by the burning grass. There he stood sharply defined, clear as a cameo, not a hundred paces from Slone. It was Wildfire.

Slone uttered an involuntary cry. Thrill on thrill shot through him. Delight and hope and fear and despair claimed him in swift, successive flashes. And then again the ruling passion of a rider held him—the sheer glory of a grand and unattainable horse. For Slone gave up Wildfire in that splendid moment. How had he ever dared to believe he could capture that wild stallion? Slone looked and looked, filling his mind, regretting nothing, sure that the moment was reward for all he had endured.

The weird lights magnified Wildfire and showed him clearly. He seemed gigantic. He shone black against the fire. His head was high, his mane flying. Behind him the fire flared and the valley-wide column of smoke rolled majestically upward, and the great monuments seemed to retreat darkly and mysteriously as the flames advanced beyond them. It was a beautiful, unearthly spectacle, with its silence the strangest feature.

But suddenly Wildfire broke that silence with a whistle which to Slone's overstrained faculties seemed a blast as piercing as the splitting sound of lightning. And with the whistle Wildfire plunged up toward the pass.

Slone yelled at the top of his lungs and fired his gun before he could terrorize the stallion and drive him back down the slope. Soon Wildfire became again a running black object, and then he disappeared.

The great line of fire had gotten beyond the monuments and now stretched unbroken across the valley from wall to slope. Wildfire could never pierce that line of flames. And now Slone saw, in the paling sky to the east, that dawn was at hand.

IV

Slone looked grimly glad when simultaneously with the first red flash of sunrise a breeze fanned his cheek. All that was needed now was a west wind. And here came the assurance of it.

The valley appeared hazy and smoky, with slow, rolling clouds low down where the line of fire moved. The coming of daylight paled the blaze of the grass, though here and there Slone caught flickering glimpses of dull red flame. The wild stallion kept to the center of the valley, restlessly facing this way and that, but never toward the smoke. Slone made sure that Wildfire gradually gave ground as the line of smoke slowly worked toward him.

Every moment the breeze freshened, grew steadier and stronger, until Slone saw that it began to clear the valley of the low-hanging smoke. There came a time when once more the blazing line extended across from slope to slope.

Wildfire was cornered, trapped. Many times Slone nervously uncoiled and recoiled his lasso. Presently the great chance of his life would come—the hardest and most important throw he would ever have with a rope. He did not miss often, but then he missed sometimes, and here he must be swift and sure. It annoyed him that his hands perspired and trembled and that something weighty seemed to obstruct his breathing. He muttered that he was pretty much worn out, not in the best of condition for a hard fight with a wild horse. Still he would capture Wildfire; his mind was unalterably set there. He anticipated that the stallion would make a final and desperate rush past him; and he had his plan of action all outlined. What worried him was the possibility of Wildfire's doing some unforeseen feat at the very last. Slone was prepared for hours of strained watching, and then a desperate effort, and then a shock that might kill Wildfire and cripple Nagger, or a long race and fight.

But he soon discovered that he was wrong about the long watch and wait. The wind had grown strong and was driving the fire swiftly. The flames, fanned by the breeze, leaped to a formidable barrier. In less than an hour, though the time seemed only a few moments to the excited Slone, Wildfire had been driven down toward the narrowing neck of the valley, and he had begun to run, to and fro, back and forth. Any moment, then, Slone expected him to grow terrorized and to come tearing up toward the pass.

Wildfire showed evidence of terror, but he did not attempt to make the pass. Instead he went at the right-hand slope of the valley and began to climb. The slope was steep and soft, yet the stallion climbed up and up. The dust flew in clouds; the gravel rolled down, and the sand followed in long streams. Wildfire showed his keenness by zigzagging up the slope.

"Go ahead, you red devil!" yelled Slone. He was much elated. In that soft bank Wildfire would tire out while not hurting himself.

Slone watched the stallion in admiration and pity and exultation. Wildfire did not make much headway, for he slipped back almost as much as he gained. He attempted one place after another where he failed. There was a bank of clay, some few feet high, and he could not round it at either end or surmount it in the middle. Finally he literally pawed and cut a path, much as if he were digging in the sand for water. When he got over that he was not much better off. The slope above was endless and grew steeper, more difficult toward the top. Slone knew absolutely that no horse could climb over it. He grew apprehensive, however, for Wildfire might stick up there on the slope until the line of fire passed. The horse apparently shunned any near proximity to the fire, and performed prodigious efforts to escape.

"He'll be ridin' an avalanche pretty soon," muttered Slone.

Long sheets of sand and gravel slid down to spill thinly over the low bank. Wildfire, now sinking to his knees, worked steadily upward till he had reached a point halfway up the slope, at the head of a long, yellow bank of treacherous-looking sand. Here he was halted by a low bulge, which he might have surmounted had his feet been free. But he stood deep in the sand. For the first time he looked down at the sweeping fire, and then at Slone.

Suddenly the bank of sand began to slide with him. He snorted in fright. The avalanche started slowly and was evidently no mere surface slide. It was deep. It stopped—then started again—and again stopped. Wildfire appeared to be sinking deeper and deeper. His struggles only embedded him more firmly. Then the bank of sand, with an ominous, low roar, began to move once more. This time it slipped swiftly. The dust rose in a cloud, almost obscuring the horse. Long streams of gravel rattled down, and waterfalls of sand waved over the steppes of the slope.

Just as suddenly the avalanche stopped again. Slone saw, from the great oval hole it had left above, that it was indeed deep. That was the reason it did not slide readily. When the dust cleared away Slone saw the stallion, sunk to his flanks in the sand, utterly helpless.

With a wild whoop Slone leaped off Nagger, and, a lasso in each hand, he ran down the long bank. The fire was perhaps a quarter of a mile distant, and, since the grass was thinning out, it was not coming so fast as it had been. The position of the stallion was halfway between the fire and Slone, and a hundred yards up the slope.

Like a madman Slone climbed up through the dragging, loose sand. He was beside himself with a fury of excitement. He fancied his eyes were failing him, that it was not possible the great horse really was up there, helpless in the sand. Yet every huge stride Slone took brought him closer to a fact he could not deny. In his eagerness he slipped, and fell, and crawled, and leaped, until he reached the slide which held Wildfire prisoner.

The stallion might have been fast in quicksand, up to his body, for all the movement he could make. He could move only his head. He held that up, his eyes wild, showing the whites, his foaming mouth wide open, his teeth gleaming. A sound like a scream rent the air. Terrible fear and hate were expressed in that piercing neigh. And shaggy, wet, dusty red, with all of brute savageness in the look and action of his head, he appeared hideous.

As Slone leaped within roping distance the avalanche slipped a foot or two, halted, slipped once more, and slowly started again with that low roar. He did not care whether it slipped or stopped. Like a wolf he leaped closer, whirling his rope. The loop hissed round his head and whistled as he flung it. And when fiercely he jerked back on the rope, the noose closed tight round Wildfire's neck.

"I—got—a rope—on him!" cried Slone, in hoarse pants.

He stared, unbelieving. It was unreal, that sight—unreal like the slow, grinding movement of the avalanche under him. Wildfire's head seemed a demon head of hate. It reached out, mouth agape, to bite, to rend. That horrible scream could not be the scream of a horse.

Slone was a wild-horse hunter, a rider, and when that second of incredulity flashed by, then came the moment of triumph. No moment could ever equal that one, when he realized he stood there with a rope around that grand stallion's neck. All the days and the miles and the toil and the endurance and the hopelessness and the hunger were paid for in that moment. His heart seemed too large for his breast.

"I tracked—you!" he cried, savagely. "I stayed—with you! An' I got a rope—on you! An'—I'll ride you—you red devil!"

The passion of the man was intense. That endless, racking pursuit had brought out all the hardness the desert had engendered in him. Almost hate, instead of love, spoke in Slone's words. He hauled on the lasso, pulling the stallion's head down and down. The action was the lust of capture as well as the rider's instinctive motive to make the horse fear him. Life was unquenchably wild and strong in that stallion; it showed in the terror which made him hideous. And man and beast somehow resembled each other in that moment which was inimical to noble life.

The avalanche slipped with little jerks, as if treacherously loosing its hold for a long plunge. The line of fire below ate at the bleached grass and the long column of smoke curled away on the wind.

Slone held the taut lasso with his left hand, and with the right he swung the other rope, catching the noose round Wildfire's nose. Then letting go of the first rope he hauled on the other, pulling the head of the stallion far down. Hand over hand Slone closed in on the horse. He leaped on Wildfire's head, pressed it down, and, holding it down on the sand with his knees, with swift fingers he tied the nose in a hackamore—an improvised halter. Then, just as swiftly, he bound his scarf tight round Wildfire's head, blindfolding him.

"All so easy!" exclaimed Slone, under his breath. "Who would believe it! Is it a dream?"

He rose and let the stallion have a free head.

"Wildfire, I got a rope on you—an' a hackamore—an' a blinder," said Slone. "An' if I had a bridle I'd put that on you. Who'd ever believe you'd catch yourself, draggin' in the sand?"

Slone, finding himself falling on the sand, grew alive to the augmented movement of the avalanche. It had begun to slide, to heave and bulge and crack. Dust rose in clouds from all around. The sand appeared to open and let him sink to his knees. The rattle of gravel was drowned in a soft roar. Then he shot down swiftly, holding the lassos, keeping himself erect, and riding as if in a boat. He felt the successive steppes of the slope, and then the long incline below, and then the checking and rising and spreading of the avalanche as it slowed down on the level. All movement then was checked violently. He appeared to be half buried in sand. While he struggled to extricate himself the thick dust blew away and, settled so that he could see. Wildfire lay before him, at the edge of the slide, and now he was not so deeply embedded as he had been up on the slope. He was struggling and probably soon would have been able to get out. The line of fire was close now, but Slone did not fear that.

At his shrill whistle Nagger bounded toward him, obedient, but snorting, with ears laid back. He halted. A second whistle started him again. Slone finally dug himself out of the sand, pulled the lassos out, and ran the length of them toward Nagger. The black showed both fear and fight. His eyes rolled and he half shied away.

"Come on!" called Slone, harshly.

He got a hand on the horse, pulled him round, and, mounting in a flash, wound both lassos round the pommel of the saddle.

"Haul him out, Nagger, old boy!" cried Slone, and he dug spurs into the black.

One plunge of Nagger's slid the stallion out of the sand. Snorting, wild, blinded, Wildfire got up, shaking in every limb. He could not see his enemies. The blowing smoke, right in his nose, made scent impossible. But in the taut lassos he sensed the direction of his captors. He plunged, rearing at the end of the plunge, and struck out viciously with his hoofs. Slone, quick with spur and bridle, swerved Nagger aside and Wildfire, off his balance, went down with a crash. Slone dragged him, stretched him out, pulled him over twice before he got forefeet planted. Once up, he reared again, screeching his rage, striking wildly with his hoofs. Slone wheeled aside and toppled him over again.

"Wildfire, it's no fair fight," he called, grimly. "But you led me a chase. An' you learn right now I'm boss!"

III.—THE HYDROPHOBIC SKUNK[3]

By Irvin S. Cobb

THE Hydrophobic Skunk resides at the extreme bottom of the Grand Cañon and, next to a Southern Republican who never asked for a Federal office, is the rarest of living creatures. He is so rare that nobody ever saw him—that is, nobody except a native. I met plenty of tourists who had seen people who had seen him, but never a tourist who had seen him with his own eyes. In addition to being rare, he is highly gifted.

I think almost anybody will agree with me that the common, ordinary skunk has been most richly dowered by Nature. To adorn a skunk with any extra qualifications seems as great a waste of the raw material as painting the lily or gilding refined gold. He is already amply equipped for outdoor pursuits. Nobody intentionally shoves him round; everybody gives him as much room as he seems to need. He commands respect—nay, more than that, respect and veneration—wherever he goes. Joy riders never run him down and foot passengers avoid crowding him into a corner. You would think Nature had done amply well by the skunk; but no—the Hydrophobic Skunk comes along and upsets all these calculations. Besides carrying the traveling credentials of an ordinary skunk, he is rabid in the most rabidissimus form. He is not mad just part of the time, like one's relatives by marriage—and not mad most of the time, like the old-fashioned railroad ticket agent—but mad all the time—incurably, enthusiastically and unanimously mad! He is mad and he is glad of it.

We made the acquaintance of the Hydrophobic Skunk when we rode down Hermit Trail. The casual visitor to the Grand Cañon first of all takes the rim drive; then he essays Bright Angel Trail, which is sufficiently scary for his purposes until he gets used to it; and after that he grows more adventurous and tackles Hermit Trail, which is a marvel of corkscrew convolutions, gimleting its way down this red abdominal wound of a cañon to the very gizzard of the world. Here, Johnny, our guide, felt moved to speech, and we hearkened to his words and hungered for more, for Johnny knows the ranges of the Northwest as a city dweller knows his own little side street. In the fall of the year Johnny comes down to the Cañon and serves as a guide a while; and then, when he gets so he just can't stand associating with tourists any longer, he packs his war bags and journeys back to the Northern Range and enjoys the company of cows a spell. Cows are not exactly exciting, but they don't ask fool questions.

A highly competent young person is Johnny and a cow-puncher of parts. Most of the Cañon guides are cow-punchers—accomplished ones, too, and of high standing in the profession. With a touch of reverence Johnny pointed out to us Sam Scovel, the greatest bronco buster of his time, now engaged in piloting tourists.

"Can he ride?" echoed Johnny in answer to our question. "Scovel could ride an earthquake if she stood still long enough for him to mount! He rode Steamboat—not Young Steamboat, but Old Steamboat! He rode Rocking Chair, and he's the only man that ever did that and was not called on in a couple of days to attend his own funeral."

We went on and on at a lazy mule trot, hearing the unwritten annals of the range from one who had seen them enacted at first hand. Pretty soon we passed a herd of burros with mealy, dusty noses and spotty hides, feeding on prickly pears and rock lichens; and just before sunset we slid down the last declivity out upon the plateau and came to a camp as was a camp!

This was roughing it de luxe with a most de-luxey vengeance! Here were three tents, or rather three canvas houses, with wooden half walls; and they were spick-and-span inside and out, and had glass windows in them and doors and matched wooden floors. . . . The mess tent was provided with a table with a clean cloth to go over it, and there were china dishes and china cups and shiny knives, forks and spoons. . . . Bill was in charge of the camp—a dark, rangy, good-looking leading man of a cowboy, wearing his blue shirt and his red neckerchief with an air.

That Johnny certainly could cook! Served on china dishes upon a cloth-covered table, we had mounds of fried steaks and shoals of fried bacon; and a bushel, more or less, of sheepherder potatoes; and green peas and sliced peaches out of cans; and sour-dough biscuits as light as kisses and much more filling; and fresh butter and fresh milk; and coffee as black as your hat and strong as sin. How easy it is for civilized man to become primitive and comfortable in his way of eating, especially if he has just ridden ten miles on a buckboard and nine more on a mule and is away down at the bottom of the Grand Cañon—and there is nobody to look on disapprovingly when he takes a bite that would be a credit to a steam shovel!

Despite all reports to the contrary, I wish to state that it is no trouble at all to eat green peas off a knife-blade—you merely mix them in with potatoes for a cement; and fried steak—take it from an old steak eater—tastes best when eaten with those tools of Nature's own providing, both hands and your teeth. An hour passed—busy, yet pleasant—and we were both gorged to the gills and had reared back with our cigars lit to enjoy a third jorum of black coffee apiece, when Johnny, speaking in an offhand way to Bill, who was still hiding away biscuits inside of himself like a parlor prestidigitator, said:

"Seen any of them old Hydrophobies the last day or two?"

"Not so many," said Bill casually. "There was a couple out last night pirootin' round in the moonlight. I reckon, though, there'll be quite a flock of 'em out to-night. A new moon always seems to fetch 'em up from the river."

Both of us quit blowing on our coffee and we put the cups down. I think I was the one who spoke.

"I beg your pardon," I asked, "but what did you say would be out to-night?"

"We were just speakin' to one another about them Hydrophoby Skunks," said Bill apologetically. "This here Cañon is where they mostly hang out and frolic 'round."

I laid down my cigar, too. I admit I was interested.

"Oh!" I said softly—like that. "Is it? Do they?"

"Yes," said Johnny. "I reckin there's liable to be one come shovin' his old nose into that door any minute. Or probably two—they mostly travels in pairs—sets, as you might say."

"You'd know one the minute you saw him, though," said Bill. "They're smaller than a regular skunk and spotted where the other kind is striped. And they got little red eyes. You won't have no trouble at all recognizin' one."

It was at this juncture that we both got up and moved back by the stove. It was warmer there and the chill of evening seemed to be settling down noticeably.

"Funny thing about Hydrophoby Skunks," went on Johnny after a moment of pensive thought—"mad, you know!"

"What makes them mad?" The two of us asked the question together.

"Born that way!" explained Bill—"mad from the start, and won't never do nothin' to get shut of it."

"Ahem—they never attack humans, I suppose?"

"Don't they?" said Johnny, as if surprised at such ignorance. "Why, humans is their favorite pastime! Humans is just pie to a Hydrophoby Skunk. It ain't really any fun to be bit by a Hydrophoby Skunk neither." He raised his coffee cup to his lips and imbibed deeply.

"Which you certainly said something then, Johnny," stated Bill. "You see," he went on, turning to us, "they aim to catch you asleep and they creep up right soft and take holt of you—take holt of a year usually—and clamp their teeth and just hang on for further orders. Some says they hang on till it thunders, same as snappin' turtles. But that's a lie, I judge, because there's weeks on a stretch down here when it don't thunder. All the cases I ever heard of they let go at sunup."

"It is right painful at the time," said Johnny, taking up the thread of the narrative; "and then in nine days you go mad yourself. Remember that fellow the Hydrophoby Skunk bit down here by the rapids, Bill? Let's see now—what was that hombre's name?"

"Williams," supplied Bill—"Heck Williams. I saw him at Flagstaff when they took him there to the hospital. That guy certainly did carry on regardless. First he went mad and his eyes turned red, and he got so he didn't have no real use for water—well, them prospectors don't never care much about water anyway—and then he got to snappin' and bitin' and foamin' so's they had to strap him down to his bed. He got loose though."

"Broke loose, I suppose?" I said.

"No, he bit loose," said Bill with the air of one who would not deceive you even in a matter of small details.

"Do you mean to say he bit those leather straps in two?"

"No, sir; he couldn't reach them," explained Bill, "so he bit the bed in two. Not in one bite, of course," he went on. "It took him several. I saw him after he was laid out. He really wasn't no credit to himself as a corpse."

I'm not sure, but I think my companion and I were holding hands by now. Outside we could hear that little lost echo laughing to itself. It was no time to be laughing either. Under certain circumstances I don't know of a lonelier place anywhere on earth than that Grand Cañon.

Presently my friend spoke, and it seemed to me his voice was a mite husky. Well, he had a bad cold.

"You said they mostly attack persons who are sleeping out, didn't you?"

"That's right, too," said Johnny, and Bill nodded in affirmation.

"Then, of course, since we sleep indoors everything will be all right," I put in.

"Well, yes and no," answered Johnny. "In the early part of the evening a Hydrophoby is liable to do a lot of prowlin' round outdoors; but toward mornin' they like to get into camps—they dig up under the side walls or come up through the floor—and they seem to prefer to get in bed with you. They're cold-blooded, I reckin, same as rattlesnakes. Cool nights always do drive 'em in, seems like."

"It's going to be sort of coolish to-night," said Bill casually.

It certainly was. I don't remember a chillier night in years. My teeth were chattering a little—from cold—before we turned in. I retired with all my clothes on, including my boots and leggings, and I wished I had brought along my ear muffs. I also buttoned my watch into my lefthand shirt pocket, the idea being if for any reason I should conclude to move during the night I would be fully equipped for traveling. The door would not stay closely shut—the door-jamb had sagged a little and the wind kept blowing the door ajar. But after a while we dozed off.

It was one twenty-seven A. M. when I woke with a violent start. I know this was the exact time because that was when my watch stopped. I peered about me in the darkness. The door was wide open—I could tell that. Down on the floor there was a dragging, scuffling sound, and from almost beneath me a pair of small red eyes peered up phosphorescently.

"He's here!" I said to my companion as I emerged from my blankets; and he, waking instantly, seemed instinctively to know whom I meant. I used to wonder at the ease with which a cockroach can climb a perfectly smooth wall and run across the ceiling. I know now that to do this is the easiest thing in the world—if you have the proper incentive behind you. I had gone up one wall of the tent and had crossed over and was in the act of coming down the other side when Bill burst in, his eyes blurred with sleep, a lighted lamp in one hand and a gun in the other.

I never was so disappointed in my life because it wasn't a Hydrophobic Skunk at all. It was a pack rat, sometimes called a trade rat, paying us a visit. The pack or trade rat is also a denizen of the Grand Cañon. He is about four times as big as an ordinary rat and has an appetite to correspond. He sometimes invades your camp and makes free with your things, but he never steals anything outright—he merely trades with you; hence his name. He totes off a side of meat or a bushel of meal and brings a cactus stalk in; or he will confiscate your saddlebags and leave you in exchange a nice dry chip. He is honest, but from what I can gather he never gets badly stuck on a deal.

Next morning at breakfast Johnny and Bill were doing a lot of laughing between them over something or other.

IV.—THE OLE VIRGINIA[4]

By Stewart Edward White

THE ring around the sun had thickened all day long, and the turquoise blue of the Arizona sky had filmed. Storms in the dry countries are infrequent, but heavy; and this surely meant storm.

We had ridden since sunup over broad mesas, down and out of deep cañons, along the base of the mountains in the wildest parts of the territory. The cattle were winding leisurely toward the high country; the jack rabbits had disappeared; the quail lacked; we did not see a single antelope in the open.

"It's a case of hold up," the Cattleman ventured his opinion. "I have a ranch over in the Double R. Charley and Windy Bill hold it down. We'll tackle it. What do you think?"

The four cowboys agreed. We dropped into a low, broad watercourse, ascended its bed to big cottonwoods and flowing water, followed it into box cañons between rim rock carved fantastically and painted like a Moorish façade, until at last in a widening below a rounded hill, we came upon an adobe house, a fruit tree, and a round corral. This was the Double R.

Charley and Windy Bill welcomed us with soda biscuits. We turned our horses out, spread our beds on the floor, filled our pipes, and squatted on our heels. Various dogs of various breeds investigated us. It was very pleasant, and we did not mind the ring around the sun.

"Somebody else coming," announced the Cattleman finally.

"Uncle Jim," said Charley, after a glance.

A hawk-faced old man with a long white beard and long white hair rode out from the cottonwoods. He had on a battered broad hat abnormally high of crown, carried across his saddle a heavy "eight square" rifle, and was followed by a half-dozen lolloping hounds.

The largest and fiercest of the latter, catching sight of our group, launched himself with lightning rapidity at the biggest of the ranch dogs, promptly nailed that canine by the back of the neck, shook him violently a score of times, flung him aside, and pounced on the next. During the ensuing few moments that hound was the busiest thing in the West. He satisfactorily whipped four dogs, pursued two cats up a tree, upset the

Dutch oven and the rest of the soda biscuits, stampeded the horses, and raised a cloud of dust adequate to represent the smoke of battle. We others were too paralyzed to move. Uncle Jim sat placidly on his white horse, his thin knees bent to the ox-bow stirrups, smoking.

In ten seconds the trouble was over, principally because there was no more trouble to make. The hound returned leisurely, licking from his chops the hair of his victims. Uncle Jim shook his head.

"Trailer," said he sadly, "is a little severe."

We agreed heartily, and turned in to welcome Uncle Jim with a fresh batch of soda biscuits.

The old man was one of the typical "long hairs." He had come to the Galiuro Mountains in '69, and since '69 he had remained in the Galiuro Mountains, spite of man or the devil. At present he possessed some hundreds of cattle, which he was reputed to water, in a dry season, from an ordinary dish pan. In times past he had prospected.

That evening, the severe Trailer having dropped to slumber, he held forth on big-game hunting and dogs, quartz claims and Apaches.

"Did you ever have any very close calls?" I asked.

He ruminated a few moments, refilled his pipe with some awful tobacco, and told the following experience:

"In the time of Geronimo I was living just about where I do now; and that was just about in line with the raiding. You see, Geronimo, and Ju, and old Loco used to pile out of the reservation at Camp Apache, raid south to the line, slip over into Mexico when the soldiers got too promiscuous, and raid there until they got ready to come back. Then there was always a big medicine talk. Says Geronimo:

"'I am tired of the warpath. I will come back from Mexico with all my warriors, if you will escort me with soldiers and protect my people.'

"'All right,' says the General, being only too glad to get him back at all.

"So, then, in ten minutes there wouldn't be a buck in camp, but next morning they shows up again, each with about fifty head of hosses.

"'Where'd you get those hosses?' asks the General, suspicious.

"'Had 'em pastured in the hills,' answers Geronimo.

"'I can't take all those hosses with me; I believe they're stolen!' says the General.

"'My people cannot go without their hosses,' says Geronimo.

"So, across the line they goes, and back to the reservation. In about a week there's fifty-two frantic Greasers wanting to know where's their hosses. The army is nothing but an importer of stolen stock, and knows it, and can't help it.

"Well, as I says, I'm between Camp Apache and the Mexican line, so that every raiding party goes right on past me. The point is that I'm a thousand feet or so above the valley, and the renegades is in such a hurry about that time that they never stop to climb up and collect me. Often I've watched them trailing down the valley in a cloud of dust. Then, in a day or two, a squad of soldiers would come up and camp at my spring for a while. They used to send soldiers to guard every water hole in the country so the renegades couldn't get water. After a while, from not being bothered none, I got to thinking I wasn't worth while with them.

"Me and Johnny Hooper were pecking away at the Ole Virginia mine then. We'd got down about sixty feet, all timbered, and was thinking of crosscutting. One day Johnny went to town, and that same day I got in a hurry and left my gun at camp.

"I worked all the morning down at the bottom of the shaft, and when I see by the sun it was getting along towards noon, I put in three good shots, tamped 'em down, lit the fuses, and started to climb out.

"It ain't noways pleasant to light a fuse in a shaft, and then have to climb out a fifty-foot ladder, with it burning behind you. I never did get used to it. You keep thinking, 'Now, suppose there's a flaw in that fuse, or something, and she goes off in six seconds instead of two minutes? Where'll you be then?' It would give you a good boost towards your home on high, anyway.

"So I climbed fast, and stuck my head out the top without looking—and then I froze solid enough. There, about fifty feet away, climbing up the hill on mighty tired hosses, was a dozen of the ugliest Chiricahuas you ever don't want to meet, and in addition a Mexican renegade named Maria, who was worse than any of 'em. I see at once their hosses was tired out, and they had a notion of camping at my water hole, not knowing nothing about the Ole Virginia mine.

"For two bits I'd have let go all holts and dropped backwards, trusting to my thick head for easy lighting. Then I heard a little fizz and sputter from below. At that my hair riz right up so I could feel the breeze blow under my hat. For about six seconds I stood there like an imbecile, grinning amiably. Then one of the Chiricahuas made a sort of grunt, and I sabed that they'd seen the original exhibit your Uncle Jim was making of himself.

"Then that fuse gave another sputter and one of the Apaches said, 'Un dah.' That means 'white man.' It was harder to turn my head than if I'd had a stiff neck; but I managed to do it, and I see that my ore dump wasn't more than ten foot away. I mighty near overjumped it; and the next I knew I was on one side of it and those Apaches on the other. Probably I flew; leastways I don't seem to remember jumping.

"That didn't seem to do me much good. The renegades were grinning and laughing to think how easy a thing they had; and I couldn't rightly think up any arguments against the notion—at least from their standpoint. They were chattering away to each other in Mexican for the benefit of Maria. Oh, they had me all distributed, down to my suspender buttons! And me squatting behind that ore dump about as formidable as a brush rabbit!

"Then, all at once, one of my shots went off down in the shaft.

"'Boom!' says she, plenty big; and a slather of rocks and stones come out of the mouth, and began to dump down promiscuous on the scenery. I got one little one in the shoulder blade, and found time to wish my ore dump had a roof. But those renegades caught it square in the thick of trouble. One got knocked out entirely for a minute, by a nice piece of country rock in the head.

"'Otra vez!' yells I, which means 'again.'

"'Boom!' goes the Ole Virginia prompt as an answer.

"I put in my time dodging, but when I gets a chance to look, the Apaches has all got to cover and is looking scared.

"'Otra vez!' yells I again.

"'Boom!' says the Ole Virginia.

"This was the biggest shot of the lot, and she surely cut loose. I ought to have been halfway up the hill watching things from a safe distance, but I wasn't. Lucky for me the shaft was a little on the drift, so she didn't quite shoot my way. But she distributed about a ton over those renegades. They sort of half got to their feet uncertain.

"'Otra vez!' yells I once more, as bold as if I could keep her shooting all day.

"It was just a cold, raw blazer; and if it didn't go through I could see me as an Apache parlor ornament. But it did. Those Chiricahuas give one yell and skipped. It was surely a funny sight, after they got aboard their war ponies, to see them trying to dig out on horses too tired to trot.

"I didn't stop to get all the laughs, though. In fact, I give one jump off that ledge, and I lit a-running. A quarter-hoss couldn't have beat me to that shack. There I grabbed my good old gun, old Meat-in-the-pot, and made a climb for the tall country."

Uncle Jim stopped with an air of finality, and began lazily to refill his pipe. From the open mud fireplace he picked a coal. Outside, the rain, faithful to the prophecy of the wide-ringed sun, beat fitfully against the roof.

"That was the closest call I ever had," said he at last.

V.—THE WEIGHT OF OBLIGATION[5]

By Rex Beach

This is the story of a burden, the tale of a load that irked a strong man's shoulders. To those who do not know the North it may seem strange, but to those who understand the humors of men in solitude, and the extravagant vagaries that steal in upon their minds, as fog drifts with the night, it will not appear unusual. There are spirits in the wilderness, eerie forces which play pranks; some droll or whimsical, others grim.

Johnny Cantwell and Mortimer Grant were partners, trail mates, brothers in soul if not in blood. The ebb and flood of frontier life had brought them together, its hardships had united them until they were as one. They were something of a mystery to each other, neither having surrendered all his confidence, and because of this they retained their mutual attraction. They had met by accident, but they remained together by desire.

The spirit of adventure bubbled merrily within them, and it led them into curious byways. It was this which sent them northward from the States in the dead of winter, on the heels of the Stony River strike; it was this which induced them to land at Katmai instead of Illiamna, whither their land journey should have commenced.

"There are two routes over the coast range," the captain of the *Dora* told them, "and only two. Illiamna Pass is low and easy, but the distance is longer than by way of Katmai. I can land you at either place."

"Katmai is pretty tough, isn't it?" Grant inquired.

"We've understood it's the worst pass in Alaska." Cantwell's eyes were eager.

"It's awful! Nobody travels it except natives, and they don't like it. Now, Illiamna—"

"We'll try Katmai. Eh, Mort?"

"Sure! They don't come hard enough for us, Cap. We'll see if it's as bad as it's painted."

So, one gray January morning they were landed on a frozen beach, their outfit was flung ashore through the surf, the lifeboat pulled away, and the *Dora* disappeared after a farewell toot of her whistle. Their last glimpse of her showed the captain waving good-by and the purser flapping a red tablecloth at them from the after-deck.

"Cheerful place, this," Grant remarked, as he noted the desolate surroundings of dune and hillside.

The beach itself was black and raw where the surf washed it, but elsewhere all was white, save for the thickets of alder and willow which protruded nakedly. The bay was little more than a hollow scooped out of the Alaskan range; along the foothills behind there was a belt of spruce and cottonwood and birch. It was a lonely and apparently unpeopled wilderness in which they had been set down.

"Seems good to be back in the North again, doesn't it?" said Cantwell, cheerily. "I'm tired of the booze, and the street cars, and the dames, and all that civilized stuff. I'd rather be broke in Alaska—with you—than a banker's son, back home."

Soon a globular Russian half-breed, the Katmai trader, appeared among the dunes, and with him were some native villagers. That night the partners slept in a snug log cabin, the roof of which was chained down with old ships' cables. Petellin, the fat little trader, explained that roofs in Katmai had a way of sailing off to seaward when the wind blew. He listened to their plan of crossing the divide and nodded.

It could be done, of course, he agreed, but they were foolish to try it, when the Illiamna route was open. Still, now that they were here, he would find dogs for them, and a guide. The village hunters were out after meat, however, and until they returned the white men would need to wait in patience.

There followed several days of idleness, during which Cantwell and Grant amused themselves around the village, teasing the squaws, playing games with the boys, and flirting harmlessly with the girls, one of whom, in particular, was not unattractive. She was perhaps three-quarters Aleut, the other quarter being plain coquette, and, having been educated at the town of Kodiak, she knew the ways and the wiles of the white man.

Cantwell approached her, and she met his extravagant advances more than halfway. They were getting along nicely together when Grant, in a spirit of fun, entered the game and won her fickle smiles for himself. He joked his partner unmercifully, and Johnny accepted defeat gracefully, never giving the matter a second thought.

When the hunters returned, dogs were bought, a guide was hired, and, a week after landing, the friends were camped at timber line awaiting a favorable moment for their dash across the range. Above them, white hillsides rose in irregular leaps to the gash in the saw-toothed barrier which formed the pass; below them a short valley led down to Katmai and the sea. The day was bright, the air clear, nevertheless after the guide had stared up at the peaks for a time he shook his head, then reëntered the tent and lay down. The mountains were "smoking"; from their tops streamed a gossamer veil which the travelers knew to be drifting snow clouds carried by the wind. It meant delay, but they were patient.

They were up and going on the following morning, however, with the Indian in the lead. There was no trail; the hills were steep; in places they were forced to unload the sled and hoist their outfit by means of ropes, and as they mounted higher the snow deepened. It lay like loose sand, only lighter; it shoved ahead of the sled in a feathery mass; the dogs wallowed in it and were unable to pull, hence the greater part of the work devolved upon the men. Once above the foothills and into the range proper, the going became more level, but the snow remained knee-deep.

The Indian broke trail stolidly; the partners strained at the sled, which hung back like a leaden thing. By afternoon the dogs had become disheartened and refused to heed the whip. There was neither fuel nor running water, and therefore the party did not pause for luncheon. The men were sweating profusely from their exertions and had long since become parched with thirst, but the dry snow was like chalk and scoured their throats.

Cantwell was the first to show the effects of his unusual exertions, for not only had he assumed a lion's share of the work, but the last few months of easy living had softened his muscles, and in consequence his vitality was quickly spent. His undergarments were drenched; he was fearfully dry inside; a terrible thirst seemed to penetrate his whole body; he was forced to rest frequently.

Grant eyed him with some concern, finally inquiring, "Feel bad, Johnny?"

Cantwell nodded. Their fatigue made both men economical of language.

"What's the matter?"

"Thirsty!" The former could barely speak.

"There won't be any water till we get across. You'll have to stand it."

They resumed their duties; the Indian "swish-swished" ahead, as if wading through a sea of swan's-down; the dogs followed listlessly; the partners leaned against the stubborn load.

A faint breath finally came out of the north, causing Grant and the guide to study the sky anxiously. Cantwell was too weary to heed the increasing cold. The snow on the slopes above began to move; here and there, on exposed ridges, it rose in clouds and puffs; the cleancut outlines of the hills became obscured as by a fog; the languid wind bit cruelly.

After a time Johnny fell back upon the sled and exclaimed: "I'm—all in, Mort. Don't seem to have the—guts." He was pale, his eyes were tortured. He scooped a mitten full of snow and raised it to his lips, then spat it out, still dry.

"Here! Brace up!" In a panic of apprehension at this collapse Grant shook him; he had never known Johnny to fail like this. "Take a drink; it'll do you good." He drew a bottle from one of the dunnage bags and Cantwell seized it avidly. It was wet; it would quench his thirst, he thought. Before Mort could check him he had drunk a third of the contents.

The effect was almost instantaneous, for Cantwell's stomach was empty and his tissues seemed to absorb the liquor like a dry sponge; his fatigue fell away, he became suddenly strong and vigorous again. But before he had gone a hundred yards the reaction followed. First his mind grew thick, then his limbs became unmanageable and his muscles flabby. He was drunk. Yet it was a strange and dangerous intoxication, against which he struggled desperately. He fought it for perhaps a quarter of a mile before it mastered him; then he gave up.

Both men knew that stimulants are never taken on the trail, but they had never stopped to reason why, and even now they did not attribute Johnny's breakdown to the brandy. After a while he stumbled and fell, then, the cool snow being grateful to his face, he sprawled there motionless until Mort dragged him to the sled. He stared at his partner in perplexity and laughed foolishly. The wind was increasing, darkness was near, they had not yet reached the Bering slope.

Something in the drunken man's face frightened Grant and, extracting a ship's biscuit from the grub box, he said, hurriedly: "Here, Johnny. Get something under your belt, quick."

Cantwell obediently munched the hard cracker, but there was no moisture on his tongue; his throat was paralyzed; the crumbs crowded themselves from the corners of his lips. He tried with limber fingers to stuff them down, or to assist the muscular action of swallowing, but finally expelled them in a cloud. Mort drew the parka hood over his partner's head, for the wind cut like a scythe and the dogs were turning tail to it, digging holes in the snow for protection. The air about them was like yeast; the light was fading.

The Indian snowshoed his way back, advising a quick camp until the storm abated, but to this suggestion Grant refused to listen, knowing only too well the peril of such a course. Nor did he dare take Johnny on the sled, since the fellow was half asleep already, but instead whipped up the dogs and urged his companion to follow as best he could.

When Cantwell fell, for a second time, he returned, dragged him forward, and tied his wrists firmly, yet loosely, to the load.

The storm was pouring over them now, like water out of a spout; it seared and blinded them; its touch was like that of a flame. Nevertheless they struggled on into the smother, making what headway they could. The Indian led, pulling at the end of a rope; Grant strained at the sled and hoarsely encouraged the dogs; Cantwell stumbled and lurched in the rear like an unwilling prisoner. When he fell his companion lifted him, then beat him, cursed him, tried in every way to rouse him from his lethargy.

After an interminable time they found they were descending and this gave them heart to plunge ahead more rapidly. The dogs began to trot as the sled overran them; they rushed blindly into gullies, fetching up at the bottom in a tangle, and Johnny followed in a nerveless, stupefied condition. He was dragged like a sack of flour for his legs were limp and he lacked muscular control, but every dash, every fall, every quick descent drove the sluggish blood through his veins and cleared his brain momentarily. Such moments were fleeting, however; much of the time his mind was a blank, and it was only by a mechanical effort that he fought off unconsciousness.

He had vague memories of many beatings at Mort's hands, of the slippery clean-swept ice of a stream over which he limply skidded, of being carried into a tent where a candle flickered and a stove roared. Grant was holding something hot to his lips, and then—

It was morning. He was weak and sick; he felt as if he had awakened from a hideous dream. "I played out, didn't I?" he queried, wonderingly.

"You sure did," Grant laughed. "It was a tight squeak, old boy. I never thought I'd get you through."

"Played out! I—can't understand it." Cantwell prided himself on his strength and stamina, therefore the truth was unbelievable. He and Mort had long been partners, they had given and taken much at each other's hands, but this was something altogether different. Grant had saved his life, at risk of his own; the older man's endurance had been the greater and he had used it to good advantage. It embarrassed Johnny tremendously to realize that he had proved unequal to his share of the work, for he had never before experienced such an obligation. He apologized repeatedly during the few days he lay sick, and meanwhile Mort waited upon him like a mother.

Cantwell was relieved when at last they had abandoned camp, changed guides at the next village, and were on their way along the coast, for somehow he felt very sensitive about his collapse. He was, in fact, extremely ashamed of himself.

Once he had fully recovered he had no further trouble, but soon rounded into fit condition and showed no effects of his ordeal. Day after day he and Mort traveled through the solitudes, their isolation broken only by occasional glimpses of native villages, where they rested briefly and renewed their supply of dog feed.

But although the younger man was now as well and strong as ever, he was uncomfortably conscious that his trail mate regarded him as the weaker of the two and shielded him in many ways. Grant performed most of the unpleasant tasks, and occasionally cautioned Johnny about overdoing. This protective attitude at first amused, then offended Cantwell, it galled him until he was upon the point of voicing his resentment, but reflected that he had no right to object, for, judging by past performances, he had proved his inferiority. This uncomfortable realization forever arose to prevent open rebellion, but he asserted himself secretly by robbing Grant of his self-appointed tasks. He rose first in the mornings, he did the cooking, he lengthened his turns ahead of the dogs, he mended harness after the day's hike had ended. Of course the older man objected, and for a time they had a good-natured rivalry as to who should work and who should rest—only it was not quite so good-natured on Cantwell's part as he made it appear.

Mort broke out in friendly irritation one day: "Don't try to do everything, Johnny. Remember I'm no cripple."

"Humph! You proved that. I guess it's up to me to do your work."

"Oh, forget that day on the pass, can't you?"

Johnny grunted a second time, and from his tone it was evident that he would never forget, unpleasant though the memory remained. Sensing his sullen resentment, the other tried to rally him, but made a bad job of it. The humor of men in the open is not delicate; their wit and their words become coarsened in direct proportion as they revert to the primitive; it is one effect of the solitudes.

Grant spoke extravagantly, mockingly, of his own superiority in a way which ordinarily would have brought a smile to Cantwell's lips, but the latter did not smile. He taunted Johnny humorously on his lack of physical prowess, his lack of good looks and manly qualities—something which had never failed to result in a friendly exchange of badinage; he even teased him about his defeat with the Katmai girl.

Cantwell did respond finally, but afterward he found himself wondering if Mort could have been in earnest. He dismissed the thought with some impatience. But men on the trail have too much time for their thoughts; there is nothing in the monotonous routine of the day's work to distract them, so the partner who had played out dwelt more and more upon his debt and upon his friend's easy assumption of preëminence. The weight of obligation began to chafe him, lightly at first, but with ever-increasing discomfort. He began to think that Grant honestly considered himself the better man, merely because chance had played into his hands.

It was silly, even childish, to dwell on the subject, he reflected, and yet he could not banish it from his mind. It was always before him, in one form or another. He felt the strength in his lean muscles, and sneered at the thought that Mort should be deceived. If it came to a physical test he felt sure he could break his slighter partner with his bare hands, and as for endurance—well, he was hungry for a chance to demonstrate it.

They talked little; men seldom converse in the wastes, for there is something about the silence of the wilderness which discourages speech. And no land is so grimly silent, so hushed and soundless, as the frozen North. For days they marched through desolation, without glimpse of human habitation, without sight of track or trail, without sound of a human voice to break the monotony. There was no game in the country, with the exception of an occasional bird or rabbit, nothing but the white hills, the fringe of alder tops along the watercourses, and the thickets of gnarled, unhealthy spruce in the smothered valleys.

Their destination was a mysterious stream at the headwaters of the unmapped Kuskokwim, where rumor said there was gold, and whither they feared other men were hastening from the mining country far to the north.

Now it is a penalty of the White Country that men shall think of women; Cantwell began to brood upon the Katmai girl, for she was the last; her eyes were haunting and distance had worked its usual enchantment. He reflected that Mort had shouldered him aside and won her favor, then boasted of it. Johnny awoke one night with a dream of her, and lay quivering.

"She was only a squaw," he said, half aloud. "If I'd really tried—"

Grant lay beside him, snoring, the heat of their bodies intermingled. The waking man tried to compose himself, but his partner's stertorous breathing irritated him beyond measure; for a long time he remained motionless, staring into the gray blurr of the tent top. He had played out. He owed his life to the man who had cheated him of the Katmai girl, and that man knew it. He had become a weak, helpless thing, dependent upon another's strength, and that other now accepted his superiority as a matter of course. The obligation was insufferable, and—it was unjust. The North had played him a devilish trick, it had betrayed him, it had bound him to his benefactor with chains of gratitude which were irksome. Had they been real chains they could have galled him no more than at this moment.

As time passed the men spoke less frequently to each other. Grant joshed his mate roughly, once or twice, masking beneath an assumption of jocularity his own vague irritation at the change that had come over them. It was as if he had probed at an open wound with clumsy fingers.

Cantwell had by this time assumed most of those petty camp tasks which provoke tired trailers, those humdrum duties which are so trying to exhausted nerves, and of course they wore upon him as they wear upon every man. But, once he had taken them over, he began to resent Grant's easy relinquishment; it rankled him to realize how willingly the other allowed him to do the cooking, the dish-washing, the fire-building, the bed-making. Little monotonies of this kind form the hardest part of winter travel, they are the rocks upon which friendships founder and partnerships are wrecked. Out on the trail, nature equalizes the work to a great extent, and no man can shirk unduly, but in camp, inside the cramped confines of a tent pitched on boughs laid over the snow, it is very different. There one must busy himself while the other rests and keeps his legs out of the way if possible. One man sits on the bedding at the rear of the shelter, and shivers, while the other squats over a tantalizing fire of green wood, blistering his face and parboiling his limbs inside his sweaty clothing. Dishes must be passed, food divided, and it is poor food, poorly prepared at best. Sometimes men criticize and voice longings for better grub and better cooking. Remarks of this kind have been known to result in tragedies, bitter words and flaming curses—then, perhaps, wild actions, memories of which the later years can never erase.

It is but one prank of the wilderness, one grim manifestation of its silent forces.

Had Grant been unable to do his part Cantwell would have willingly accepted the added burden, but Mort was able, he was nimble and "handy," he was the better cook of the two; in fact, he was the better man in every way—or so he believed. Cantwell sneered at the last thought, and the memory of his debt was like bitter medicine.

His resentment—in reality nothing more than a phase of insanity begot of isolation and silence—could not help but communicate itself to his companion, and there resulted a mutual antagonism, which grew into a dislike, then festered into something more, something strange, reasonless, yet terribly vivid and amazingly potent for evil. Neither man ever mentioned it—their tongues were clenched between their teeth and they held themselves in check with harsh hands—but it was constantly in their minds, nevertheless. No man who has not suffered the manifold irritations of such an intimate association can appreciate the gnawing canker of animosity like this. It was dangerous because there was no relief from it: the two were bound together as by gyves; they shared each other's every action and every plan; they trod in each other's tracks, slept in the same bed, ate from the same plate. They were like prisoners ironed to the same staple.

Each fought the obsession in his own way, but it is hard to fight the impalpable, hence their sick fancies grew in spite of themselves. Their minds needed food to prey upon, but found none. Each began to criticize the other silently, to sneer at his weaknesses, to meditate derisively upon his peculiarities. After a time they no longer resisted the advance of these poisonous thoughts, but welcomed it.

On more than one occasion the embers of their wrath were upon the point of bursting into flame, but each realized that the first ill-considered word would serve to slip the leash from those demons that were straining to go free, and so managed to restrain himself.

The crisis came one crisp morning when a dog team whirled around a bend in the river and a white man hailed them. He was the mail carrier, on his way out from Nome, and he brought news of the "inside."

"Where are you boys bound for?" he inquired when greetings were over and gossip of the trail had passed.

"We're going to the Stony River strike," Grant told him.

"Stony River? Up the Kuskokwim?"

"Yes!"

The mail man laughed. "Can you beat that? Ain't you heard about Stony River?"

"No!"

"Why, it's a fake—no such place."

There was a silence; the partners avoided each other's eyes.

"MacDonald, the fellow that started it, is on his way to Dawson. There's a gang after him, too, and if he's caught it'll go hard with him. He wrote the letters—to himself—and spread the news just to raise a grubstake. He cleaned up big before they got onto him. He peddled his tips for real money."

"Yes!" Grant spoke quietly. "Johnny bought one. That's what brought us from Seattle. We went out on the last boat and figured we'd come in from this side before the break-up. So—fake!"

"Gee! You fellers bit good." The mail carrier shook his head. "Well! You'd better keep going now; you'll get to Nome before the season opens. Better take dogfish from Bethel—it's four bits a pound on the Yukon. Sorry I didn't hit your camp last night; we'd 'a' had a visit. Tell the gang that you saw me." He shook hands ceremoniously, yelled at his panting dogs, and went swiftly on his way, waving a mitten on high as he vanished around the next bend.

The partners watched him go, then Grant turned to Johnny, and repeated: "Fake! MacDonald stung you."

Cantwell's face went as white as the snow behind him, his eyes blazed. "Why did you tell him I bit?" he demanded harshly.

"Hunh! *Didn't* you bite? Two thousand miles afoot; three months of Hades; for nothing. That's biting some."

"*Well!*" The speaker's face was convulsed, and Grant's flamed with an answering anger. They glared at each other for a moment. "Don't blame me. You fell for it, too."

"I— —" Mort checked his rushing words.

"Yes, *you!* Now, what are you going to do about it? Welsh?"

"I'm going through to Nome." The sight of his partner's rage had set Mort to shaking with a furious desire to fly at his throat, but fortunately, he retained a spark of sanity.

"Then shut up, and quit chewing the rag. You—talk too much."

Mort's eyes were bloodshot; they fell upon the carbine under the sled lashings, and lingered there, then wavered. He opened his lips, reconsidered, spoke softly to the team, then lifted the heavy dog whip and smote the Malemutes with all his strength.

The men resumed their journey without further words, but each was cursing inwardly.

"So! I talk too much," Grant thought. The accusation struck in his mind and he determined to speak no more.

"He blames me," Cantwell reflected, bitterly. "I'm in wrong again and he couldn't keep his mouth shut. A fine partner, he is!"

All day they plodded on, neither trusting himself to speak. They ate their evening meal like mutes; they avoided each other's eyes. Even the guide noticed the change and looked on curiously.

There were two robes and these the partners shared nightly, but their hatred had grown so during the past few hours that the thought of lying side by side, limb to limb, was distasteful.

Yet neither dared suggest a division of the bedding, for that would have brought further words and resulted in the crash which they longed for, but feared. They stripped off their furs, and lay down beside each other with the same repugnance they would have felt had there been a serpent in the couch.

This unending malevolent silence became terrible. The strain of it increased, for each man now had something definite to cherish in the words and the looks that had passed. They divided the camp work with scrupulous nicety, each man waited upon himself and asked no favors. The knowledge of his debt forever chafed Cantwell; Grant resented his companion's lack of gratitude.

Of course they spoke occasionally—it was beyond human endurance to remain entirely dumb—but they conversed in monosyllables, about trivial things, and their voices were throaty, as if the effort choked them. Meanwhile they continued to glow inwardly at a white heat.

Cantwell no longer felt the desire merely to match his strength against Grant's; the estrangement had become too wide for that; a physical victory would have been flat and tasteless; he craved some deeper satisfaction. He began to think of the ax—just how or when or why he never knew. It was a thin-bladed, polished thing of frosty steel, and the more he thought of it the stronger grew his impulse to rid himself once for all of that presence which exasperated him. It would be very easy, he reasoned; a sudden blow, with the weight of his shoulders behind it—he fancied he could feel the bit sink into Grant's flesh, cleaving bone and cartilages in its course—a slanting downward stroke, aimed at the neck where it joined the body, and he would be forever satisfied. It would be ridiculously simple. He practiced in the gloom of evening as he felled spruce trees for firewood; he guarded the ax religiously; it became a living thing which urged him on to violence. He saw it standing by the tent fly when he closed his eyes to sleep; he dreamed of it; he sought it out with his eyes when he first awoke. He slid it loosely under the sled lashings every morning, thinking that its use could not long be delayed.

As for Grant, the carbine dwelt forever in his mind, and his fingers itched for it. He secretly slipped a cartridge into the chamber, and when an occasional ptarmigan offered itself for a target he saw the white spot on the breast of Johnny's reindeer parka, dancing ahead of the Lyman bead.

The solitude had done its work; the North had played its grim comedy to the final curtain, making sport of men's affections and turning love to rankling hate. But into the mind of each man crept a certain craftiness. Each longed to strike, but feared to face the consequences. It was lonesome, here among the white hills and the deathly silences, yet they reflected that it would be still more lonesome if they were left to keep step with nothing more substantial than a memory. They determined, therefore, to wait until civilization was nearer, meanwhile rehearsing the moment they knew was inevitable. Over and over in their thoughts each of them enacted the scene, ending it always with the picture of a prostrate man in a patch of trampled snow which grew crimson as the other gloated.

They paused at Bethel Mission long enough to load with dried salmon, then made the ninety-mile portage over lake and tundra to the Yukon. There they got their first touch of the "inside" world. They camped in a barabora where white men had slept a few nights before, and heard their own language spoken by native tongues. The time was growing short now, and they purposely dismissed their guide, knowing that the trail was plain from there on. When they hitched up, on the next morning, Cantwell placed the ax, bit down, between the tarpaulin and the sled rail, leaving the helve projecting where his hand could reach it. Grant thrust the barrel of the rifle beneath a lashing, with the butt close by the handle-bars, and it was loaded.

A mile from the village they were overtaken by an Indian and his squaw, traveling light behind hungry dogs. The natives attached themselves to the white men and hung stubbornly to their heels, taking advantage of their tracks. When night came they camped alongside, in the hope of food. They announced that they were bound for St. Michaels, and in spite of every effort to shake them off they remained close behind the partners until that point was reached.

At St. Michaels there were white men, practically the first Johnny and Mort had encountered since landing at Katmai, and for a day at least they were sane. But there were still three hundred miles to be traveled, three hundred miles of solitude and haunting thoughts. Just as they were about to start, Cantwell came upon Grant and the A. C. agent, and heard his name pronounced, also the word "Katmai." He noted that Mort fell silent at his approach, and instantly his anger blazed afresh. He decided that the latter had been telling the story of their experience on the pass and boasting of his service. So much the better, he thought, in a blind rage; that which he planned doing would appear all the more like an accident, for who would dream that a man could kill the person to whom he owed his life?

That night he waited for a chance.

They were camped in a dismal hut on a wind-swept shore; they were alone. But Grant was waiting also, it seemed. They lay down beside each other, ostensibly to sleep; their limbs touched; the warmth from their bodies intermingled, but they did not close their eyes.

They were up and away early, with Nome drawing rapidly nearer. They had skirted an ocean, foot by foot; Bering Sea lay behind them, now, and its northern shore swung westward to their goal. For two months they had lived in silent animosity, feeding on bitter food while their elbows rubbed.

Noon found them floundering through one of those unheralded storms which make coast travel so hazardous. The morning had turned off gray, the sky was of a leaden hue which blended perfectly with the snow underfoot, there was no horizon, it was impossible to see more than a few yards in any direction. The trail soon became obliterated and their eyes began to play tricks. For all they could distinguish, they might have been suspended in space; they seemed to be treading the measures of an endless dance in the center of a whirling cloud. Of course it was cold, for the wind off the open sea was damp, but they were not men to turn back.

They soon discovered that their difficulty lay not in facing the storm, but in holding to the trail. That narrow, two-foot causeway, packed by a winter's travel and frozen into a ribbon of ice by a winter's frosts, afforded their only avenue of progress, for the moment they left it the sled plowed into the loose snow, well-nigh disappearing and bringing the dogs to a standstill. It was the duty of the driver, in such case, to wallow forward, right the load if necessary, and lift it back into place. These mishaps were forever occurring, for it was impossible to distinguish the trail beneath its soft covering. However, if the driver's task was hard it was no more trying than that of the man ahead, who was compelled to feel out and explore the ridge of hardened snow and ice with his feet, after the fashion of a man walking a plank in the dark. Frequently he lunged into the drifts with one foot, or both; his glazed mukluk soles slid about, causing him to bestride the invisible hogback, or again his legs crossed awkwardly, throwing him off his balance. At times he wandered away from the path entirely and had to search it out again. These exertions were very wearing and they were dangerous, also, for joints are easily dislocated, muscles twisted, and tendons strained.

Hour after hour the march continued, unrelieved by any change, unbroken by any speck or spot of color. The nerves of their eyes, wearied by constant nearsighted peering at the snow, began to jump so that vision became untrustworthy. Both travelers appreciated the necessity of clinging to the trail, for, once they lost it, they knew they might wander about indefinitely until they chanced to regain it or found their way to the shore, while always to seaward was the menace of open water, of air holes, or cracks which might gape beneath their feet like jaws. Immersion in this temperature, no matter how brief, meant death.

The monotony of progress through this unreal, leaden world became almost unbearable. The repeated strainings and twistings they suffered in walking the slippery ridge reduced the men to weariness; their legs grew clumsy and their feet uncertain. Had they found a camping place they would have stopped, but they dared not forsake the thin thread that linked them with safety to go and look for one, not knowing where the shore lay. In storms of this kind men have lain in their sleeping bags for days within a stone's throw of a road-house or village. Bodies have been found within a hundred yards of shelter after blizzards have abated.

Cantwell and Grant had no choice, therefore, except to bore into the welter of drifting flakes.

It was late in the afternoon when the latter met with an accident. Johnny, who had taken a spell at the rear, heard him cry out, saw him stagger, struggle to hold his footing, then sink into the snow. The dogs paused instantly, lay down, and began to strip the ice pellets from between their toes.

Cantwell spoke harshly, leaning upon the handle-bars: "Well! What's the idea?"

It was the longest sentence of the day.

"I've—hurt myself." Mort's voice was thin and strange; he raised himself to a sitting posture, and reached beneath his parka, then lay back weakly. He writhed, his face was twisted with pain. He continued to lie there, doubled into a knot of suffering. A groan was wrenched from between his teeth.

"Hurt? How?" Johnny inquired, dully.

It seemed very ridiculous to see that strong man kicking around in the snow.

"I've ripped something loose—here." Mort's palms were pressed in upon his groin, his fingers were clutching something. "Ruptured—I guess." He tried again to rise, but sank back. His cap had fallen off and his forehead glistened with sweat.

Cantwell went forward and lifted him. It was the first time in many days that their hands had touched, and the sensation affected him strangely. He struggled to repress a devilish mirth at the thought that Grant had played out—it amounted to that and nothing less; the trail had delivered him into his enemy's hands, his hour had struck. Johnny determined to square the debt now, once for all, and wipe his own mind clean of that poison which corroded it. His muscles were strong, his brain clear, he had never felt his strength so irresistible as at this moment, while Mort, for all his boasted superiority, was nothing but a nerveless thing hanging limp against his breast. Providence had arranged it all. The younger man was impelled to give raucous voice to his glee, and yet—his helpless burden exerted an odd effect upon him.

He deposited his foe upon the sled and stared at the face he had not met for many days. He saw how white it was, how wet and cold, how weak and dazed, then as he looked he cursed inwardly, for the triumph of his moment was spoiled.

The ax was there, its polished bit showed like a piece of ice, its helve protruded handily, but there was no need of it now; his fingers were all the weapons Johnny needed; they were more than sufficient, in fact, for Mort was like a child.

Cantwell was a strong man, and, although the North had coarsened him, yet underneath the surface was a chivalrous regard for all things weak, and this the trail madness had not affected. He had longed for this instant, but now that it had come he felt no enjoyment, since he could not harm a sick man and waged no war on cripples. Perhaps, when Mort had rested, they could settle their quarrel; this was as good a place as any. The storm hid them, they would leave no traces, there could be no interruption.

But Mort did not rest. He could not walk; movement brought excruciating pain.

Finally Cantwell heard himself saying: "Better wrap up and lie still for a while. I'll get the dogs underway." His words amazed him dully. They were not at all what he had intended to say.

The injured man demurred, but the other insisted gruffly, then brought him his mittens and cap, slapping the snow out of them before rousing the team to motion. The load was very heavy now, the dogs had no footprints to guide them, and it required all of Cantwell's efforts to prevent capsizing. Night approached swiftly, the whirling snow particles continued to flow past upon the wind, shrouding the earth in an impenetrable pall.

The journey soon became a terrible ordeal, a slow, halting progress that led nowhere and was accomplished at the cost of tremendous exertion. Time after time Johnny broke trail, then returned and urged the huskies forward to the end of his tracks. When he lost the path he sought it out, laboriously hoisted the sledge back into place, and coaxed his four-footed helpers to renewed effort. He was drenched with perspiration, his inner garments were steaming, his outer ones were frozen into a coat of armor; when he paused he chilled rapidly. His vision was untrustworthy, also, and he felt snow blindness coming on. Grant begged him more than once to unroll the bedding and prepare to sleep out the storm; he even urged Johnny to leave him and make a dash for his own safety, but at this the younger man cursed and told him to hold his tongue.

Night found the lone driver slipping, plunging, lurching ahead of the dogs, or shoving at the handle-bars and shouting at the dogs. Finally, during a pause for rest he heard a sound which roused him. Out of the gloom to the right came the faint complaining howl of a malemute; it was answered by his own dogs, and the next moment they had caught a scent which swerved them shoreward and led them scrambling through the drifts. Two hundred yards, and a steep bank loomed above, up and over which they rushed, with Cantwell yelling encouragement; then a light showed, and they were in the lee of a low-roofed hut.

A sick native, huddled over a Yukon stove, made them welcome to his mean abode, explaining that his wife and son had gone to Unalaklik for supplies.

Johnny carried his partner to the one unoccupied bunk and stripped his clothes from him. With his own hands he rubbed the warmth back into Mortimer's limbs, then swiftly prepared hot food, and, holding him in the hollow of his aching arm, fed him, a little at a time. He was like to drop from exhaustion, but he made no complaint. With one folded robe he made the hard boards comfortable, then spread the other as a covering. For himself he sat beside the fire and fought his weariness. When he dozed off and the cold awakened him, he renewed the fire; he heated beef tea, and, rousing Mort, fed it to him with a teaspoon. All night long, at intervals, he tended the sick man, and Grant's eyes followed him with an expression that brought a fierce pain to Cantwell's throat.

"You're mighty good—after the rotten way I acted," the former whispered once.

And Johnny's big hand trembled so that he spilled the broth.

His voice was low and tender as he inquired, "Are you resting easier now?"

The other nodded.

"Maybe you're not hurt badly, after—all. God! That would be awful——" Cantwell choked, turned away, and, raising his arms against the log wall, buried his face in them.

The morning broke clear; Grant was sleeping. As Johnny stiffly mounted the creek bank with a bucket of water he heard a jingle of sleighbells and saw a sled with two white men swing in toward the cabin.

"Hello!" he called, then heard his own name pronounced.

"Johnny Cantwell, by all that's holy!"

The next moment he was shaking hands vigorously with two old friends from Nome.

"Martin and me are bound for Saint Mikes," one of them explained. "Where the deuce did you come from, Johnny?"

"The 'outside.' Started for Stony River, but—"

"Stony River!" The newcomers began to laugh loudly and Cantwell joined them. It was the first time he had laughed for weeks. He realized the fact with a start, then recollected also his sleeping partner, and said:

"Sh-h! Mort's inside, asleep!"

During the night everything had changed for Johnny Cantwell; his mental attitude, his hatred, his whole reasonless insanity. Everything was different now, even his debt was canceled, the weight of obligation was removed, and his diseased fancies were completely cured.

"Yes! Stony River," he repeated, grinning broadly. "I bit!"

Martin burst forth, gleefully: "They caught MacDonald at Holy Cross and ran him out on a limb. He'll never start another stampede. Old man Baker gun-branded him."

"What's the matter with Mort?" inquired the second traveler.

"He's resting up. Yesterday, during the storm he—" Johnny was upon the point of saying "played out," but changed it to "had an accident. We thought it was serious, but a few days' rest'll bring him around all right. He saved me at Katmai, coming in. I petered out and threw up my tail, but he got me through. Come inside and tell him the news."

"Sure thing."

"Well, well!" Martin said. "So you and Mort are still partners, eh?"

"*Still* partners?" Johnny took up the pail of water. "Well, rather! We'll always be partners." His voice was young and full and hearty as he continued: "Why, Mort's the best fellow in the world. I'd lay down my life for him."

VI.—THAT SPOT[6]

By Jack London

I DON'T think much of Stephen Mackaye any more, though I used to swear by him. I know that in those days I loved him more than my brother. If ever I meet Stephen Mackaye again, I shall not be responsible for my actions. It passes beyond me that a man with whom I shared food and blanket, and with whom I mushed over the Chilcoot Trail, should turn out the way he did. I always sized Steve up as a square man, a kindly comrade, without an iota of anything vindictive or malicious in his nature. I shall never trust my judgment in men again. Why, I nursed that man through typhoid fever; we starved together on the headwaters of the Stewart; and he saved my life on the Little Salmon. And now, after the years we were together, all I can say of Stephen Mackaye is that he is the meanest man I ever knew.

We started for the Klondike in the fall rush of 1897, and we started too late to get over Chilcoot Pass before the freeze-up. We packed our outfit on our backs part way over, when the snow began to fly, and then we had to buy dogs in order to sled it the rest of the way. That was how we came to get that Spot. Dogs were high, and we paid one hundred and ten dollars for him. He looked worth it. I say *looked*, because he was one of the finest-appearing dogs I ever saw. He weighed sixty pounds, and he had all the lines of a good sled animal. We never could make out his breed. He wasn't husky, nor Malemute, nor Hudson Bay; he looked like all of them and he didn't look like any of them; and on top of it all he had some of the white man's dog in him, for on one side, in the thick of the mixed yellow-brown-red-and-dirty-white that was his prevailing color, there was a spot of coal-black as big as a water bucket. That was why we called him Spot.

He was a good looker all right. When he was in condition his muscles stood out in bunches all over him. And he was the strongest-looking brute I ever saw in Alaska, also the most intelligent-looking. To run your eyes over him, you'd think he could outpull three dogs of his own weight. Maybe he could, but I never saw it. His intelligence didn't run that way. He could steal and forage to perfection; he had an instinct that was positively gruesome for divining when work was to be done and for making a sneak accordingly; and for getting lost and not staying lost he was nothing short of inspired. But when it came to work, the way that intelligence dribbled out of him and left him a mere clot of wobbling, stupid jelly would make your heart bleed.

There are times when I think it wasn't stupidity. Maybe, like some men I know, he was too wise to work. I shouldn't wonder if he put it all over us with that intelligence of his. Maybe he figured it all out and decided that a licking now and again and no work was a whole lot better than work all the time and no licking. He was intelligent enough for such a computation. I tell you, I've sat and looked into that dog's eyes till the shivers ran up and down my spine and the marrow crawled like yeast, what of the intelligence I saw shining out. I can't express myself about that intelligence. It is beyond mere words. I saw it, that's all. At times it was like gazing into a human soul, to look into his eyes; and what I saw there frightened me and started all sorts of ideas in my own mind of reincarnation and all the rest. I tell you I sensed something big in that brute's eyes; there was a message there, but I wasn't big enough myself to catch it. Whatever it was (I know I'm making a fool of myself)—whatever it was, it baffled me. I can't give an inkling of what I saw in that brute's eyes; it wasn't light, it wasn't color; it was something that moved, away back, when the eyes themselves weren't moving. And I guess I didn't see it move, either; I only sensed that it moved. It was an expression,—that's what it was,—and I got an impression of it. No; it was different from a mere expression; it was more than that. I don't know what it was, but it gave me a feeling of kinship just the same. Oh, no, not sentimental kinship. It was, rather, a kinship of equality. Those eyes never pleaded like a deer's eyes. They challenged. No, it wasn't defiance. It was just a calm assumption of equality. And I don't think it was deliberate. My belief is that it was unconscious on his part. It was there because it was there, and it couldn't help shining out. No, I don't mean shine. It didn't shine; it *moved*. I know I'm talking rot, but if you'd looked into that animal's eyes the way I have, you'd understand. Steve was affected the same way I was. Why, I tried to kill that Spot once—he was no good for anything; and I fell down on it. I led him out into the brush, and he came along slow and unwilling. He knew what was going on. I stopped in a likely place, put my foot on the rope, and pulled my big Colt's. And that dog sat down and looked at me. I tell you he didn't plead. He just looked. And I saw all kinds of incomprehensible things moving, yes, *moving*, in those eyes of his. I didn't really see them move; I thought I saw them, for, as I said before, I guess I only sensed them. And I want to tell you right now that it got beyond me. It was like killing a man, a conscious, brave man who looked calmly into your gun as much as to say, "Who's afraid?" Then, too, the message seemed so near that, instead of pulling the trigger quick, I stopped to see if I could catch the message. There it was, right before me, glimmering all around in those eyes of his. And then it was too late. I got scared. I was trembly all over, and my stomach generated a nervous palpitation that made me seasick. I just sat down and looked at that dog, and he looked at me, till I thought I was going crazy. Do you want to know what I did? I threw down the gun and ran back to camp with the fear of God in my heart. Steve laughed at me. But I notice that Steve led Spot into the woods, a week later, for the same purpose, and that Steve came back alone, and a little later Spot drifted back, too.

At any rate, Spot wouldn't work. We paid a hundred and ten dollars for him from the bottom of our sack, and he wouldn't work. He wouldn't even tighten the traces. Steve spoke to him the first time we put him in harness, and he sort of shivered, that was all. Not an ounce on the traces. He just stood still and wobbled, like so much jelly. Steve touched him with the whip. He yelped, but not an ounce. Steve touched him again, a bit harder, and he howled—the regular long wolf howl. Then Steve got mad and gave him half a dozen, and I came on the run from the tent.

I told Steve he was brutal with the animal, and we had some words—the first we'd ever had. He threw the whip down in the snow and walked away mad. I picked it up and went to it. That Spot trembled and wobbled and cowered before ever I swung the lash, and with the first bite of it he howled like a lost soul. Next he lay down in the snow. I started the rest of the dogs, and they dragged him along, while I threw the whip into him. He rolled over on his back and bumped along, his four legs waving in the air, himself howling as though he was going through a sausage machine. Steve came back and laughed at me, and I apologized for what I'd said.

There was no getting any work out of that Spot; and to make up for it, he was the biggest pig-glutton of a dog I ever saw. On top of that, he was the cleverest thief. These was no circumventing him. Many a breakfast we went without our bacon because Spot had been there first. And it was because of him that we nearly starved to death up the Stewart. He figured out the way to break into our meat cache, and what he didn't eat, the rest of the team did. But he was impartial. He stole from everybody. He was a restless dog, always very busy snooping around or going somewhere. And there was never a camp within five miles that he didn't raid. The worst of it was that they always came back on us to pay his board bill, which was just, being the law of the land; but it was mighty hard on us, especially that first winter on the Chilcoot, when we were busted, paying for whole hams and sides of bacon that we never ate. He could fight, too, that Spot. He could do everything but work. He never pulled a pound, but he was the boss of the whole team. The way he made those dogs stand around was an education. He bullied them, and there was always one or more of them fresh-marked with his fangs. But he was more than a bully. He wasn't afraid of anything that walked on four legs; and I've seen him march, single-handed, into a strange team, without any provocation whatever, and put the *kibosh* on the whole outfit. Did I say he could eat? I caught him eating the whip once. That's straight. He started in at the lash, and when I caught him he was down to the handle, and still going.

But he was a good looker. At the end of the first week we sold him for seventy-five dollars to the Mounted Police. They had experienced dog drivers, and we knew that by the time he'd covered the six hundred miles to Dawson he'd be a good sled dog. I say we *knew*, for we were just getting acquainted with that Spot. A little later we were not brash enough to know anything where he was concerned. A week later we woke up in the morning to the dangedest dog fight we'd ever heard. It was that Spot come back and knocking the team into shape. We ate a pretty depressing breakfast, I can tell you; but cheered up two hours afterward when we sold him to an official courier, bound in to Dawson with government dispatches. That Spot was only three days in coming back, and, as usual, celebrated his arrival with a rough-house.

We spent the winter and spring, after our own outfit was across the pass, freighting other people's outfits; and we made a fat stake. Also, we made money out of Spot. If we sold him once, we sold him twenty times. He always came back, and no one asked for their money. We didn't want the money. We'd have paid handsomely for any one to take him off our hands for keeps. We had to get rid of him, and we couldn't give him away, for that would have been suspicious. But he was such a fine looker that we never had any difficulty in selling him. "Unbroke," we'd say, and they'd pay any old price for him. We sold him as low as twenty-five dollars, and once we got a hundred and fifty for him. That particular party returned him in person, refused to take his money back, and the way he abused us was something awful. He said it was cheap at the price to tell us what he thought of us; and we felt he was so justified that we never talked back. But to this day I've never quite regained all the old self-respect that was mine before that man talked to me.

When the ice cleared out of the lakes and river, we put our outfit in a Lake Bennet boat and started for Dawson. We had a good team of dogs, and of course we piled them on top the outfit. That Spot was along—there was no losing him; and a dozen times, the first day, he knocked one or another of the dogs overboard in the course of fighting with them. It was close quarters, and he didn't like being crowded.

"What that dog needs is space," Steve said the second day. "Let's maroon him."

We did, running the boat in at Caribou Crossing for him to jump ashore. Two of the other dogs, good dogs, followed him; and we lost two whole days trying to find them. We never saw those two dogs again; but the quietness and relief we enjoyed made us decide, like the man who refused his hundred and fifty, that it was cheap at the price. For the first time in months Steve and I laughed and whistled and sang. We were as happy as clams. The dark days were over. The nightmare had been lifted. That Spot was gone.

Three weeks later, one morning, Steve and I were standing on the river bank at Dawson. A small boat was just arriving from Lake Bennett. I saw Steve give a start, and heard him say something that was not nice and that was not under his breath. Then I looked; and there, in the bow of the boat, with ears pricked up, sat Spot. Steve and I sneaked immediately, like beaten curs, like cowards, like absconders from justice. It was this last that the lieutenant of police thought when he saw us sneaking. He surmised that there were law officers in the boat who were after us. He didn't wait to find out, but kept us in sight, and in the M.&.M. saloon got us in a corner. We had a merry time explaining, for we refused to go back to the boat and meet Spot; and finally he held us under guard of another policeman while he went to the boat. After we got clear of him, we started for the cabin, and when we arrived, there was that Spot sitting on the stoop waiting for us. Now how did he know we lived there? There were forty thousand people in Dawson that summer, and how did he *savvy* our cabin out of all the cabins? How did he know we were in Dawson, anyway? I leave it to you. But don't forget what I have said about his intelligence and that immortal something I have seen glimmering in his eyes.

There was no getting rid of him any more. There were too many people in Dawson who had bought him up on Chilcoot, and the story got around. Half a dozen times we put him on board steamboats going down the Yukon; but he merely went ashore at the first landing and trotted back up the bank. We couldn't sell him, we couldn't kill him (both

Steve and I had tried), and nobody else was able to kill him. He bore a charmed life. I've seen him go down in a dog fight on the main street with fifty dogs on top of him, and when they were separated, he'd appear on all his four legs, unharmed, while two of the dogs that had been on top of him would be lying dead.

I saw him steal a chunk of moose meat from Major Dinwiddie's cache so heavy that he could just keep one jump ahead of Mrs. Dinwiddie's squaw cook, who was after him with an ax. As he went up the hill, after the squaw gave out, Major Dinwiddie himself came out and pumped his Winchester into the landscape. He emptied his magazine twice, and never touched that Spot. Then a policeman came along and arrested him for discharging firearms inside the city limits. Major Dinwiddie paid his fine, and Steve and I paid him for the moose meat at the rate of a dollar a pound, bones and all. That was what he paid for it. Meat was high that year.

I am only telling what I saw with my own eyes. And now I'll tell you something, also. I saw that Spot fall through a water hole. The ice was three and a half feet thick, and the current sucked him under like a straw. Three hundred yards below was the big water hole used by the hospital. Spot crawled out of the hospital water hole, licked off the water, bit out the ice that had formed between his toes, trotted up the bank, and whipped a big Newfoundland belonging to the Gold Commissioner.

In the fall of 1898, Steve and I poled up the Yukon on the last water, bound for Stewart River. We took the dogs along, all except Spot. We figured we'd been feeding him long enough. He'd cost us more time and trouble and money and grub than we'd got by selling him on the Chilcoot—especially grub. So Steve and I tied him down in the cabin and pulled our freight. We camped that night at the mouth of Indian River, and Steve and I were pretty facetious over having shaken him. Steve was a funny cuss, and I was just sitting up in the blankets and laughing when a tornado hit camp. The way that Spot walked into those dogs and gave them what-for was hair-raising. Now how did he get loose? It's up to you. I haven't any theory. And how did he get across the Klondike River? That's another facer. And anyway, how did he know we had gone up the Yukon? You see, we went by water, and he couldn't smell our tracks. Steve and I began to get superstitious about that dog. He got on our nerves, too; and, between you and me, we were just a mite afraid of him.

The freeze-up came on when we were at the mouth of Henderson Creek, and we traded him off for two sacks of flour to an outfit that was bound up White River after copper. Now that whole outfit was lost. Never trace nor hide nor hair of men, dogs, sleds, or anything was ever found. They dropped clean out of sight. It became one of the mysteries of the country. Steve and I plugged away up the Stewart, and six weeks afterward that Spot crawled into camp. He was a perambulating skeleton, and could just drag along; but he got there. And what I want to know is who told him we were up the Stewart? We could have gone a thousand other places. How did he know? You tell me, and I'll tell you.

No losing him. At the Mayo he started a row with an Indian dog. The buck who owned the dog took a swing at Spot with an ax, missed him, and killed his own dog. Talk about magic and turning bullets aside—I, for one, consider it a blamed sight harder to turn an ax aside with a big buck at the other end of it. And I saw him do it with my own eyes. That buck didn't want to kill his own dog. You've got to show me.

I told you about Spot breaking into our meat cache. It was nearly the death of us. There wasn't any more meat to be killed, and meat was all we had to live on. The moose had gone back several hundred miles and the Indians with them. There we were. Spring was on, and we had to wait for the river to break. We got pretty thin before we decided to eat the dogs, and we decided to eat Spot first. Do you know what that dog did? He sneaked. Now how did he know our minds were made up to eat him? We sat up nights laying for him, but he never came back, and we ate the other dogs. We ate the whole team.

And now for the sequel. You know what it is when a big river breaks up and a few billion tons of ice go out, jamming and milling and grinding. Just in the thick of it, when the Stewart went out, rumbling and roaring, we sighted Spot out in the middle. He'd got caught as he was trying to cross up above somewhere. Steve and I yelled and shouted and ran up and down the bank, tossing our hats in the air. Sometimes we'd stop and hug each other, we were that boisterous, for we saw Spot's finish. He didn't have a chance in a million. He didn't have any chance at all. After the ice-run, we got into a canoe and paddled down to the Yukon, and down the Yukon to Dawson, stopping to feed up for a week at the cabins at the mouth of Henderson Creek. And as we came in to the bank at Dawson, there sat that Spot, waiting for us, his ears pricked up, his tail wagging, his mouth smiling, extending a hearty welcome to us. Now how did he get out of that ice? How did he know we were coming to Dawson, to the very hour and minute, to be out there on the bank waiting for us?

The more I think of that Spot, the more I am convinced that there are things in this world that go beyond science. On no scientific grounds can that Spot be explained. It's psychic phenomena, or mysticism, or something of that sort, I guess, with a lot of theosophy thrown in. The Klondike is a good country. I might have been there yet, and become a millionaire, if it hadn't been for Spot. He got on my nerves. I stood him for two years altogether, and then I guess my stamina broke. It was the summer of 1899 when I pulled out. I didn't say anything to Steve. I just sneaked. But I fixed it up all right. I wrote Steve a note, and enclosed a package of "rough-on-rats," telling him what to do with it. I was worn down to skin and bone by that Spot, and I was that nervous that I'd jump and look around when there wasn't anybody within hailing distance. But it was astonishing the way I recuperated when I got quit of him. I got back twenty pounds before I arrived in San Francisco, and by the time I'd crossed the ferry to Oakland I was my old self again, so that even my wife looked in vain for any change in me.

Steve wrote to me once, and his letter seemed irritated. He took it kind of hard because I'd left him with Spot. Also, he said he'd used the "rough-on-rats," per directions, and that there was nothing doing. A year went by. I was back in the office and prospering in all ways—even getting a bit fat. And then Steve arrived. He didn't look me up. I read his name in the steamer list, and wondered why. But I didn't wonder long. I got up one morning and found that Spot chained to the gate-post and holding up the milkman. Steve went north to Seattle, I learned, that very morning. I didn't put on any more weight. My wife made me buy him a collar and tag, and within an hour he showed his gratitude by killing her pet Persian cat. There is no getting rid of that Spot. He will be with me until I die, for he'll never die. My appetite is not so good since he arrived, and my wife says I am looking peaked. Last night that Spot got into Mr. Harvey's hen house (Harvey is my next door neighbor) and killed nineteen of his fancy-bred chickens. I shall have to pay for them. My neighbors on the other side quarreled with my wife and then moved out. Spot was the cause of it. And that is why I am disappointed in Stephen Mackaye. I had no idea he was so mean a man.

VII.—WHEN LINCOLN LICKED A BULLY[7]

By Irving Bacheller

In "A Man For the Ages" Irving Bacheller tells the story of Abraham Lincoln's life and career in the form of a novel. He represents that the book is written by the grandson of one Samson Traylor, who is presented as a friend of Lincoln's. The story that follows is an abbreviation of the account of the journey of Samson Traylor and his wife and two children and their dog, Sambo, in 1831, from Vergennes, Vermont, to the Illinois country; and the part "Abe" Lincoln, a clerk in Denton Offut's store at New Salem, had in building a log cabin for them upon their arrival there; and concludes by telling how Lincoln licked a bully.—THE EDITOR.

IN the early summer of 1831 Samson Traylor and his wife, Sarah, and two children left their old home near the village of Vergennes, Vermont, and began their travels toward the setting sun with four chairs, a bread board and rolling-pin, a feather bed and blankets, a small looking-glass, a skillet, an ax, a pack basket with a pad of sole leather on the same, a water pail, a box of dishes, a tub of salt pork, a rifle, a teapot, a sack of meal, sundry small provisions and a violin, in a double wagon drawn by oxen. . . . A young black shepherd dog with tawny points and the name of Sambo followed the wagon or explored the fields and woods it passed.

The boy Josiah—familiarly called Joe—sits beside his mother. He is a slender, sweet-faced boy. He is looking up wistfully at his mother. The little girl Betsey sits between him and her father.

That evening they stopped at the house of an old friend some miles up the dusty road to the north.

"Here we are—goin' west," Samson shouted to the man at the doorstep.

He alighted and helped his family out of the wagon.

"You go right in—I'll take care o' the oxen," said the man.

Samson started for the house with the girl under one arm and the boy under the other. A pleasant-faced woman greeted them with a hearty welcome at the door.

"You poor man! Come right in," she said.

"Poor! I'm the richest man in the world," said he. "Look at the gold on that girl's head—curly, fine gold, too—the best there is. She's Betsey—

my little toy woman—half past seven years old—blue eyes—helps her mother get tired every day. Here's my toy man Josiah—yes, brown hair and brown eyes like Sarah—heart o' gold—helps his mother, too—six times one year old."

"What pretty faces!" said the woman as she stooped and kissed them.

"Yes, ma'am. Got 'em from the fairies," Samson went on. "They have all kinds o' heads for little folks, an' I guess they color 'em up with the blood o' roses an' the gold o' buttercups an' the blue o' violets. Here's this wife o' mine. She's richer'n I am. She owns all of us. We're her slaves."

"Looks as young as she did the day she was married—nine years ago," said the woman.

"Exactly!" Samson exclaimed. "Straight as an arrow and proud! I don't blame her. She's got enough to make her proud I say. I fall in love again every time I look into her big brown eyes."

The talk and laughter brought the dog into the house.

"There's Sambo, our camp follower," said Samson. "He likes us, one and all, but he often feels sorry for us because we cannot feel the joy that lies in buried bones and the smell of a liberty pole or a gate post."

They had a joyous evening and a restful night with these old friends and resumed their journey soon after daylight. They ferried across the lake at Burlington and fared away over the mountains and through the deep forest on the Chateaugay trail. . . .

They had read a little book called *The Country of the Sangamon*. The latter was a word of the Pottawatomies meaning "land of plenty." It was the name of a river in Illinois draining "boundless, flowery meadows of unexampled beauty and fertility, belted with timber, blessed with shady groves, covered with game and mostly level, without a stick or a stone to vex the plowman." Thither they were bound to take up a section of government land.

They stopped for a visit with Elisha Howard and his wife, old friends of theirs, who lived in the village of Malone, which was in Franklin County, New York. There they traded their oxen for a team of horses. They were large gray horses named Pete and Colonel. The latter was fat and good-natured. His chief interest in life was food. Pete was always looking for food and perils. Colonel was the near horse. Now and then Samson threw a sheepskin over his back and put the boy on it and tramped along within arm's reach of Joe's left leg. This was a great delight to the little lad.

They proceeded at a better pace to the Black River country, toward which, in the village of Canton, they tarried again for a visit with Captain Moody and Silas Wright, both of whom had taught school in the town of Vergennes.

They proceeded through DeKalb, Richville and Gouverneur and Antwerp and on to the Sand Plains. They had gone far out of their way for a look at these old friends of theirs.

Every day the children would ask many questions, as they rode along, mainly about the beasts and birds in the dark shadows of the forest through which they passed. These were answered patiently by their father and mother and every answer led to other queries.

"You're a funny pair," said their father one day. "You have to turn over every word we say to see what's under it. I used to be just like ye, used to go out in the lot and tip over every stick and stone I could lift to see the bugs and crickets run. You're always hopin' to see a bear or a panther or a fairy run out from under my remarks."

"Wonder why we don't see no bears?" Joe asked.

"'Cause they always see us first or hear us comin'," said his father. "If you're goin' to see ol' Uncle Bear ye got to pay the price of admission."

"What's that?" Joe asked.

"Got to go still and careful so you'll see him first. If this old wagon didn't talk so loud and would kind o' go on its tiptoes maybe we'd see him. He don't like to be seen. Seems so he was kind o' shamed of himself, an' I wouldn't wonder if he was. He's done a lot o' things to be 'shamed of."

"What's he done?" Joe asked.

"Ketched sheep and pigs and fawns and run off with 'em."

"What does he do with 'em?"

"Eats 'em up. Now you quit. Here's a lot o' rocks and mud and I got to tend to business. You tackle yer mother and chase her up and down the hills a while and let me get my breath."

On the twenty-ninth day after their journey began they came in sight of the beautiful green valley of the Mohawk. As they looked from the hills they saw the roof of the forest dipping down to the river shores and stretching far to the east and west and broken, here and there, by small clearings. Soon they could see the smoke and spires of the thriving village of Utica.

Here they bought provisions and a tin trumpet for Joe, and a doll with a real porcelain face for Betsey, and turned into the great main thoroughfare of the north leading eastward to Boston and westward to a shore of the midland seas. This road was once the great trail of the Iroquois, by them called the Long House, because it had reached from the Hudson to Lake Erie, and in their day had been well roofed with foliage. Here the travelers got their first view of a steam engine. The latter stood puffing and smoking near the village of Utica, to the horror and amazement of the team and the great excitement of those in the wagon. The boy clung to his father for fear of it.

Samson longed to get out of the wagon and take a close look at the noisy monster, but his horses were rearing in their haste to get away, and even a short stop was impossible. Sambo, with his tail between his legs, ran ahead, in a panic, and took refuge in some bushes by the roadside.

"What was that, father?" the boy asked when the horses had ceased to worry over this new peril.

"A steam engyne," he answered. "Sarah, did ye get a good look at it?"

"Yes; if that don't beat all the newfangled notions I ever heard of," she exclaimed.

"It's just begun doin' business," said Samson.

"What does it do?" Joe asked.

"On a railroad track it can grab hold of a house full o' folks and run off with it. Goes like the wind, too."

"Does it eat 'em up?" Joe asked.

"No. It eats wood and oil and keeps yellin' for more. I guess it could eat a cord o' wood and wash it down with half a bucket o' castor oil in about five minutes. It snatches folks away to some place and drops 'em. I guess it must make their hair stand up and their teeth chatter."

"Does it hurt anybody?" Joe asked hopefully.

"Well, sir, if anybody wanted to be hurt and got in its way, I rather guess he'd succeed purty well. It's powerful. Why, if a man was to ketch hold of the tail of a locomotive, and hang on, it would jerk the toe nails right off him."

Joe began to have great respect for locomotives.

Soon they came in view of the famous Erie Canal, hard by the road. Through it the grain of the far West had just begun moving eastward in a tide that was flowing from April to December. Big barges, drawn by mules and horses on its shore, were cutting the still waters of the canal. They stopped and looked at the barges and the long tow ropes and the tugging animals.

"There is a real artificial river, hundreds o' miles long, handmade of the best material, water tight, no snags or rocks or other imperfections, durability guaranteed," said Samson. "It has made the name of DeWitt Clinton known everywhere."

"I wonder what next!" Sarah exclaimed.

They met many teams and passed other movers going west, and some prosperous farms on a road wider and smoother than any they had traveled. They camped that night, close by the river, with a Connecticut family on its way to Ohio with a great load of household furniture on one wagon and seven children in another. There were merry hours for the young, and pleasant visiting between the older folk that evening at the fireside. There was much talk among the latter about the great Erie Canal.

So they fared along through Canandaigua and across the Genesee to the village of Rochester and on through Lewiston and up the Niagara River to the Falls, and camped where they could see the great water flood and hear its muffled thunder. . . .

"Children," said Samson, "I want you to take a good look at that. It's the most wonderful thing in the world and maybe you'll never see it again."

"The Indians used to think that the Great Spirit was in this river," said Sarah.

"Kind o' seems to me they were right," Samson remarked thoughtfully. "Kind o' seems as if the great spirit of America was in that water. It moves on in the way it wills and nothing can stop it. Everything in its current goes along with it. . . ."

They had the lake view and its cool breeze on their way to Silver Creek, Dunkirk and Erie, and a rough way it was in those days.

They fared along through Indiana and over the wide savannas of Illinois, and on the ninety-seventh day of their journey they drove through rolling, grassy, flowering prairies and up a long, hard hill to the small log cabin settlement of New Salem, Illinois, on the shore of the Sangamon. They halted about noon in the middle of this little prairie village, opposite a small clapboarded house. A sign hung over its door which bore the rudely lettered words: "Rutledge's Tavern."

A long, slim, stoop-shouldered young man sat in the shade of an oak tree that stood near a corner of the tavern, with a number of children playing around him. He had sat leaning against the tree trunk reading a book. He had risen as they came near and stood looking at them, with the book under his arm. . . .

He wore a hickory shirt without a collar or coat or jacket. One suspender held up his coarse, linsey trousers, the legs of which fitted closely and came only to a blue yarn zone above his heavy cowhide shoes. Samson writes that he "fetched a sneeze and wiped his big nose with a red handkerchief" as he stood surveying them in silence, while Dr. John Allen, who had sat on the doorstep reading a paper—a kindly-faced man of middle age with a short white beard under his chin—greeted them cheerfully.

The withering sunlight of a day late in August fell upon the dusty street, now almost deserted. Faces at the doors and windows of the little houses were looking out at them. Two ragged boys and a ginger-colored dog came running toward the wagon. The latter and Sambo surveyed each other with raised hair and began scratching the earth, straight-legged, whining meanwhile, and in a moment began to play together. A man in blue jeans who sat on the veranda of a store opposite, leaning against its wall, stopped whittling and shut his jacknife.

"Where do ye hail from?" the Doctor asked.

"Vermont," said Samson.

"All the way in that wagon?"

"Yes, sir."

"I guess you're made o' the right stuff," said the Doctor. "Where ye bound?"

"Don't know exactly. Going to take up a claim somewhere."

"There's no better country than right here. This is the Canaan of America. We need people like you. Unhitch your team and have some dinner and we'll talk things over after you're rested. I'm the doctor here and I ride all over this part o' the country. I reckon I know it pretty well."

A woman in a neat calico dress came out of the door—a strong built and rather well favored woman with blond hair and dark eyes.

"Mrs. Rutledge, these are travelers from the East," said the Doctor. "Give 'em some dinner, and if they can't pay for it, I can. They've come all the way from Vermont."

"Good land! Come right in an' rest yerselves. Abe, you show the gentleman where to put his horses an' lend him a hand."

Abe extended his long arm toward Samson and said "Howdy" as they shook hands.

"When his big hand got hold of mine, I kind of felt his timber," Samson writes. "I says to myself, 'There's a man it would be hard to tip over in a rassle.'"

"What's yer name? How long ye been travelin'? My conscience! Ain't ye wore out?" the hospitable Mrs. Rutledge was asking as she went into the house with Sarah and the children. "You go and mix up with the little ones and let yer mother rest while I git dinner," she said to Joe and Betsey, and added as she took Sarah's shawl and bonnet: "You lop down an' rest yerself while I'm flyin' around the fire."

"Come all the way from Vermont?" Abe asked as he and Samson were unhitching.

"Yes, sir."

"By jing!" the slim giant exclaimed. "I reckon you feel like throwin' off yer harness an' takin' a roll in the grass."

The tavern was the only house in New Salem with stairs in it. Stairs so steep, as Samson writes, that "they were first cousins to the ladder." There were four small rooms above them. Two of these were parted by a partition of cloth hanging from the rafters. In each was a bed and bedstead and smaller beds on the floor. In case there were a number of adult guests the bedstead was screened with sheets hung upon strings.

In one of these rooms the travelers had a night of refreshing sleep.

After riding two days with the Doctor, Samson bought the claim of one Isaac Gollaher to a half section of land a little more than a mile from the western end of the village. He chose a site for his house on the edge of an open prairie.

"Now we'll go over and see Abe," said Dr. Allen, after the deal was made. "He's the best man with an ax and a saw in this part of the country. He clerks for Mr. Offut. Abe Lincoln is one of the best fellows that ever lived—a rough diamond just out of the great mine of the West, that only needs to be cut and polished."

Denton Offut's store was a small log structure about twenty by twenty which stood near the brow of the hill east of Rutledge's Tavern. When they entered it Abe lay at full length on the counter, his head resting on a bolt of blue denim as he studied a book in his hand. He wore the same shirt and one suspender and linsey trousers which he had worn in the dooryard of the tavern, but his feet were covered only by his blue yarn socks.

Abe laid aside his book and rose to a sitting posture.

"Mr. Traylor," said Doctor Allen, "has just acquired an interest in all our institutions. He has bought the Gollaher tract and is going to build a house and some fences. Abe, couldn't you help get the timber out in a hurry so we can have a raising within a week? You know the art of the ax better than any of us."

Abe looked at Samson.

"I reckon he and I would make a good team with the ax," he said. "He looks as if he could push a house down with one hand and build it up with the other. You can bet I'll be glad to help in any way I can."

Next morning at daylight two parties went out in the woods to cut timber for the home of the newcomers. In one party were Harry Needles carrying two axes and a well-filled luncheon pail; Samson with a saw in his hand and the boy Joe on his back; Abe with saw and ax and a small jug of root beer and a book tied in a big red handkerchief and slung around his neck. When they reached the woods Abe cut a pole for the small boy and carried him on his shoulder to the creek and said:

"Now you sit down here and keep order in this little frog city. If you hear a frog say anything improper you fetch him a whack. Don't allow any nonsense. We'll make you Mayor of Frog City."

The men fell to with axes and saws while Harry limbed the logs and looked after the Mayor. Their huge muscles flung the sharp axes into the timber and gnawed through it with a saw. Many big trees fell before noontime when they stopped for luncheon. While they were eating Abe said:

"I reckon we better saw out a few boards this afternoon. Need 'em for the doors. We'll tote a couple of logs up on the side o' that knoll, put 'em on skids an' whip 'em up into boards with the saw."

Samson took hold of the middle of one of the logs and raised it from the ground.

"I guess we can carry 'em," he said.

"Can ye shoulder it?" Abe asked.

"Easy," said Samson as he raised an end of the log, stepped beneath it and, resting its weight on his back, soon got his shoulder near its center and swung it clear of the ground and walked with it to the knollside where he let it fall with a resounding thump that shook the ground. Abe stopped eating and watched every move in this remarkable performance. The ease with which the big Vermonter had so defied the law of gravitation with that unwieldly stick amazed him.

"That thing'll weigh from seven to eight hundred pounds," said he. "I reckon you're the stoutest man in this part o' the state an' I'm quite a man myself. I've lifted a barrel o' whisky and put my mouth to the bung hole. I never drink it."

"Say," he added as he sat down and began eating a doughnut. "If you ever hit anybody take a sledge hammer or a crowbar. It wouldn't be decent to use your fist."

"Don't talk when you've got food in your mouth," said Joe who seemed to have acquired a sense of responsibility for the manners of Abe.

"I reckon you're right," Abe laughed. "A man's ideas ought not to be mingled with cheese and doughnuts."

"Once in a while I like to try myself in a lift," said Samson. "It feels good. I don't do it to show off. I know there's a good many men stouter than I be. I guess you're one of 'em."

"No, I'm too stretched out—my neck is too far from the ground," Abe answered. "I'm like a crowbar. If I can get my big toe or my fingers under anything I can pry some."

After luncheon he took off his shoes and socks.

"When I'm working hard I always try to give my feet a rest and my brain a little work at noontime," he remarked. "My brain is so far behind the procession I have to keep putting the gad on it. Give me twenty minutes of Kirkham and I'll be with you again."

He lay down on his back under a tree with his book in hand and his feet resting on the tree trunk well above him. Soon he was up and at work again.

When they were getting ready to go home that afternoon Joe got into a great hurry to see his mother. It seemed to him that ages had elapsed since he had seen her—a conviction which led to noisy tears.

Abe knelt before him and comforted the boy. Then he wrapped him in his jacket and swung him in the air and started for home with Joe astride his neck.

Samson says in his diary: "His tender play with the little lad gave me another look at the man Lincoln."

"Some one proposed once that we should call that stream the Minnehaha," said Abe as he walked along. "After this Joe and I are going to call it the Minneboohoo."

The women of the little village had met at a quilting party at ten o'clock with Mrs. Martin Waddell. There Sarah had had a seat at the frame and heard all the gossip of the countryside. . . .

So the day passed with them and was interrupted by the noisy entrance of Joe, soon after candlelight, who climbed on the back of his mother's chair and kissed her and in breathless eagerness began to relate the history of his own day.

That ended the quilting party and Sarah and Mrs. Rutledge and her daughter Ann joined Samson and Abe and Harry Needles who were waiting outside and walked to the tavern with them.

John McNeil, whom the Traylors had met on the road near Niagara Falls and who had shared their camp with them, arrived on the stage that evening. . . . Abe came in, soon after eight o'clock, and was introduced to the stranger. All noted the contrast between the two young men as they greeted each other. Abe sat down for a few minutes and looked sadly into the fire but said nothing. He rose presently, excused himself and went away.

Soon Samson followed him. Over at Offut's store he did not find Abe, but Bill Berry was drawing liquor from the spigot of a barrel set on blocks in a shed connected with the rear end of the store and serving it to a number of hilarious young Irishmen. The young men asked Samson to join them.

"No, thank you. I never touch it," he said.

"We'll come over here an' learn ye how to enjoy yerself some day," one of them said.

"I'm pretty well posted on that subject now," Samson answered.

It is likely that they would have begun his schooling at once but when they came out into the store and saw the big Vermonter standing in the candlelight their laughter ceased for a moment. Bill was among them with a well-filled bottle in his hand.

He and the others got into a wagon which had been waiting at the door and drove away with a wild Indian whoop from the lips of one of the young men.

Samson sat down in the candlelight and Abe in a moment arrived.

"I'm getting awful sick o' this business," said Abe.

"I kind o' guess you don't like the whisky part of it," Samson remarked, as he felt a piece of cloth.

"I hate it," Abe went on. "It don't seem respectable any longer."

"Back in Vermont we don't like the whisky business."

"You're right, it breeds deviltry and disorder. In my youth I was surrounded by whisky. Everybody drank it. A bottle or a jug of liquor was thought to be as legitimate a piece of merchandise as a pound of tea or a yard of calico. That's the way I've always thought of it. But lately I've begun to get the Yankee notion about whisky. When it gets into bad company it can raise the devil."

Soon after nine o'clock Abe drew a mattress filled with corn husks from under the counter, cleared away the bolts of cloth and laid it where they had been and covered it with a blanket.

"This is my bed," said he. "I'll be up at five in the morning. Then I'll be making tea here by the fireplace to wash down some jerked meat and a hunk o' bread. At six or a little after I'll be ready to go with you again. Jack Kelso is going to look after the store to-morrow."

He began to laugh.

"Ye know when I went out of the tavern that little vixen stood peekin' into the window—Bim, Jack's girl," said Abe. "I asked her why she didn't go in and she said she was scared. 'Who you 'fraid of?' I asked. 'Oh, I reckon that boy,' says she. And honestly her hand trembled when she took hold of my arm and walked to her father's house with me."

Abe snickered as he spread another blanket. "What a cut-up she is! Say, we'll have some fun watching them two I reckon," he said.

The logs were ready two days after the cutting began. Martin Waddell and Samuel Hill sent teams to haul them. John Cameron and Peter Lukins had brought the window sash and some clapboards from Beardstown in a small flat boat. Then came the day of the raising—a clear, warm day early in September. All the men from the village and the near farms gathered to help make a home for the newcomers. Samson and Jack Kelso went out for a hunt after the cutting and brought in a fat buck and many grouse for the bee dinner, to which every woman of the neighborhood made a contribution of cake or pie or cookies or doughnuts.

"What will be my part?" Samson had inquired of Kelso.

"Nothing but a jug of whisky and a kind word and a house warming," Kelso had answered.

They notched and bored the logs and made pins to bind them and cut those that were to go around the fireplace and window spaces. Strong, willing and well-trained hands hewed and fitted the logs together. Alexander Ferguson lined the fireplace with a curious mortar made of clay in which he mixed grass for a binder. This mortar he rolled into layers called "cats," each eight inches long and three inches thick. Then he laid them against the logs and held them in place with a woven network of sticks. The first fire—a slow one—baked the clay into a rigid stonelike sheath inside the logs and presently the sticks were burned away. The women had cooked the meats by an open fire and spread the dinner on a table of rough boards resting on poles set in crotches. At noon one of them sounded a conch shell. Then with shouts of joy the men hurried to the fireside and for a moment there was a great spluttering over the wash basins. Before they ate every man except Abe and Samson "took a pull at the jug—long or short"—to quote a phrase of the time.

It was a cheerful company that sat down upon the grass around the table with loaded plates. Their food had its extra seasoning of merry jests and loud laughter. Sarah was a little shocked at the forthright directness of their eating, no knives or forks or napkins being needed in that process. Having eaten, washed and packed away their dishes the women went home at two. Before they had gone Samson's ears caught a thunder of horses' feet in the distance. Looking in its direction he saw a cloud of dust in the road and a band of horsemen riding toward them at full speed. Abe came to him and said:

"I see the boys from Clary's Grove are coming. If they get mean let me deal with 'em. It's my responsibility. I wouldn't wonder if they had some of Offut's whisky with them."

The boys arrived in a cloud of dust and a chorus of Indian whoops and dismounted and hobbled their horses. They came toward the workers, led by burly Jack Armstrong, a stalwart, hard-faced blacksmith of about twenty-two with broad, heavy shoulders, whose name has gone into history. They had been drinking some but no one of them was in the least degree off his balance. They scuffled around the jug for a moment in perfect good nature and then Abe and Mrs. Waddell provided them with the best remnants of the dinner. They were rather noisy. Soon they went up on the roof to help with the rafters and the clapboarding. They worked well a few minutes and suddenly they came scrambling down for another pull at the jug. They were out for a spree and Abe knew it and knew further that they had reached the limit of discretion.

"Boys, there are ladies here and we've got to be careful," he said. "Did I ever tell you what Uncle Jerry Holman said of his bull calf? He said the calf was such a *suckcess* that he didn't leave any milk for the family and that while the calf was growin' fat the children was growin' poor. In my opinion you're about fat enough for the present. Let's stick to the job till four o'clock. Then we'll knock off for refreshments."

The young revelers gathered in a group and began to whisper together. Samson writes that it became evident then they were going to make trouble and says:

"We had left the children at Rutledge's in the care of Ann. I went to Sarah and told her she had better go on and see if they were all right.

"'Don't you get in any fight,' she said, which shows that the women knew what was in the air.

"Sarah led the way and the others followed her."

Those big, brawny fellows from the grove when they got merry were looking always for a chance to get mad at some man and turn him into a plaything. A victim had been a necessary part of their sprees. Many a poor fellow had been fastened in a barrel and rolled down hill or nearly drowned in a ducking for their amusement. A chance had come to get mad and they were going to make the most of it. They began to growl with resentment. Some were wigging their leader Jack Armstrong to fight Abe. One of them ran to his horse and brought a bottle from his saddlebag. It began passing from mouth to mouth. Jack Armstrong got the bottle before it was half emptied, drained it and flung it high in the air. Another called him a hog and grappled him around the waist and there was a desperate struggle which ended quickly. Armstrong got a hold on the neck of his assailant and choked him until he let go. This was not enough for the sturdy bully of Clary's Grove. He seized his follower and flung him so roughly on the ground that the latter lay for a moment stunned. Armstrong had got his blood warm and was now ready for action. With a wild whoop he threw off his coat, unbuttoned his right shirtsleeve and rolled it to the shoulder and declared in a loud voice, as he swung his arm in the air, that he could "outjump, outhop, outrun, throw down, drag out an' lick any man in New Salem."

In a letter to his father Samson writes:

"Abe was working at my elbow. I saw him drop his hammer and get up and make for the ladder. I knew something was going to happen and I followed him. In a minute every one was off the roof and out of the building. I guess they knew what was coming. The big lad stood there swinging his arm and yelling like an Injun. It was a big arm and muscled and corded up some but I guess if I'd shoved the calico off mine and held it up he'd a pulled down his sleeve. I suppose the feller's arm had a kind of a mule's kick in it, but, good gracious! If he'd a seen as many arms as you an' I have that have growed up on a hickory helve he'd a known that his was nothing to brag of. I didn't know just how good a man Abe was and I was kind o' scairt for a minute. I never found it so hard work to do nothin' as I did then. Honest my hands kind o' ached. I wanted to go an' cuff that feller's ears an' grab hold o' him an' toss him over the ridge pole. Abe went right up to him an' said:

"'Jack, you ain't half so bad or half so cordy as ye think ye are. You say you can throw down any man here. I reckon I'll have to show ye that you're mistaken. I'll rassle with ye. We're friends an' we won't talk about lickin' each other. Le's have a friendly rassle.'

"In a second the two men were locked together. Armstrong had lunged at Abe with a yell. There was no friendship in the way he took hold. He was going to do all the damage he could in any way he could. He tried to butt with his head and ram his knee into Abe's stomach as soon as they came together. Half-drunk Jack is a man who would bite your ear off. It was no rassle; it was a fight. Abe moved like lightning. He acted awful limber an' well-greased. In a second he had got hold of the feller's neck with his big right hand and hooked his left into the cloth on his hip. In that way he held him off and shook him as you've seen our dog shake a woodchuck. Abe's blood was hot. If the whole crowd had piled on him I guess he would have come out all right, for when he's roused there's something in Abe more than bones and muscles. I suppose it's what I feel when he speaks a piece. It's a kind of lightning. I guess it's what our minister used to call the power of the spirit. Abe said to me afterwards that he felt as if he was fighting for the peace and honor of New Salem.

"A friend of the bully jumped in and tried to trip Abe. Harry Needles stood beside me. Before I could move he dashed forward and hit that feller in the middle of his forehead and knocked him flat. Harry had hit Bap McNoll the cock fighter. I got up next to the kettle then and took the scum off it. Fetched one of them devils a slap with the side of my hand that took the skin off his face and rolled him over and over.

When I looked again Armstrong was going limp. His mouth was open and his tongue out. With one hand fastened to his right leg and the other on the nape of his neck Abe lifted him at arm's length and gave him a toss in the air. Armstrong fell about ten feet from where Abe stood and lay there for a minute. The fight was all out of him and he was kind of dazed and sick. Abe stood up like a giant and his face looked awful solemn.

"'Boys, if there's any more o' you that want trouble you can have some off the same piece,' he said.

"They hung their heads and not one of them made a move or said a word. Abe went to Armstrong and helped him up.

"'Jack, I'm sorry that I had to hurt you,' he said. 'You get on to your horse and go home.'

"'Abe, you're a better man than me,' said the bully, as he offered his hand to Abe. 'I'll do anything you say.'"

So the Clary's Grove gang was conquered. They were to make more trouble but not again were they to imperil the foundations of law and order in the little community of New Salem.

VIII.—THE END OF THE TRAIL[8]

By Clarence E. Mulford

Buck Peters, foreman of Bar-20 Ranch had many cowboys; Pete Wilson, Red Connors, Billy Williams, Johnny Nelson, and a goodly number more, but chief among them was Hopalong Cassidy. Many interesting stories are told about him in "Bar-20 Days" but none of his thrilling experiences ever ended as did the one recited in this most unusual story, "The End of the Trail."—THE EDITOR.

WHEN one finds on his ranch the carcasses of two cows on the same day, and both are skinned, there can be only one conclusion. The killing and skinning of two cows out of herds that are numbered by thousands need not, in themselves, bring lines of worry to any foreman's brow; but there is the sting of being cheated, the possibility of the losses going higher unless a sharp lesson be given upon the folly of fooling with a very keen and active buzz-saw,—and it was the determination of the outfit of the Bar-20 to teach that lesson, and as quickly as circumstances would permit.

It was common knowledge that there was a more or less organized band of shiftless malcontents making its headquarters in and near Perry's Bend, some distance up the river, and the deduction in this case was easy. The Bar-20 cared very little about what went on at Perry's Bend—that was a matter which concerned only the ranches near that town—so long as no vexatious happenings sifted too far south. But they had so sifted, and Perry's Bend, or rather the undesirable class hanging out there, was due to receive a shock before long.

About a week after the finding of the first skinned cows, Pete Wilson tornadoed up to the bunk house with a perforated arm. Pete was on foot, having lost his horse at the first exchange of shots, which accounts for the expression describing his arrival. Pete hated to walk, he hated still more to get shot, and most of all he hated to have to admit that his rifle-shooting was so far below par. He had seen the thief at work and, too eager to work up close to the cattle skinner before announcing his displeasure, had missed the first shot. When he dragged himself out from under his deceased horse the scenery was undisturbed save for a small cloud of dust hovering over a distant rise to the north of him. After delivering a short and bitter monologue he struck out for the ranch and arrived in a very hot and wrathful condition. It was contagious, that condition, and before long the entire outfit was in the saddle and pounding north, Pete overjoyed because his wound was so slight as not to bar him from the chase. The shock was on the way, and as events proved, was to be one long to linger in the minds of the inhabitants of Perry's Bend and the surrounding range.

The patrons of the Oasis liked their tobacco strong. The pungent smoke drifted in sluggish clouds along the low, black ceiling, following its upward slant toward the east wall and away from the high bar at the other end. This bar, rough and strong, ran from the north wall to within a scant two feet of the south wall, the opening bridged by a hinged board which served as an extension to the counter. Behind the bar was a rear door, low and double, the upper part barred securely—the lower part was used most. In front of and near the bar was a large round table, at which four men played cards silently, while two smaller tables were located along the north wall. Besides dilapidated chairs there were half a dozen low wooden boxes partly filled with sand, and attention was directed to the existence and purpose of these by a roughly lettered sign on the wall, reading: "Gents will look for a box first," which the "gents" sometimes did. The majority of the "gents" preferred to aim at various knotholes in the floor and bet on the result, chancing the outpouring of the proprietor's wrath if they missed.

On the wall behind the bar was a smaller and neater request: "Leave your guns with the bartender.—Edwards." This, although a month old, still called forth caustic and profane remarks from the regular frequenters of the saloon, for hitherto restraint in the matter of carrying weapons had been unknown. They forthwith evaded the order in a manner consistent with their characteristics—by carrying smaller guns where they could not be seen. The majority had simply sawed off a generous part of the long barrels of their Colts and Remingtons, which did not improve their accuracy.

Edwards, the new marshal of Perry's Bend, had come direct from Kansas and his reputation as a fighter had preceded him. When he took up his first day's work he was kept busy proving that he was the rightful owner of it and that it had not been exaggerated in any manner or degree. With the exception of one instance the proof had been bloodless, for he reasoned that gun-play should give way, whenever possible, to a crushing "right" or "left" to the point of the jaw or the pit of the stomach. His proficiency in the manly art was polished and thorough and bespoke earnest application. The last doubting Thomas to be convinced came to five minutes after his diaphragm had been rudely and suddenly raised several inches by a low right hook, and as he groped for his bearings and got his wind back again he asked, very feebly, where "Kansas" was; and the name stuck.

The marshal did not like the Oasis; indeed, he went further and cordially hated it. Harlan's saloon was a thorn in his side and he was only waiting for a good excuse to wipe it off the local map. He was the Law, and behind him were the range riders, who would be only too glad to have the nest of rustlers wiped out and its gang of ne'er-do-wells scattered to the four winds. Indeed, he had been given to understand in a most polite and diplomatic way that if this were not done lawfully, they would try to do it themselves, and they had great faith in their ability to handle the situation in a thorough and workmanlike manner. This would not do in a law-abiding community, as he called the town, and so he had replied that the work was his, and that it would be performed as soon as he believed himself justified to act. Harlan and his friends were fully conversant with the feeling against them and had become a little more cautious, alertly watching out for trouble.

On the evening of the day which saw Pete Wilson's discomfiture most of the *habitués* had assembled in the Oasis where, besides the card-players already mentioned, eight men lounged against the bar. There was some laughter, much subdued talking, and a little whispering. More whispering went on under that roof than in all the other places in town put together; for here rustling was planned, wayfaring strangers were "trimmed" in "frame-up" at cards, and a hunted man was certain to find assistance. Harlan had once boasted that no fugitive had ever been taken from his saloon, and he was behind the bar and standing on the trap door which led to the six-by-six cellar when he made the assertion. It was true, for only those in his confidence knew of the place of refuge under the floor: it had been dug at night and the dirt carefully disposed of.

It had not been dark very long before talking ceased and card-playing was suspended while all looked up as the front door crashed open and two punchers entered, looking the crowd over with critical care.

"Stay here, Johnny," Hopalong told his youthful companion, and then walked forward, scrutinizing each scowling face in turn, while Johnny stood with his back to the door, keenly alert, his right hand resting lightly on his belt not far from the holster.

Harlan's thick neck grew crimson and his eyes hard. "Lookin' fer something?" he asked with bitter sarcasm, his hands under the bar. Johnny grinned hopefully and a sudden tenseness took possession of him as he watched for the first hostile move.

"Yes," Hopalong replied coolly, appraising Harlan's attitude and look in one swift glance, "but it ain't here, now. Johnny, get out," he ordered, backing after his companion, and safely outside, the two walked towards Jackson's store, Johnny complaining about the little time spent in the Oasis.

As they entered the store they saw Edwards, whose eyes asked a question.

"No; he ain't in there yet," Hopalong replied.

"Did you look all over? Behind th' bar?" Edwards asked, slowly. "He can't get out of town through that cordon you've got strung around it, an' he ain't nowhere else. Leastwise, I couldn't find him."

"Come on back!" excitedly exclaimed Johnny, turning towards the door. "You didn't look behind th' bar! Come on—bet you ten dollars that's where he is!"

"Mebby yo're right, Kid," replied Hopalong, and the marshal's nodding head decided it.

In the saloon there was strong language, and Jack Quinn, expert skinner of other men's cows, looked inquiringly at the proprietor. "What's up now, Harlan?"

The proprietor laughed harshly but said nothing—taciturnity was his one redeeming trait. "Did you say cigars?" he asked, pushing a box across the bar to an impatient customer. Another beckoned to him and he leaned over to hear the whispered request, a frown struggling to show itself on his face. "Nix; you know my rule. No trust in here."

But the man at the far end of the line was unlike the proprietor and he prefaced his remarks with a curse. "*I* know what's up! They want Jerry Brown, that's what! An' I hopes they don't get him, th' bullies!"

"What did he do? Why do they want him?" asked the man who had wanted trust.

"Skinning. He was careless or crazy, working so close to their ranch houses. Nobody that had any sense would take a chance like that," replied Boston, adept at sleight-of-hand with cards and very much in demand when a frame-up was to be rung in on some unsuspecting stranger. His one great fault in the eyes of his partners was that he hated to divvy his winnings and at times had to be coerced into sharing equally.

"Aw, them big ranches make me mad," announced the first speaker. "Ten years ago there was a lot of little ranchers, an' every one of 'em had his own herd, an' plenty of free grass an' water fer it. Where are th' little herds now? Where are th' cows that we used to own?" he cried, hotly. "What happens to a maverick-hunter, nowadays? If a man helps hisself to a pore, sick dogie he's hunted down! It can't go on much longer, an' that's shore."

Slivers Lowe leaped up from his chair. "Yo're right, Harper! Dead right! *I* was a little cattle owner onct, so was you, an' Jerry, an' most of us!" Slivers found it convenient to forget that fully half of his small herd had perished in the bitter and long winter of five years before, and that the remainder had either flowed down his parched throat or been lost across the big round table near the bar. Not a few of his cows were banked in the East under Harlan's name.

The rear door opened slightly and one of the loungers looked up and nodded. "It's all right Jerry. But get a move on!"

"Here, *you!*" called Harlan, quickly bending over the trap door, "*Lively!*"

Jerry was halfway to the proprietor when the front door swung open and Hopalong, closely followed by the marshal, leaped into the room, and immediately thereafter the back door banged open and admitted Johnny. Jerry's right hand was in his side coat pocket and Johnny, young and self-confident, and with a lot to learn, was certain that he could beat the fugitive on the draw.

"I reckon you won't blot no more brands!" he cried, triumphantly, watching both Jerry and Harlan.

The card-players had leaped to their feet and at a signal from Harlan they surged forward to the bar and formed a barrier between Johnny and his friends; and as they did so that puncher jerked at his gun, twisting to half face the crowd. At that instant fire and smoke spurted from Jerry's side coat pocket and the odor of burning cloth arose. As Johnny fell, the rustler ducked low and sprang for the door. A gun roared twice in the front of the room and Jerry staggered a little and cursed as he gained the opening, but he plunged into the darkness and threw himself into the saddle on the first horse he found in the small corral.

When the crowd massed, Hopalong leaped at it and strove to tear his way to the opening at the end of the bar, while the marshal covered Harlan and the others. Finding that he could not get through, Hopalong sprang on the shoulder of the nearest man and succeeded in winging the fugitive at the first shot, the other going wild. Then, frantic with rage and anxiety, he beat his way through the crowd, hammering mercilessly at heads with the butt of his Colt, and knelt at his friend's side.

Edwards, angered almost to the point of killing, ordered the crowd to stand against the wall, and laughed viciously when he saw two men senseless on the floor. "Hope he beat in yore heads!" he gritted, savagely. "Harlan, put yore paws up in sight or I'll drill you clean! Now climb over an' get in line—quick!"

Johnny moaned and opened his eyes. "Did—did I—get him?"

"No; but he gimleted you, all right," Hopalong replied. "You'll come 'round if you keep quiet." He arose, his face hard with the desire to kill. "I'm coming back for *you*, Harlan, after I get yore friend! An' all th' rest of you pups, too!"

"Get me out of here," whispered Johnny.

"Shore enough, Kid; but keep quiet," replied Hopalong, picking him up in his arms and moving carefully towards the door. "We'll get him, Johnny; an' all th' rest, too, when"—the voice died out in the direction of Jackson's and the marshal, backing to the front door, slipped out and to one side, running backward, his eyes on the saloon.

"Yore day's about over, Harlan," he muttered.

"There's going to be some few funerals around here before many hours pass."

When he reached the store he found the owner and two Double-Arrow punchers taking care of Johnny. "Where's Hopalong?" he asked.

"Gone to tell his foreman," replied Jackson. "Hey, youngster, you let them bandages alone! Hear me?"

"Hullo, Kansas," remarked John Bartlett, foreman of the Double-Arrow. "I come nigh getting yore man; somebody rode past me like a streak in th' dark, so I just ups an' lets drive for luck, an' so did he. I heard him cuss an' I emptied my gun after him."

The rain slanted down in sheets and the broken plain, thoroughly saturated, held the water in pools or sent it down the steep side of the cliff to feed the turbulent flood which swept along the bottom, foam-flecked and covered with swiftly moving driftwood. Around a bend where the angry water flung itself against the ragged bulwark of rock and flashed away in a gleaming line of foam, a horseman appeared, bending low in the saddle for better protection against the storm. He rode along the edge of the stream on the farther bank, opposite the steep bluff on the northern side, forcing his wounded and jaded horse to keep fetlock deep in the water which swirled and sucked about its legs. He was trying his hardest to hide his trail. Lower down the hard, rocky ground extended to the water's edge, and if he could delay his pursuers for an hour or so, he felt that, even with his tired horse, he would have more than an even chance.

But they had gained more than he knew. Suddenly above him on the top of the steep bluff across the torrent a man loomed up against the clouds, peered intently and then waved his sombrero to an unseen companion. A puff of smoke flashed from his shoulder and streaked away, the report of the shot lost in the gale. The fugitive's horse reared and plunged into the deep water and with its rider was swept rapidly towards the bend, the way they had come.

"That makes th' fourth time I've missed that coyote!" angrily exclaimed Hopalong as Red Connors joined him.

The other quickly raised his rifle and fired; and the horse, spilling its rider out of the saddle, floated away tail first. The fugitive, gripping his rifle, bobbed and whirled at the whim of the greedy water as shots struck near him. Making a desperate effort, he staggered up the bank and fell exhausted behind a bowlder.

"Well, th' coyote is afoot, anyhow," said Red, with great satisfaction.

"Yes; but how are we going to get to him?" asked Hopalong. "We can't get th' cayuses down here, an' we can't swim *that* water without them. And if we could, he'd pot us easy."

"There's a way out of it somewhere," Red replied, disappearing over the edge of the bluff to gamble with Fate.

"Hey! Come back here, you chump!" cried Hopalong, running forward. "He'll get you, shore!"

"That's a chance I've got to take if I get him," was the reply.

A puff of smoke sailed from behind the bowlder on the other bank and Hopalong, kneeling for steadier aim, fired and then followed his friend. Red was downstream casting at a rock across the torrent but the wind toyed with the heavy, water-soaked *reata* as though it were a string. As Hopalong reached his side a piece of driftwood ducked under the water and an angry humming sound died away downstream. As the report reached their ears a jet of water spurted up into Red's face and he stepped back involuntarily.

"He's some shaky," Hopalong remarked, looking back at the wreath of smoke above the bowlder. "I reckon I must have hit him harder than I thought in Harlan's. Gee! he's wild as blazes!" he ejaculated as a bullet hummed high above his head and struck sharply against the rock wall.

"Yes," Red replied, coiling the rope. "I was trying to rope that rock over there. If I could anchor to that, th' current would push us over quick. But it's too far with this wind blowing."

"We can't do nothing here 'cept get plugged. He'll be getting steadier as he rests from his fight with th' water," Hopalong remarked, and added quickly, "Say, remember that meadow back there a ways? We can make her from there, all right."

"Yo're right; that's what we've got to do. He's sending 'em nearer every shot—Gee! I could 'most feel th' wind of that one. An' blamed if it ain't stopped raining. Come on."

They clambered up the slippery, muddy bank to where they had left their horses, and cantered back over their trail. Minute after minute passed before the cautious skulker among the rocks across the stream could believe in his good fortune. When he at last decided that he was alone again he left his shelter and started away, with slowly weakening stride, over cleanly washed rock where he left no trail.

It was late in the afternoon before the two irate punchers appeared upon the scene, and their comments, as they hunted slowly over the hard ground, were numerous and bitter. Deciding that it was hopeless in that vicinity, they began casting in great circles on the chance of crossing the trail further back from the river. But they had little faith in their success. As Red remarked, snorting like a horse in his disgust, "I'll bet four dollars an' a match he's swum down th' river just to have th' laugh on us." Red had long since given it up as a bad job, though continuing to search, when a shout from the distant Hopalong sent him forward on a run.

"Hey, Red!" cried Hopalong, pointing ahead of them. "Look there! Ain't that a house?"

"Naw; course not! It's a—it's a ship!" Red snorted sarcastically. "What did you think it might be?"

"G'wan!" retorted his companion. "It's a mission."

"Ah, g'wan yorself! What's a mission doing up here?" Red snapped.

"What do you think they do? What do they do anywhere?" hotly rejoined Hopalong, thinking about Johnny. "There! See th' cross?"

"Shore enough!"

"An' there's tracks at last—mighty wobbly, but tracks just th' same. Them rocks couldn't go on forever. Red, I'll bet he's cashed in by this time."

"Cashed nothing! Them fellers don't."

"Well, if he's in that joint we might as well go back home. We won't get him, not nohow," declared Hopalong.

"Huh! You wait an' see!" replied Red, pugnaciously.

"Reckon you never run up agin' a mission real hard," Hopalong responded, his memory harking back to the time he had disagreed with a convent, and they both meant about the same to him as far as winning out was concerned.

"Think I'm a fool kid?" snapped Red, aggressively.

"Well, you ain't no *kid*."

"You let *me* do th' talking; *I'll* get him."

"All right; an' I'll do th' laughing," snickered Hopalong, at the door. "Sic 'em, Red!"

The other boldly stepped into a small vestibule, Hopalong close at his heels. Red hitched his holster and walked heavily into a room at his left. With the exception of a bench, a table, and a small altar, the room was devoid of furnishings, and the effect of these was lost in the dim light from the narrow windows. The peculiar, not unpleasant odor of burning incense and the dim light awakened a latent reverence and awe in Hopalong, and he sneaked off his sombrero, an inexplicable feeling of guilt stealing over him. There were three doors in the walls, deeply shrouded in the dusk of the room, and it was very hard to watch all three at once. . . .

Red listened intently and then grinned. "Hear that? They're playing dominoes in there—come on!"

"Aw, you chump! 'Dominee' means 'mother' in Latin, which is what they speaks."

"How do you know?"

"Hanged if I can tell—I've heard it somewhere, that's all."

"Well, I don't care what it means. This is a frame-up so that coyote can get away. I'll bet they gave him a cayuse an' started him off while we've been losing time in here. I'm going inside an' ask some questions."

Before he could put his plan into execution, Hopalong nudged him and he turned to see his friend staring at one of the doors. There had been no sound, but he would swear that a monk stood gravely regarding them, and he rubbed his eyes. He stepped back suspiciously and then started forward again.

"Look here, stranger," he remarked, with quiet emphasis, "we're after that cow-lifter, an' we mean to get him. Savvy?"

The monk did not appear to hear him, so he tried another trick. "*Habla española?*" he asked, experimentally.

"You have ridden far?" replied the monk in perfect English.

"All th' way from th' Bend," Red replied, relieved. "We're after Jerry Brown. He tried to kill Johnny, judgin' from th' tracks."

"And if you capture him?"

"He won't have no more use for no side pocket shooting."

"I see; you will kill him."

"Shore's it's wet outside."

"I'm afraid you are doomed to disappointment."

"Ya-as?" asked Red with a rising inflection.

"You will not want him now," replied the monk.

Red laughed sarcastically and Hopalong smiled.

"There ain't a-going to be no argument about it. Trot him out," ordered Red, grimly.

The monk turned to Hopalong. "Do you, too, want him?"

Hopalong nodded.

"My friends, he is safe from your punishment."

Red wheeled instantly and ran outside, returning in a few moments, smiling triumphantly. "There are tracks coming in, but there ain't none going away. He's here. If you don't lead us to him we'll shore have to rummage around an' poke him out for ourselves: which is it?"

"You are right—he is here, and he is not here."

"We're waiting," Red replied, grinning.

"When I tell you that you will not want him, do you still insist on seeing him?"

"We'll see him, an' we'll want him, too."

As the rain poured down again the sound of approaching horses was heard, and Hopalong ran to the door in time to see Buck Peters swing off his mount and step forward to enter the building. Hopalong stopped him and briefly outlined the situation, begging him to keep the men outside. The monk met his return with a grateful smile and, stepping forward, opened the chapel door, saying, "Follow me."

The unpretentious chapel was small and nearly dark, for the usual dimness was increased by the lowering clouds outside. The deep, narrow window openings, fitted with stained glass, ran almost to the rough-hewn rafters supporting the steep-pitched roof, upon which the heavy rain beat again with a sound like that of distant drums. Gusts of rain and the water from the roof beat against the south windows, while the wailing wind played its mournful cadences about the eaves, and the stanch timbers added their creaking notes to swell the dirgelike chorus.

At the farther end of the room two figures knelt and moved before the white altar, the soft light of flickering candles playing fitfully upon them and glinting from the altar ornaments, while before a rough coffin, which rested upon two pedestals, stood a third, whose rich, sonorous Latin filled the chapel with impressive sadness. "Give eternal rest to them, O Lord,"—the words seeming to become a part of the room. The ineffably sad, haunting melody of the mass whispered back from the roof between the assaults of the enraged wind, while from the altar came the responses in a low Gregorian chant, and through it all the clinking of the censer chains added intermittent notes. Aloft streamed the vapor of the incense, wavering with the air currents, now lost in the deep twilight of the sanctuary, and now faintly revealed by the glow of the candles, perfuming the air with its aromatic odor.

As the last deep-toned words died away the celebrant moved slowly around the coffin, swinging the censer over it and then, sprinkling the body and making the sign of the cross above its head, solemnly withdrew.

From the shadows along the side walls other figures silently emerged and grouped around the coffin. Raising it they turned it slowly around and carried it down the dim aisle in measured tread, moving silently as ghosts.

"He is with God, Who will punish according to his sins," said a low voice, and Hopalong started, for he had forgotten the presence of the guide. "God be with you, and may you die as he died—repentant and in peace."

Buck chafed impatiently before the chapel door leading to a small, well-kept graveyard, wondering what it was that kept quiet for so long a time his two most assertive men, when he had momentarily expected to hear more or less turmoil and confusion.

C-r-e-a-k! He glanced up, gun in hand and raised as the door swung slowly open. His hand dropped suddenly and he took a short step forward; six black-robed figures shouldering a long box stepped slowly past him, and his nostrils were assailed by the pungent odor of the incense. Behind them came his fighting punchers, humble, awed, reverent, their sombreros in their hands, and their heads bowed.

"What in blazes!" exclaimed Buck, wonder and surprise struggling for the mastery as the others cantered up.

"He's cashed," Red replied, putting on his sombrero and nodding toward the procession.

Buck turned like a flash and spoke sharply: "Skinny! Lanky! Follow that glory-outfit, an' see what's in that box!"

Billy Williams grinned at Red. "Yo're shore pious, Red."

"Shut up!" snapped Red, anger glinting in his eyes, and Billy subsided.

Lanky and Skinny soon returned from accompanying the procession.

"I had to look twict to be shore it was him. His face was plumb happy, like a baby. But he's gone, all right," Lanky reported.

"All right—he knowed how he'd finish when he began. Now for that dear Mr. Harlan," Buck replied, vaulting into the saddle. He turned and looked at Hopalong, and his wonder grew. "Hey, *you!* Yes, *you!* Come out of that an' put on yore lid! Straddle leather—we can't stay here all night."

Hopalong started, looked at his sombrero and silently obeyed. As they rode down the trail and around a corner he turned in his saddle and looked back; and then rode on, buried in thought.

Billy, grinning, turned and playfully punched him in the ribs. "Gettin' glory, Hoppy?"

Hopalong raised his head and looked him steadily in the eyes; and Billy, losing his curiosity and the grin at the same instant, looked ahead,

whistling softly.

IX.—Dey Ain't No Ghosts[9]

By Ellis Parker Butler

ONCE 'pon a time dey was a li'l black boy whut he name was Mose. An' whin he come erlong to be 'bout knee-high to a mewel, he 'gin to git powerful 'fraid ob ghosts, 'ca'se dey's a grabeyard in de hollow, an' a buryin'-ground on de hill, an' a cemuntary in betwixt an' between, an' dey ain't nuffin' but trees nowhar in de clearin' by de shanty an' down de hollow whar de pumpkin-patch am.

An' whin de night come erlong, dey ain't no sounds at all whut kin be heard in dat locality but de rain-doves, whut mourn out, "Oo-*oo*-o-o-o!" jes dat trembulous an' scary, an' de owls, whut mourn out, "Whut-*whoo*-o-o-o!" more trembulous an' scary dan dat, an' de wind, whut mourn out, "You-*you*-o-o-o!" mos' scandalous, trembulous an' scary ob all. Dat a powerful onpleasant locality for a li'l black boy whut he name was Mose.

'Ca'se dat li'l black boy he so specially black he can't be seen in de dark *at* all 'cept by de whites ob he eyes. So whin he go outen de house at night, he ain't dast shut he eyes, 'ca'se den ain't nobody can see him in de least. He jest as invidsible as nuffin'! An' who know but whut a great, big ghost bump right into him 'ca'se it can't see him? An' dat shore w'u'd scare dat li'l black boy powerful bad, 'ca'se yever'body knows whut a cold, damp pussonality a ghost is.

So whin dat li'l black Mose go' outen de shanty at night, he keep he eyes wide open, you may be shore. By day he eyes 'bout de size ob butter-pats, an' come sundown he eyes 'bout de size ob saucers; but whin he go outer de shanty at night, he eyes am de size ob de white chiny plate whut set on de mantel; an' it powerful hard to keep eyes whut am de size ob dat from a-winkin' an' a-blinkin'.

So whin Hallowe'en come erlong, dat li'l black Mose he jes mek up he mind he ain't gwine outen de shack at all. He cogitate he gwine stay right snug in de shack wid he pa an' he ma, 'ca'se de rain-doves tek notice dat de ghosts are philanderin' roun' de country, 'ca'se dey mourn out, "Oo-*oo*-o-o-o!" an' de owls dey mourn out, "You-*you*-o-o-o!" De eyes ob dat li'l black Mose dey as big as de white chiny plate whut set on de mantel by side de clock, an' de sun jes a-settin'!

So dat all right. Li'l black Mose he scrooge back in de corner by de fireplace, an' he 'low he gwine stay dere till he gwine *to* bed. But bimeby Sally Ann, whut live up de road, draps in, an' Mistah Sally Ann, whut is her husban', he draps in an' Zack Badget an' de school-teacher whut board at Unc' Silas Diggs's house drap in, an' a powerful lot ob folks drap in. An' li'l black Mose he seen dat gwine be one s'prise party, an' he right down cheerful 'bout dat.

So all dem folks shake dere hands an' 'low "Howdy," an' some ob dem say: "Why, dere's li'l Mose! Howdy, li'l Mose?" An' he so please he jes grin an' grin, 'ca'se he ain't reckon whut gwine happen. So bimeby Sally Ann, whut live up de road, she say, "Ain't no sort o' Hallowe'en lest we got a jack-o'-lantern." An' de school-teacher, whut board at Unc' Silas Diggs's house, she 'low, "Hallowe'en jes no Hallowe'en *at* all 'thout we got a jack-o'-lantern." An' li'l black Mose he stop a-grinnin', an' he scrooge so far back in de corner he 'most scrooge frough de wall. But dat ain't no use, 'ca'se he ma say, "Mose, go on down to de pumpkin-patch an' fotch a pumpkin."

"I ain't want to go," say li'l black Mose.

"Go on erlong wid yo'," say he ma, right commandin'.

"I ain't want to go," say Mose ag'in.

"Why ain't yo' want to go?" he ma ask.

"'Ca'se I's afraid ob de ghosts," say li'l black Mose, an' dat de particular truth an' no mistake.

"Dey ain't no ghosts," say de school-teacher, whut board at Unc' Silas Diggs's house, right peart.

"'Co'se dey ain't no ghosts," say Zack Badget, whut dat 'feared ob ghosts he ain't dar' come to li'l black Mose's house ef de school-teacher ain't ercompany him.

"Go 'long wid your ghosts!" say li'l black Mose's ma.

"Wha' yo' pick up dat nonsense?" say he pa. "Dey ain't no ghosts."

An' dat whut all dat s'prise-party 'lows: dey ain't no ghosts. An' dey 'low dey mus' hab a jack-o'-lantern or de fun all spiled. So dat li'l black boy whut he name is Mose he done got to fotch a pumpkin from de pumpkin-patch down de hollow. So he step outen de shanty an' he stan' on de doorstep twell he get he eyes pried open as big as de bottom ob he ma's washtub, mostly, an' he say, "Dey ain't no ghosts." An' he put one foot on de ground, an' dat was de fust step.

An' de rain-dove say, "Oo-*oo*-o-o-o!"

An' li'l black Mose he tuck anudder step.

An' de owl mourn out, "Whut-*whoo*-o-o-o!"

An' li'l black Mose he tuck anudder step.

An' de wind sob out, "You-*you*-o-o-o!"

An' li'l black Mose he tuck one look ober he shoulder an' he shut he eyes so tight dey hurt round de aidges, an' he pick up he foots an' run.

Yas, sah, he run right peart fast. An' he say: "Dey ain't no ghosts. Dey ain't no ghosts." An' he run erlong de paff whut lead by de buryin'-ground on de hill, 'ca'se dey ain't no fince eround dat buryin'-ground at all.

No fince; jes de big trees whut de owls an' de rain-doves sot in an' mourn an' sob, an' whut de wind sigh an' cry frough. An' bimeby somefin' jes *brush* li'l Mose on de arm, which mek him run jest a bit more faster. An' bimeby somefin' jes *brush* li'l Mose on de cheek, which mek him run erbout as fast as he can. An' bimeby somefin' *grab* li'l Mose by de aidge of he coat, an' he fight an' struggle an' cry out: "Dey ain't no ghosts. Dey ain't no ghosts." An' dat ain't nuffin' but de wild brier whut grab him, an' dat ain't nuffin' but de leaf ob a tree whut brush he cheek, an' dat ain't nuffin' but de branch ob a hazel-bush whut brush he arm. But he downright scared jes de same, an' he ain't lost no time, 'ca'se de wind an' de owls an' de rain-doves dey signerfy whut ain't no good. So he scoot past dat buryin'-ground whut on de hill, an' dat cemuntary whut betwixt an' between, an' dat grabeyard in de hollow, twell he come to de pumpkin-patch, an' he rotch down an' tek erhold ob de bestest pumpkin whut in de patch. An' he right smart scared. He jes de mostest scared li'l black boy whut yever was. He ain't gwine open he eyes fo' nuffin', 'ca'se de wind go, "You-*you*-o-o-o!" an' de owls go, "Whut-*whoo*-o-o-o!" an' de rain-doves go, "Oo-*oo*-o-o-o!"

He jes speculate, "Dey ain't no ghosts," an' wish he hair don't stand on ind dat way. An' he jes cogitate, "Dey ain't no ghosts," an' wish he goose-pimples don't rise up dat way. An' he jes 'low, "Dey ain't no ghosts," an' wish he backbone ain't all trembulous wid chills dat way. So he rotch down, an' he rotch down, twell he git a good hold on dat pricklesome stem of dat bestest pumpkin whut in de patch, an' he jes yank dat stem wid all he might.

"*Let loosen my head!*" say a big voice all on a suddent.

Dat li'l black boy whut he name is Mose he jump 'most outen he skin. He open he eyes an' he 'gin to shake like de aspen tree, 'ca'se whut dat a-standin' right dar behind him but a 'mendjous big ghost! Yas, sah, dat de bigges', whites' ghost whut yever was. An' it ain't got no head. Ain't go no head *at* all. Li'l black Mose he jest drap on he knees an' he beg an' pray:

"Oh, 'scuse me! 'Scuse me, Mistah Ghost!" he beg. "Ah ain't mean no harm at all."

"Whut for you try to take my head?" as' de ghost in dat fearsome voice whut like de damp wind outen de cellar.

"'Scuse me! 'Scuse me!" beg li'l Mose. "Ah ain't know dat was yo' head, an' I ain't know you was dar *at* all. 'Scuse me!"

"Ah 'scuse you ef you do me dis favor," say de ghost. "Ah got somefin' powerful *im*portant to say unto you, an' Ah can't say hit 'ca'se Ah ain't got no head; an' whin Ah ain't got no head, Ah ain't got no mouf, an' whin Ah ain't got no mouf, Ah can't talk *at* all."

An' dat right logical fo' shore. Can't nobody talk whin he ain't got no mouf, an' can't nobody have no mouf whin he ain't got no head, an' whin li'l black Mose he look, he see dat ghost ain't go no head *at* all. Nary head.

So de ghost say:

"Ah come on down yere fo' to git a pumpkin fo' a head, an' Ah pick dat ixact pumpkin whut yo' gwine tek, an' Ah don't like dat one bit. No, sah. Ah feel like Ah pick yo' up an' carry yo' away, an' nobody see you no more for yever. But Ah got somefin' powerful *im*portant to say unto yo', an' if yo' pick up dat pumpkin an' sot it on de place whar my head ought to be, Ah let you off dis time, 'ca'se Ah ain't been able to talk fo' so long Ah'm right hongry to say somefin'!"

So li'l black Mose he heft up dat pumpkin, an' de ghost he bent down, an' li'l black Mose he sot dat pumpkin on dat ghostses neck. An' right off dat pumpkin head 'gin to wink an' blink like a jack-o'-lantern, an' right off dat pumpkin head 'gin to glimmer an' glow frough de mouf like a jack-o'-lantern, an' right off dat ghost start to speak. Yas, sah, dass so.

"Whut yo' want to say unto me?" *in*quire li'l black Mose.

"Ah want to tell yo'," say de ghost, "dat yo' ain't need yever be skeered of ghosts, 'ca'se dey ain't no ghosts."

An' whin he say dat de ghost jes vanish away like de smoke in July. He ain't even linger round dat locality like de smoke in Yoctober. He jes dissipate outen de air, an' he gone *in*tirely.

So li'l Mose he grab up de nex' bestest pumpkin an' he scoot. An' whin he come to de grabeyard in de hollow, he goin' erlong same as yever, on'y faster, whin he reckon, he'll pick up a club *in* case he gwine have trouble. An' he rotch down an' rotch down, an' tek hold of a lively appearin' hunk o' wood whut right dar. An' whin he grab dat hunk of wood. . . .

"*Let loosen my leg!*" say a big voice all on a suddent.

Dat li'l black boy 'most jump outen he skin, 'ca'se right dar in de paff is six 'mendjus big ghosts, an' de bigges' ain't got but one leg. So li'l black

Mose jes natchully handed dat hunk of wood to dat bigges' ghost, an' he say:

"'Scuse me, Mistah Ghost; Ah ain't know dis your leg."

An' whut dem six ghostes do but stand round an' confabulate? Yas, sah, dass so. An' whin dey do so, one say:

"'Pears like dis a mighty likely li'l black boy. Whut we gwine do fo' to *re*ward him fo' politeness?"

"Tell him whut de truth is 'bout ghosts."

So de bigges' ghost he say:

"Ah gwine tell yo' somethin' important whut yever'body don't know: Dey *ain't* no ghosts."

An' whin he say dat, de ghosts jes natchully vanish away, an' li'l black Mose he proceed up de paff. He so scared he hair jes yank at de roots, an' when de wind go "Oo-*oo*-oo-o-o," an' de owl go, "Whut-*whoo*-o-o-o!" an' de rain-doves go, "You-*you*-o-o-o!" he jes tremble an' shake. An' bimeby he come to de cemuntary whut betwixt an' between, an' he shore is mighty skeered, 'ca'se dey is a whole comp'ny of ghostes lined up along de road, an' he 'low he ain't gwine spind no more time palaverin' wid ghostes. So he step offen de road fo' to go round erbout, an' he step on a pine-stump whut lay right dar.

"*Git offen my chest!*" say a big voice all on a suddent, 'ca'se dat stump am been selected by de captain ob de ghostes for to be he chest, 'ca'se he ain't got no chest betwixt he shoulders an' he legs. An' li'l black Mose he hop offen dat stump right peart. Yes, *sah;* right peart.

"'Scuse me! 'Scuse me!" dat li'l black Mose beg an' pleed, an' de ghostes ain't know whuther to eat him all up or not, 'ca'se he step on de boss ghostes's chest dat a-way. But bimeby they 'low they let him go 'ca'se dat was an accident, an' de captain ghost he say, "Mose, you Mose, Ah gwine let you off dis time, 'ca'se you ain't nuffin' but a misabul li'l tremblin' nigger; but Ah want you should remimber one thing mos' particular'."

"Ya-yas, sah," say dat li'l black boy; "Ah'll remimber. What is dat Ah got to remimber?"

De captain ghost he swell up, an' he swell up, twell he as big as a house, an' he say in a voice whut shake de ground:

"Dey ain't no ghosts."

So li'l black Mose he bound to remimber dat, an' he rise up an' mek a bow, an' he proceed toward home right libely. He do, indeed.

An' he gwine along jes as fast as he kin whin he come to de aidge ob de buryin'-ground whut on de hill, an' right dar he bound to stop, 'ca'se de kentry round about am so populate he ain't able to go frough. Yas, sah, seem like all de ghostes in de world havin' de conferince right dar. Seem like all de ghosteses whut yever was am havin' a convintion on dat spot. An' dat li'l black Mose so skeered he jes fall down on e' old log whut dar an' screech an' moan! An' all on a suddent de log up and spoke to li'l Mose:

"*Get offen me! Get offen me!*" yell dat log.

So li'l black Mose he git offen dat log, an' no mistake.

An' soon as he git offen de log, de log uprise, an' li'l black Mose he see dat dat log am de king ob all de ghostes. An' whin de king uprise, all de congregation crowd round li'l black Mose, an' dey am about leben millium an' a few lift over. Yes, sah; dat de reg'lar annyul Hallowe'en convintion whut li'l black Mose interrup. Right dar am all de sperits in de world, an' all de ha'nts in de world, an' all de hobgoblins in de world, an' all de ghouls in de world, an' all de spicters in de world, an' all de ghostes in de world. An' whin dey see li'l black Mose, dey all gnash dey teef an' grin 'ca'se it gettin' erlong toward dey-all's lunchtime. So de king, whut he name old Skull-an'-Bones, he step on top ob li'l Mose's head, an' he say:

"Gin'l'min, de convintion will come to order. De sicretary please note who is prisint. De firs' business whut come before de convintion am: whut we gwine do to a li'l black boy whut stip on de king an' maul all ober de king an' treat de king dat disdespictful."

An' li'l black Mose jes moan an' sob:

"'Scuse me! 'Scuse me, Mistah King! Ah ain't mean no harm *at* all."

But nobody ain't pay no attintion to him at all, 'ca'se yevery one lookin' at a monstrous big ha'nt whut name Bloody Bones, whut rose up an' spoke.

"Your Honor, Mistah King, an' gin'l'min *an'* ladies," he say, "dis am a right bad case ob *lazy majesty*, 'ca'se de king been step on. Whin yevery li'l black boy whut choose gwine wander round at night an' stip on de king of ghostes, it ain't no time for to palaver, it ain't no time for to prevaricate, it ain't no time for to cogitate, it ain't no time do nuffin' but tell de truth, an' de whole truth, an' nuffin but de truth."

An' all dem ghostes sicond de motion, an' dey canfabulate out loud erbout it, an' de noise soun like de rain-doves goin', "Oo-*oo*-o-o-o!" an' de owls goin', "Whut-*whoo*-o-o-o!" an' de wind goin', "You-*you*-o-o-o!" So dat risolution am passed unanermous, an' no mistake.

So de king ob de ghosts, whut name old Skull-an'-Bones, he place he hand on de head ob li'l black Mose, an' he hand feel like a wet rag, an' he say:

"Dey ain't no ghosts."

An' one ob de hairs whut on de head ob li'l black Mose turn white.

An' de monstrous big ha'nt whut he name Bloody Bones he lay he hand on de head ob li'l black Mose, and he hand feel like a toadstool in de cool ob de day, an' he say:

"Dey ain't no ghosts."

An' anudder ob de hairs whut on de head ob li'l black Mose turn white.

An' a heejus sperit whut he name Moldy Pa'm place he hand on de head ob li'l black Mose, an' he hand feel like ye yunner side ob a lizard, an' he say:

"Dey ain't no ghosts."

An' anudder ob de hairs whut on de head ob li'l black Mose turn white *as* snow.

An' a perticklar bent-up hobgoblin he put hand on de head ob li'l black Mose, an' he mek dat same *re*mark, and dat whole convintion ob ghostes an' spicters an' ha'nts an' yever-thing, which am more 'n a millium, pass by so quick dey-all's hands feel lak de wind whut blow outen de cellar whin de day am hot, an' dey-all say, "Dey ain't no ghosts." Yas, sah, dey-all say dem wo'ds so fas' it soun like de wind whin it moan frough de turkentine-trees whut behind de cider-priss. An' yevery hair whut on li'l black Mose's head turn white. Dat whut happen whin a li'l black boy gwine meet a ghost convintion dat a-way. Dat's so he ain't gwine fergit to remimber dey ain't no ghosts. 'Ca'se ef a li'l black boy gwine imaginate dey *is* ghostes, he gwine be skeered in de dark. An' dat a foolish thing for to imaginate.

So prisintly all de ghostes am whiff away, like de fog outen de holler whin de wind blow' on it, an' li'l black Mose he ain' see 'ca'se for to remain in dat locality no longer. He rotch down, an' he raise up de pumpkin, an' he perambulate right quick to he ma's shack, an' he lift up de latch, an' he open de do', an' he yenter in. An' he say:

"Yere's de pumpkin."

An' he ma an' he pa, an' Sally Ann, whut live up de road, an' Mistah Sally Ann, whut her husban', an' Zack Badget, an' de school-teacher whut board at Unc' Silas Diggs's house, an' all de powerful lot of folks whut come to de doin's, dey all scrooged back in de cornder ob de shack, 'ca'se Zack Badget he been done tell a ghost-tale, an' de rain-doves gwine

"Ooo-*oo*-o-o-o!" an' de owls am gwine, "Whut-*whoo*-o-o-o!" and de wind it gwine, "You-*you*-o-o-o!" an' yever'body powerful skeered. 'Ca'se li'l black Mose he come a-fumblin' an' a-rattlin' at de do' jes whin dat ghost-tale mos' skeery, an' yever'body gwine imaginate dat de ghost a-fumblin' an' a-rattlin' at de do'. Yas, sah. So li'l black Mose he turn he white head, an' he look roun' an' peer roun', an' he say:

"Whut you all skeered fo'?"

'Ca'se ef anybody skeered, he want to be skeered, too. Dat's natural. But de school-teacher, whut live at Unc' Silas Diggs's house, she say:

"Fo' de lan's sake, we fought you was a ghost!"

So li'l black Mose he sort ob sniff an' he sort ob sneer, an' he 'low:

"Huh! dey ain't no ghosts."

Den he ma she powerful took back dat li'l black Mose he gwine be so upotish an' contrydict folks whut know 'rifmeticks an' algebricks an' gin'ral countin' widout fingers, like de school-teacher whut board at Unc' Silas Diggs's house knows, an' she say:

"Huh; whut you know 'bout ghosts, anner way?"

An' li'l black Mose he jes kinder stan' on one foot, an' he jes kinder suck he thumb, an' he jes kinder 'low:

"I don' know nuffin' erbout ghosts, 'ca'se dey ain't no ghosts."

So he pa gwine whop him fo' tellin' a fib 'bout dey ain't no ghosts whin yever'body know dey is ghosts; but de school-teacher, whut board at Unc' Silas Diggs's house, she tek note de hair ob li'l black Mose's head am plumb white, an' she tek note li'l black Mose's face am de color of wood-ash, so she jes retch one arm round dat li'l black boy, an' she jes snuggle him up, an' she say:

"Honey lamb, don't you be skeered; ain' nobody gwine hurt you. How you know dey ain't no ghosts?"

An' li'l black Mose he kinder lean up 'g'inst de school-teacher whut board at Unc' Silas Diggs's house, an' he 'low:

"'Ca'se—'ca'se—'ca'se I met de cap'n ghost, an' I met de gin'ral ghost, an' I met de king ghost, an' I met all de ghostes whut yever was in de whole worl', an' yevery ghost say de same thing: 'Dey ain't no ghosts.' An' if de cap'n ghost an' de gin'ral ghost an' de king ghost an' all de ghostes in de whole worl' don' know ef dar am ghostes, who does?"

"Das right; das right, honey lamb," say de school-teacher. An' she say: "I been s'picious dey ain' no ghostes dis long whiles, an' now I know. Ef all de ghostes say dey ain' no ghosts, dey *ain'* no ghosts."

So yever'body 'low dat o cep' Zack Badget, whut been tellin' de ghost-tale, an' he ain' gwine say "Yis" an' he ain' gwine say "No," 'ca'se he right sweet on de school-teacher; but he know right well he done seen plinty ghostes in he day. So he boun' to be sure fust. So he say to li'l black Mose:

"'Tain' likely you met up wid a monstrous big ha'nt whut live down de lane whut he name Bloody Bones?"

"Yas," say li'l black Mose, "I done met up wid him."

"An' did old Bloody Bones done tol' you dey ain' no ghosts?" say Zack Badget.

"Yas," say li'l black Mose, "he done tell me perzactly dat."

"Well, if *he* tol' you dey ain' no ghosts," say Zack Badget, "I got to 'low dey ain't no ghosts, 'ca'se he ain't gwine tell no lie erbout it. I know dat Bloody Bones ghost sence I was a piccaninny, an' I done met up wif him a powerful lot o' times, an' he ain't gwine tell no lie erbout it. Ef dat perticklar ghost say dey ain't no ghosts, dey ain't no ghosts."

So yever'body say:

"Das right; dey ain't no ghosts."

An' dat mek li'l black Mose feel mighty good, 'ca'se he ain' lek ghostes. He reckon he gwine be a heap mo' comfortable in he mind sence he know dey ain't no ghosts, an' he reckon he ain' gwine be skeered of nuffin' never no more. He ain't gwine min' de dark, an' he ain't gwine min' de rain-doves whut go, "Ooo-*oo*-o-o-o!" an' he ain' gwine min' de owls whut go, "Who-*who*-o-o-o!" an' he ain' gwine min' de wind whut go, "You-*you*-o-o-o!" nor nuffin, nohow. He gwine be brave as a lion, sence he know fo' sure dey ain' no ghosts. So prisintly he ma say:

"Well, time fo' a li'l black boy whut he name is Mose to be gwine up de ladder to de loft to bed."

An' li'l black Mose he 'low he gwine wait a bit. He 'low he gwine jes wait a li'l bit. He 'low he gwine be no trouble *at* all ef he jes been let wait twell he ma she gwine up de ladder to de loft to bed, too. So he ma she say:

"Git erlong wid yo'! Whut you skeered ob whin dey ain't no ghosts?"

An' li'l black Mose he scrooge, an' he twist, an' he pucker up he mouf, an' he rub he eyes, an' prisintly he say right low:

"I ain't skeered ob ghosts whut am, 'ca'se dey ain't no ghosts."

"Den what am yo' skeered ob?" ask he ma.

"Nuffin'," say de li'l black boy whut he name is Mose; "but I jes feel kinder oneasy 'bout de ghosts whut ain't."

Jes lak white folks! Jes lak white folks!

X.—THE NIGHT OPERATOR[10]

By Frank L. Packard

TODDLES, in the beginning, wasn't exactly a railroad man—for several reasons. First he wasn't a man at all; second, he wasn't, strictly speaking, on the company's pay roll; third, which is apparently irrelevant, everybody said he was a bad one; and fourth—because Hawkeye nicknamed him Toddles.

Toddles had another name—Christopher Hyslop Hoogan—but Big Cloud never lay awake at nights losing any sleep over that. On the first run that Christopher Hyslop Hoogan ever made, Hawkeye looked him over for a minute, said, "Toddles," shortlike—and, shortlike, that settled the matter so far as the Hill Division was concerned. His name was Toddles.

Piecemeal, Toddles wouldn't convey anything to you to speak of. You'd have to see Toddles coming down the aisle of a car to get him at all—and then the chances are you'd turn around after he'd gone by and stare at him, and it would be even money that you'd call him back and fish for a dime to buy something by way of excuse. Toddles got a good deal of business that way. Toddles had a uniform and a regular run all right, but he wasn't what he passionately longed to be—a legitimate, dyed-in-the-wool railroader. His pay check, plus commissions, came from the News Company down East that had the railroad concession. Toddles was a newsboy. In his blue uniform and silver buttons, Toddles used to stack up about the height of the back of the car seats as he hawked his wares along the aisles; and the only thing that was big about him was his head, which looked as though it had got a whopping big lead on his body—and didn't intend to let the body cut the lead down any. This meant a big cap, and, as Toddles used to tilt the vizor forward, the tip of his nose, bar his mouth which was generous, was about all one got of his face. Cap, buttons, magazines and peanuts, that was Toddles—all except his voice. Toddles had a voice that would make you jump if you were nervous the minute he opened the car door, and if you weren't nervous you would be before he had reached the other end of the aisle—it began low down somewhere on high G and went through you shrill as an east wind, and ended like the shriek of a brake-shoe with everything the Westinghouse equipment had to offer cutting loose on a quick stop.

Hawkeye? That was what Toddles called his beady-eyed conductor in retaliation. Hawkeye used to nag Toddles every chance he got, and, being Toddles' conductor, Hawkeye got a good many chances. In a word, Hawkeye, carrying the punch on the local passenger, that happened to be the run Toddles was given when the News Company sent him out from the East, used to think he got a good deal of fun out of Toddles—only his idea of fun and Toddles' idea of fun were as divergent as the poles, that was all.

Toddles, however, wasn't anybody's fool, not by several degrees—not even Hawkeye's. Toddles hated Hawkeye like poison; and his hate, apart from daily annoyances, was deep-seated. It was Hawkeye who had dubbed him "Toddles." And Toddles repudiated the name with his heart, his soul—and his fists.

Toddles wasn't anybody's fool, whatever the division thought, and he was right down to the basic root of things from the start. Coupled with the stunted growth that nature in a miserly mood had doled out to him, none knew better than himself that the name of "Toddles," keeping that nature stuff patently before everybody's eyes, damned him in his aspirations for a bona fide railroad career. Other boys got a job and got their feet on the ladder as call-boys, or in the roundhouse; Toddles got—a grin. Toddles pestered everybody for a job. He pestered Carleton, the super. He pestered Tommy Regan, the master mechanic. Every time that he saw anybody in authority Toddles spoke up for a job, he was in deadly earnest—and got a grin. Toddles with a basket of unripe fruit and stale chocolates and his "best-seller" voice was one thing; but Toddles as anything else was just—Toddles.

Toddles repudiated the name, and did it forcefully. Not that he couldn't take his share of a bit of guying, but because he felt that he was face to face with a vital factor in the career he longed for—so he fought. And if nature had been niggardly in one respect, she had been generous in others; Toddles, for all his size, possessed the heart of a lion and the strength of a young ox, and he used both, with black and bloody effect, on the eyes and noses of the call-boys and younger element who called him Toddles. He fought it all along the line—at the drop of the hat—at a whisper of "Toddles." There wasn't a day went by that Toddles wasn't in a row; and the women, the mothers of the defeated warriors whose eyes were puffed and whose noses trickled crimson, denounced him in virulent language over their washtubs and the back fences of Big Cloud. You see, they didn't understand him, so they called him a "bad one," and, being from the East and not one of themselves, "a New York gutter snipe."

But, for all that, the name stuck. Up and down through the Rockies it was—Toddles. Toddles, with the idea of getting a lay-over on a siding, even went to the extent of signing himself in full—Christopher Hyslop Hoogan—every time his signature was in order; but the official documents in which he was concerned, being of a private nature between himself and the News Company, did not, in the very nature of things, have much effect on the Hill Division. Certainly the big fellows never knew he had any name but Toddles—and cared less. But they knew him as Toddles, all right! All of them did, every last one of them! Toddles was everlastingly and eternally bothering them for a job. Any kind of a job, no matter what, just so it was real railroading, and so a fellow could line up with everybody else when the pay car came along, and look forward to being something some day.

Toddles, with time, of course, grew older, up to about seventeen or so, but he didn't grow any bigger—not enough to make it noticeable! Even Toddles' voice wouldn't break—it was his young heart that did all the breaking there was done. Not that he ever showed it. No one ever saw a tear in the boy's eyes. It was clenched fists for Toddles, clenched fists and passionate attack. And therein, while Toddles had grasped the basic truth that his nickname militated against his ambitions, he erred in another direction that was equally fundamental, if not more so.

And here, it was Bob Donkin, the night dispatcher, as white a man as his record after years of train-handling was white, a railroad man from the ground up if there ever was one, and one of the best, who set Toddles—but we'll come to that presently. We've got our "clearance" now, and we're off with "rights" through.

No. 83, Hawkeye's train—and Toddles'—scheduled Big Cloud on the eastbound run at 9.05; and, on the night the story opens, they were about an hour away from the little mountain town that was the divisional point, as Toddles, his basket of edibles in the crook of his arm, halted in the forward end of the second-class smoker to examine again the fistful of change that he dug out of his pants pocket with his free hand.

Toddles was in an unusually bad humor, and he scowled. With exceeding deftness he separated one of the coins from the others, using his fingers like the teeth of a rake, and dropped the rest back jingling into his pocket. The coin that remained he put into his mouth, and bit on it—

hard. His scowl deepened. Somebody had presented Toddles with a lead quarter.

It wasn't so much the quarter, though Toddles' salary wasn't so big as some people's who would have felt worse over it, it was his *amour propre* that was touched—deeply. It wasn't often that any one could put so bald a thing as lead money across on Toddles. Toddles' mind harked back along the aisles of the cars behind him. He had only made two sales that round, and he had changed a quarter each time—for the pretty girl with the big picture hat, who had giggled at him when she bought a package of chewing gum; and the man with the three-carat diamond tie-pin in the parlor car, a little more than on the edge of inebriety, who had got on at the last stop, and who had bought a cigar from him.

Toddles thought it over for a bit; decided he wouldn't have a fuss with a girl anyway, balked at a parlor car fracas with a drunk, dropped the coin back into his pocket, and went on into the combination baggage and express car. Here, just inside the door, was Toddles', or, rather, the News Company's chest. Toddles lifted the lid; and then his eyes shifted slowly and traveled up the car. Things were certainly going badly with Toddles that night.

There were four men in the car: Bob Donkin, coming back from a holiday trip somewhere up the line; MacNicoll, the baggage-master; Nulty, the express messenger—and Hawkeye. Toddles' inventory of the contents of the chest had been hurried—but intimate. A small bunch of six bananas was gone, and Hawkeye was munching them unconcernedly. It wasn't the first time the big, hulking, six-foot conductor had pilfered the boy's chest, not by many—and never paid for the pilfering. That was Hawkeye's idea of a joke.

Hawkeye was talking to Nulty, elaborately simulating ignorance of Toddles' presence—and he was talking about Toddles.

"Sure," said Hawkeye, his mouth full of banana, "he'll be a great railroad man some day! He's the stuff they're made of! You can see it sticking out all over him! He's only selling peanuts now till he grows up and——"

Toddles put down his basket and planted himself before the conductor.

"You pay for those bananas," said Toddles in a low voice—which was high.

"When'll he grow up?" continued Hawkeye, peeling more fruit. "I don't know—you've got me. The first time I saw him two years ago, I'm hanged if he wasn't bigger than he is now—guess he grows backwards. Have a banana?" He offered one to Nulty, who refused it.

"You pay for those bananas, you big stiff!" squealed Toddles belligerently.

Hawkeye turned his head slowly and turned his little beady, black eyes on Toddles, then he turned with a wink to the others, and for the first time in two years offered payment. He fished into his pocket and handed Toddles a twenty-dollar bill—there always was a mean streak in Hawkeye, more or less of a bully, none too well liked, and whose name on the pay roll, by the way, was Reynolds.

"Take fifteen cents out of that," he said, with no idea that the boy could change the bill.

For a moment Toddles glared at the yellow-back, then a thrill of unholy glee came to Toddles. He could just about make it, business all around had been pretty good that day, particularly on the run west in the morning.

Hawkeye went on with the exposition of his idea of humor at Toddles' expense; and Toddles went back to his chest and his reserve funds. Toddles counted out eighteen dollars in bills, made a neat pile of four quarters—the lead one on the bottom—another neat pile of the odd change, and returned to Hawkeye. The lead quarter wouldn't go very far toward liquidating Hawkeye's long-standing indebtedness—but it would help some.

Queer, isn't it—the way things happen? Think of a man's whole life, aspirations, hopes, ambitions, everything, pivoting on—a lead quarter! But then they say that opportunity knocks once at the door of every man; and, if that be true, let it be remarked in passing that Toddles wasn't deaf!

Hawkeye, making Toddles a target for a parting gibe, took up his lantern and started through the train to pick up the fates from the last stop. In due course he halted before the inebriated one with the glittering tie-pin in the smoking compartment of the parlor car.

"Ticket, please," said Hawkeye.

"Too busy to buysh ticket," the man informed him, with heavy confidence. "Whash fare Loon Dam to Big Cloud?"

"One-fifty," said Hawkeye curtly.

The man produced a roll of bills, and from the roll extracted a two-dollar note.

Hawkeye handed him back two quarters, and started to punch a cash-fare slip. He looked up to find the man holding out one of the quarters insistently, if somewhat unsteadily.

"What's the matter?" demanded Hawkeye brusquely.

"Bad," said the man.

A drummer grinned; and an elderly gentleman, from his magazine, looked up inquiringly over his spectacles.

"Bad!" Hawkeye brought his elbow sharply around to focus his lamp on the coin; then he leaned over and rang it on the window sill—only it wouldn't ring. It was indubitably bad. Hawkeye, however, was dealing with a drunk—and Hawkeye always did have a mean streak in him.

"It's perfectly good," he asserted gruffly.

The man rolled an eye at the conductor that mingled a sudden shrewdness and anger, and appealed to his fellow travelers. The verdict was against Hawkeye, and Hawkeye ungraciously pocketed the lead piece and handed over another quarter.

"Shay," observed the inebriated one insolently, "shay, conductor, I don't like you. You thought I was—hic!—s'drunk I wouldn't know—eh? Thash where you fooled yerself!"

"What do you mean?" Hawkeye bridled virtuously for the benefit of the drummer and the old gentleman with the spectacles.

And then the other began to laugh immoderately.

"Same ol' quarter," said he. "Same—hic!—ol' quarter back again. Great system—peanut boy—conductor—hic! Pass it off on one—other passes it off on some one else. Just passed it off on—hic!—peanut boy for a joke. Goin' to give him a dollar when he comes back."

"Oh, you did, did you!" snapped Hawkeye ominously. "And you mean to insinuate that I deliberately tried to——"

"Sure!" declared the man heartily.

"You're a liar!" announced Hawkeye, spluttering mad. "And what's more, since it came from you, you'll take it back!" He dug into his pocket for the ubiquitous lead piece.

"Not—hic!—on your life!" said the man earnestly. "You hang on to it, old top. I didn't pass it off on *you*."

"Haw!" exploded the drummer suddenly. "Haw—haw, haw!"

And the elderly gentleman smiled.

Hawkeye's face went red, and then purple.

"Go 'way!" said the man petulantly. "I don't like you. Go 'way! Go an' tell peanuts I—hic!—got a dollar for him."

And Hawkeye went—but Toddles never got the dollar. Hawkeye went out of the smoking compartment of the parlor car with the lead quarter in his pocket—because he couldn't do anything else—which didn't soothe his feelings any—and he went out mad enough to bite himself. The drummer's guffaw followed him, and he thought he even caught a chuckle from the elderly party with the magazine and spectacles.

Hawkeye was mad; and he was quite well aware, painfully well aware that he had looked like a fool, which is about one of the meanest feelings there is to feel; and, as he made his way forward through the train, he grew madder still. That change was the change from his twenty-dollar bill. He had not needed to be told that the lead quarter had come from Toddles. The only question at all in doubt was whether or not Toddles had put the counterfeit coin over on him knowingly and with malice aforethought. Hawkeye, however, had an intuition deep down inside of him that there wasn't any doubt even about that, and as he opened the door of the baggage car his intuition was vindicated. There was a grin on the faces of Nulty, MacNicoll and Bob Donkin that disappeared with suspicious celerity at sight of him as he came through the door.

There was no hesitation then on Hawkeye's part. Toddles, equipped for another excursion through the train with a stack of magazines and books that almost hid him, received a sudden and vicious clout on the side of the ear.

"You'd try your tricks on me, would you?" Hawkeye snarled. "Lead quarters—eh?" Another clout. "I'll teach you, you blasted little runt!"

And with the clouts, the stack of carefully balanced periodicals went flying over the floor; and with the clouts, the nagging, and the hectoring, and the bullying, that had rankled for close on two years in Toddles' turbulent soul, rose in a sudden all-possessing sweep of fury. Toddles was a fighter—with the heart of a fighter. And Toddles' cause was just. He couldn't reach the conductor's face—so he went for Hawkeye's legs. And the screams of rage from his high-pitched voice, as he shot himself forward, sounded like a cageful of Australian cockatoos on the rampage.

Toddles was small, pitifully small for his age; but he wasn't an infant in arms—not for a minute. And in action Toddles was as near to a wild cat as anything else that comes handy by way of illustration. Two legs and one arm he twined and twisted around Hawkeye's legs; and the other arm, with a hard and knotty fist on the end of it, caught the conductor a wicked jab in the region of the bottom button of the vest.

The brass button peeled the skin off Toddles' knuckles, but the jab doubled the conductor forward, and coincident with Hawkeye's winded grunt, the lantern in his hand sailed ceilingwards, crashed into the center lamps in the roof of the car, and down in a shower of tinkling glass, dripping oil and burning wicks, came the wreckage to the floor.

There was a yell from Nulty; but Toddles hung on like grim death. Hawkeye was bawling fluent profanity and seeing red. Toddles heard one and sensed the other—and he clung grimly on. He was all doubled up around Hawkeye's knees, and in that position Hawkeye couldn't get at him very well; and, besides, Toddles had his own plan of battle. He was waiting for an extra heavy lurch of the car.

It came. Toddles' muscles strained legs and arms and back in concert, and for an instant across the car they tottered, Hawkeye staggering in a desperate attempt to maintain his equilibrium—and then down—speaking generally, on a heterogeneous pile of express parcels; concretely, with an eloquent squnch, on a crate of eggs, thirty dozen of them, at forty cents a dozen.

Toddles, over his rage, experienced a sickening sense of disaster, but still he clung; he didn't dare let go. Hawkeye's fists, both in an effort to recover himself and in an endeavor to reach Toddles, were going like a windmill; and Hawkeye's threats were something terrifying to listen to. And now they rolled over, and Toddles was underneath; and then they rolled over again; and then a hand locked on Toddles' collar, and he was yanked, terrier-fashion, to his feet.

His face white and determined, his fists doubled, Toddles waited for Hawkeye to get up—the word "run" wasn't in Toddles' vocabulary. He hadn't long to wait.

Hawkeye lunged up, draped in the broken crate—a sight. The road always prided itself on the natty uniforms of its train crews, but Hawkeye wasn't dressed in uniform then—mostly egg yolks. He made a dash for Toddles, but he never reached the boy. Bob Donkin was between them.

"Cut it out!" said Donkin coldly, as he pushed Toddles behind him. "You asked for it, Reynolds, and you got it. Now cut it out!"

And Hawkeye "cut it out." It was pretty generally understood that Bob Donkin never talked much for show, and Bob Donkin was bigger than Toddles, a whole lot bigger, as big as Hawkeye himself. Hawkeye "cut it out."

Funny, the egg part of it? Well, perhaps. But the fire wasn't. True, they got it out with the help of the hand extinguishers before it did any serious damage, for Nulty had gone at it on the jump; but while it lasted the burning oil on the car floor looked dangerous. Anyway, it was bad enough so that they couldn't hide it when they got into Big Cloud—and Hawkeye and Toddles went on the carpet for it the next morning in the super's office.

Carleton, "Royal" Carleton, reached for a match, and, to keep his lips straight, clamped them firmly on the amber mouthpiece of his brier, and stumpy, big-paunched Tommy Regan, the master mechanic, who was sitting in a chair by the window, reached hurriedly into his back pocket for his chewing and looked out of the window to hide a grin, as the two came in and ranged themselves in front of the super's desk—Hawkeye, six feet and a hundred and ninety pounds, with Toddles trailing him, mostly cap and buttons and no weight at all.

Carleton didn't ask many questions—he'd asked them before—of Bob Donkin—and the dispatcher hadn't gone out of his way to invest the conductor with any glorified halo. Carleton, always a strict disciplinarian, said what he had to say and said it quietly; but he meant to let the conductor have the worst of it, and he did—in a way that was all Carleton's own. Two years' picking on a youngster didn't appeal to Carleton, no matter who the youngster was. Before he was half through he had the big conductor squirming. Hawkeye was looking for something else—besides a galling and matter-of-fact impartiality that accepted himself and Toddles as being on exactly the same plane and level.

"There's a case of eggs," said Carleton at the end. "You can divide up the damage between you. And I'm going to change your runs, unless you've got some good reason to give me why I shouldn't?"

He waited for an answer.

Hawkeye, towering, sullen, his eyes resting bitterly on Regan, having caught the master mechanic's grin, said nothing; Toddles, whose head barely showed over the top of Carleton's desk, and the whole of him sizing up about big enough to go into the conductor's pocket, was equally silent—Toddles was thinking of something else.

"Very good," said Carleton suavely, as he surveyed the ridiculous incongruity before him. "I'll change your runs, then. I can't have you two *men* brawling and prize-fighting every trip."

There was a sudden sound from the window, as though Regan had got some of his blackstrap juice down the wrong way.

Hawkeye's face went black as thunder.

Carleton's face was like a sphinx.

"That'll do, then," he said. "You can go, both of you."

Hawkeye stamped out of the room and down the stairs. But Toddles stayed.

"Please, Mr. Carleton, won't you give me a job on——" Toddles stopped.

So had Regan's chuckle. Toddles, the irrepressible, was at it again—and Toddles after a job, any kind of a job, was something that Regan's experience had taught him to fly from without standing on the order of his flight. Regan hurried from the room.

Toddles watched him go—kind of speculatively, kind of reproachfully. Then he turned to Carleton.

"Please give me a job, Mr. Carleton," he pleaded. "Give me a job, won't you?"

It was only yesterday on the platform that Toddles had waylaid the super with the same demand—and about every day before that as far back as Carleton could remember. It was hopelessly chronic. Anything convincing or appealing about it had gone long ago—Toddles said it parrot-fashion now. Carleton took refuge in severity.

"See here, young man," he said grimly, "you were brought into this office for a reprimand and not to apply for a job! You can thank your stars and Bob Donkin you haven't lost the one you've got. Now, get out!"

"I'd make good if you gave me one," said Toddles earnestly. "Honest, I would, Mr. Carleton."

"Get out!" said the super, not altogether unkindly. "I'm busy."

Toddles swallowed a lump in his throat—but not until after his head was turned and he'd started for the door so the super couldn't see it. Toddles swallowed the lump—and got out. He hadn't expected anything else, of course. The refusals were just as chronic as the demands. But that didn't make each new one any easier for Toddles. It made it worse.

Toddles' heart was heavy as he stepped out into the hall, and the iron was in his soul. He was seventeen now, and it looked as though he never would get a chance—except to be a newsboy all his life. Toddles swallowed another lump. He loved railroading; it was his one ambition, his one desire. If he could ever get a chance, he'd show them! He'd show them that he wasn't a joke, just because he was small!

Toddles turned at the head of the stairs to go down, when somebody called his name.

"Here—Toddles! Come here!"

Toddles looked over his shoulder, hesitated, then marched in through the open door of the dispatchers' room. Bob Donkin was alone there.

"What's your name—Toddles?" inquired Donkin, as Toddles halted before the dispatcher's table.

Toddles froze instantly—hard. His fists doubled; there was a smile on Donkin's face. Then his fists slowly uncurled; the smile on Donkin's face had broadened, but there wasn't any malice in the smile.

"Christopher Hyslop Hoogan," said Toddles, unbending.

Donkin put his hand quickly to his mouth—and coughed.

"Um-m!" said he pleasantly. "Super hard on you this morning—Hoogan?"

And with the words Toddles' heart went out to the big dispatcher: "Hoogan"—and a man-to-man tone.

"No," said Toddles cordially. "Say, I thought you were on the night trick."

"Double-shift—short-handed," replied Donkin. "Come from New York, don't you?"

"Yes," said Toddles.

"Mother and father down there still?"

It came quick and unexpected, and Toddles stared for a moment. Then he walked over to the window.

"I haven't got any," he said.

There wasn't any sound for an instant, save the clicking of the instruments; then Donkin spoke again—a little gruffly:

"When are you going to quit making a fool of yourself?"

Toddles swung from the window, hurt. Donkin, after all, was like all the rest of them.

"Well?" prompted the dispatcher.

"You go to blazes!" said Toddles bitterly, and started for the door.

Donkin halted him.

"You're only fooling yourself, Hoogan," he said coolly. "If you wanted what you call a real railroad job as much as you pretend you do, you'd get one."

"Eh?" demanded Toddles defiantly; and went back to the table.

"A fellow," said Donkin, putting a little sting into his words, "never got anywhere by going around with a chip on his shoulder fighting everybody because they called him Toddles, and making a nuisance of himself with the Big Fellows until they got sick of the sight of him."

It was a pretty stiff arraignment. Toddles choked over it, and the angry blood flushed to his cheeks.

"That's all right for you!" he spluttered out hotly. "You don't look too small for the train crews or the roundhouse, and they don't call you Toddles so's nobody'll forget it. What'd *you* do?"

"I'll tell you what I'd do," said Donkin quietly. "I'd make everybody on the division wish their own name was Toddles before I was through with them, and I'd *make* a job for myself."

Toddles blinked helplessly.

"Getting right down to a cash fare," continued Donkin, after a moment, as Toddles did not speak, "they're not so far wrong, either, about you sizing up pretty small for the train crews or the roundhouse, are they?"

"No-o," admitted Toddles reluctantly; "but——"

"Then why not something where there's no handicap hanging over you?" suggested the dispatcher—and his hand reached out and touched the sender. "The key, for instance?"

"But I don't know anything about it," said Toddles, still helplessly.

"That's just it," returned Donkin smoothly. "You never tried to learn."

Toddles' eyes widened, and into Toddles' heart leaped a sudden joy. A new world seemed to open out before him in which aspirations, ambitions, longings all were a reality. A key! That *was* real railroading, the top-notch of railroading, too. First an operator, and then a dispatcher, and—and—and then his face fell, and the vision faded.

"How'd I get a chance to learn?" he said miserably. "Who'd teach me?"

The smile was back on Donkin's face as he pushed his chair from the table, stood up, and held out his hand—man-to-man fashion.

"I will," he said. "I liked your grit last night, Hoogan. And if you want to be a railroad man, I'll make you one—before I'm through. I've some old instruments you can have to practice with, and I've nothing to do in my spare time. What do you say?"

Toddles didn't say anything. For the first time since Toddles' advent to the Hill Division, there were tears in Toddles' eyes for some one else to see.

Donkin laughed.

"All right, old man, you're on. See that you don't throw me down. And keep your mouth shut; you'll need all your wind. It's work that counts, and nothing else. Now chase yourself! I'll dig up the things you'll need, and you can drop in here and get them when you come off your run to-night."

Spare time! Bob Donkin didn't have any spare time those days! But that was Donkin's way. Spence sick, and two men handling the dispatching where three had handled it before, didn't leave Bob Donkin much spare time—not much. But a boost for the kid was worth a sacrifice. Donkin went at it as earnestly as Toddles did—and Toddles was in deadly earnest.

When Toddles left the dispatcher's office that morning with Donkin's promise to teach him the key, Toddles had a hazy idea that Donkin had wings concealed somewhere under his coat and was an angel in disguise; and at the end of two weeks he was sure of it. But at the end of a month Bob Donkin was a god! Throw Bob Donkin down! Toddles would have sold his soul for the dispatcher.

It wasn't easy, though; and Bob Donkin wasn't an easy-going taskmaster, not by long odds. Donkin had a tongue, and on occasions could use it. Short and quick in his explanations, he expected his pupil to get it short and quick; either that, or Donkin's opinion of him. But Toddles stuck. He'd have crawled on his knees for Donkin anywhere, and he worked like a major—not only for his own advancement, but for what he came to prize quite as much, if not more, Donkin's approval.

Toddles, mindful of Donkin's words, didn't fight so much as the days went by, though he found it difficult to swear off all at once; and on his runs he studied his Morse code, and he had the "calls" of every station on the division off by heart right from the start. Toddles mastered the "sending" by leaps and bounds; but the "taking" came slower, as it does for everybody—but even at that, at the end of six weeks, if it wasn't thrown at him too fast and hard, Toddles could get it after a fashion.

Take it all around, Toddles felt like whistling most of the time; and, pleased with his own progress, looked forward to starting in presently as a full-fledged operator.

He mentioned the matter to Bob Donkin—once. Donkin picked his words and spoke fervently. Toddles never brought the subject up again.

And so things went on. Late summer turned to early fall, and early fall to still sharper weather, until there came the night that the operator at Blind River muddled his orders and gave No. 73, the westbound fast freight, her clearance against the second section of the eastbound Limited that doomed them to meet somewhere head-on in the Glacier Cañon; the night that Toddles—but there's just a word or two that comes before.

When it was all over, it was up to Sam Beale, the Blind River operator, straight enough. Beale blundered. That's all there was to it; that covers it all—he blundered. It would have finished Beale's railroad career forever and a day—only Beale played the man, and the instant he realized what he had done, even while the tail lights of the freight were disappearing down the track and he couldn't stop her, he was stammering the tale of his mistake over the wire, the sweat beads dripping from his wrist, his face gray with horror, to Bob Donkin under the green-shaded lamp in the dispatchers' room at Big Cloud, miles away.

Donkin got the miserable story over the chattering wire—got it before it was half told—cut Beale out and began to pound the Gap call. And as though it were before him in reality, that stretch of track, fifteen miles of it, from Blind River to the Gap, unfolded itself like a grisly panorama before his mind. There wasn't a half mile of tangent at a single stretch in the whole of it. It swung like the writhings of a snake, through cuts and tunnels, hugging the cañon walls, twisting this way and that. Anywhere else there might be a chance, one in a thousand even, that they would see each other's headlights in time—here it was disaster quick and absolute.

Donkin's lips were set in a thin, straight line. The Gap answered him; and the answer was like the knell of doom. He had not expected anything else; he had only hoped against hope. The second section of the Limited had pulled out of the Gap, eastbound, two minutes before. The two trains were in the open against each other's orders.

In the next room, Carleton and Regan, over their pipes, were at their nightly game of pedro. Donkin called them—and his voice sounded strange to himself. Chairs scraped and crashed to the floor, and an instant later the super and the master mechanic were in the room.

"What's wrong, Bob?" Carleton flung the words from him in a single breath.

Donkin told them. But his fingers were on the key again as he talked. There was still one chance, worse than the thousand-to-one shot; but it was the only one. Between the Gap and Blind River, eight miles from the Gap, seven miles from Blind River, was Cassil's Siding. But there was no night man at Cassil's, and the little town lay a mile from the station. It was ten o'clock—Donkin's watch lay face up on the table before him—the day man at Cassil's went off at seven—the chance was that the day man *might* have come back to the station for something or other!

Not much of a chance? No—not much! It was a possibility, that was all; and Donkin's fingers worked—the seventeen, the life and death—calling, calling on the night trick to the day man at Cassil's Siding.

Carleton came and stood at Donkin's elbow, and Regan stood at the other; and there was silence now, save only for the key that, under Donkin's fingers, seemed to echo its stammering appeal about the room like the sobbing of a human soul.

"CS—CS—CS," Donkin called; and then, "the seventeen," and then, "hold second Number Two." And then the same thing over and over again.

And there was no answer.

It had turned cold that night and there was a fire in the little heater. Donkin had opened the draft a little while before, and the sheet-iron sides now began to purr red-hot. Nobody noticed it. Regan's kindly, good-humored face had the stamp of horror in it, and he pulled at his scraggly brown mustache, his eyes seemingly fascinated by Donkin's fingers. Everybody's eyes, the three of them, were on Donkin's fingers and the key. Carleton was like a man of stone, motionless, his face set harder than face was ever carved in marble.

It grew hot in the room; but Donkin's fingers were like ice on the key, and, strong man though he was, he faltered.

"Oh, my God!" he whispered—and never a prayer rose more fervently from lips than those three broken words.

Again he called, and again, and again. The minutes slipped away. Still he called—with the life and death—the "seventeen"—called and called. And there was no answer save that echo in the room that brought the perspiration streaming down from Regan's face, a harder light into Carleton's eyes and a chill like death into Donkin's heart.

Suddenly Donkin pushed back his chair; and his fingers, from the key, touched the crystal of his watch.

"The second section will have passed Cassil's now," he said in a curious, unnatural, matter-of-fact tone. "It'll bring them together about a mile east of there—in another minute."

And then Carleton spoke—master railroader, "Royal" Carleton, it was up to him then, all the pity of it, the ruin, the disaster, the lives out, all the bitterness to cope with as he could. And it was in his eyes, all of it. But his voice was quiet. It rang quick, peremptory, his voice—but quiet.

"Clear the line, Bob," he said. "Plug in the roundhouse for the wrecker—and tell them to send uptown for the crew."

Toddles? What did Toddles have to do with this? Well, a good deal, in one way and another. We're coming to Toddles now. You see, Toddles, since his fracas with Hawkeye, had been put on the Elk River local run that left Big Cloud at 9.45 in the morning for the run west, and scheduled Big Cloud again on the return trip at 10.10 in the evening.

It had turned cold that night, after a day of rain. Pretty cold—the thermometer can drop on occasions in the late fall in the mountains—and by eight o'clock, where there had been rain before, there was now a thin sheeting of ice over everything—very thin—you know the kind—rails and telegraph wires glistening like the decorations on a Christmas tree—very pretty—and also very nasty running on a mountain grade. Likewise, the rain, in a way rain has, had dripped from the car roofs to the platforms—the local did not boast any closed vestibules—and had also been blown upon the car steps with the sweep of the wind, and, having frozen, it stayed there. Not a very serious matter; annoying, perhaps, but not serious, demanding a little extra caution, that was all.

Toddles was in high fettle that night. He had been getting on famously of late; even Bob Donkin had admitted it. Toddles, with his stack of books and magazines, an unusually big one, for a number of the new periodicals were out that day, was dreaming rosy dreams to himself as he started from the door of the first-class smoker to the door of the first-class coach. In another hour now he'd be up in the dispatcher's room at Big Cloud for his nightly sitting with Bob Donkin. He could see Bob Donkin there now; and he could hear the big dispatcher growl at him in his bluff way: "Use your head—use your head—*Hoogan!*" It was always "Hoogan," never "Toddles." "Use your head"—Donkin was everlastingly drumming that into him; for the dispatcher used to confront him suddenly with imaginary and hair-raising emergencies, and demand Toddles' instant solution. Toddles realized that Donkin was getting to the heart of things, and that some day he, Toddles, would be a great dispatcher—like Donkin. "Use your head, Hoogan"—that's the way Donkin talked—"anybody can learn a key, but that doesn't make a railroad man think quick and think *right*. Use your——"

Toddles stepped out on the platform—and walked on ice. But that wasn't Toddles' undoing. The trouble with Toddles was that he was walking on air at the same time. It was treacherous running, they were nosing a curve, and in the cab, Kinneard, at the throttle, checked with a little jerk at the "air." And with the jerk, Toddles slipped; and with the slip, the center of gravity of the stack of periodicals shifted, and they bulged ominously from the middle. Toddles grabbed at them—and his heels went out from under him. He ricocheted down the steps, snatched desperately at the handrail, missed it, shot out from the train, and, head, heels, arms and body going every which way at once, rolled over and over down the embankment. And, starting from the point of Toddles' departure from the train, the right of way for a hundred yards was strewn with "the latest magazines" and "new books just out to-day."

Toddles lay there, a little, curled, huddled heap, motionless in the darkness. The tail lights of the local disappeared. No one aboard would miss Toddles until they got into Big Cloud—and found him gone. Which is Irish for saying that no one would attempt to keep track of a newsboy's idiosyncrasies on a train; it would be asking too much of any train crew; and, besides, there was no mention of it in the rules.

It was a long while before Toddles stirred; a very long while before consciousness crept slowly back to him. Then he moved, tried to get up—and fell back with a quick, sharp cry of pain. He lay still, then, for a moment. His ankle hurt him frightfully, and his back, and his shoulder, too. He put his hand to his face where something seemed to be trickling warm—and brought it away wet. Toddles, grim little warrior, tried to think. They hadn't been going very fast when he fell off. If they had, he would have been killed. As it was, he was hurt, badly hurt, and his head swam, nauseating him.

Where was he? Was he near any help? He'd have to get help somewhere, or—or with the cold and—and everything he'd probably die out here before morning. Toddles shouted out—again and again. Perhaps his voice was too weak to carry very far; anyway, there was no reply.

He looked up at the top of the embankment, clamped his teeth, and started to crawl. If he got up there, perhaps he could tell where he was. It had taken Toddles a matter of seconds to roll down; it took him ten minutes of untold agony to get up. Then he dashed his hand across his eyes where the blood was, and cried a little with the surge of relief. East, down the track, only a few yards away, the green eye of a switch lamp winked at him.

Where there was a switch lamp there was a siding, and where there was a siding there was promise of a station. Toddles, with the sudden uplift upon him, got to his feet and started along the track—two steps—and went down again. He couldn't walk, the pain was more than he could bear—his right ankle, his left shoulder, and his back—hopping only made it worse—it was easier to crawl.

And so Toddles crawled.

It took him a long time even to pass the switch light. The pain made him weak, his senses seemed to trail off giddily every now and then, and he'd find himself lying flat and still beside the track. It was a white, drawn face that Toddles lifted up each time he started on again—miserably white, except where the blood kept trickling from his forehead.

And then Toddles' heart, stout as it was, seemed to snap. He had reached the station platform, wondering vaguely why the little building that loomed ahead was dark—and now it came to him in a flash, as he recognized the station. It was Cassil's Siding—*and there was no night man at Cassil's Siding!* The switch lights were lighted before the day man left, of course. Everything swam before Toddles' eyes. There—there was no help here. And yet—yet perhaps—desperate hope came again—perhaps there might be. The pain was terrible—all over him. And—and he'd got so weak now—but it wasn't far to the door.

Toddles squirmed along the platform, and reached the door finally—only to find it shut and fastened. And then Toddles fainted on the threshold.

When Toddles came to himself again, he thought at first that he was up in the dispatcher's room at Big Cloud with Bob Donkin pounding away on the battered old key they used to practice with—only there seemed to be something the matter with the key, and it didn't sound as loud as it usually did—it seemed to come from a long way off somehow. And then, besides, Bob was working it faster than he had ever done before when they were practicing. "Hold second"—second something—Toddles couldn't make it out. Then the "seventeen"—yes, he knew that—that was the life and death. Bob was going pretty quick, though. Then "CS—CS—CS"—Toddles' brain fumbled a bit over that—then it came to him. CS was the call for Cassil's Siding. *Cassil's Siding!* Toddles' head came up with a jerk.

A little cry burst from Toddles' lips—and his brain cleared. He wasn't at Big Cloud at all—he was at Cassil's Siding—and he was hurt—and that was the sounder inside calling, calling frantically for Cassil's Siding—where he was.

The life and death—*the seventeen*—it sent a thrill through Toddles' pain-twisted spine. He wriggled to the window. It, too, was closed, of course, but he could hear better there. The sounder was babbling madly.

"Hold second——"

He missed it again—and as, on top of it, the "seventeen" came pleading, frantic, urgent, he wrung his hands.

"Hold second"—he got it this time—"Number Two."

Toddles' first impulse was to smash in the window and reach the key. And then, like a dash of cold water over him, Donkin's words seemed to ring in his ears: "Use your head."

With the "seventeen" it meant a matter of minutes, perhaps even seconds. Why smash the window? Why waste the moment required to do it simply to answer the call? The order stood for itself—"Hold second Number Two." That was the second section of the Limited, eastbound. Hold her! How? There was nothing—not a thing to stop her with. "Use your head," said Donkin in a far-away voice to Toddles' wobbling brain.

Toddles looked up the track—west—where he had come from—to where the switch light twinkled green at him—and, with a little sob, he started to drag himself back along the platform. If he could throw the switch, it would throw the light from green to red, and—and the Limited would take the siding. But the switch was a long way off.

Toddles half fell, half bumped from the end of the platform to the right of way. He cried to himself with low moans as he went along. He had the heart of a fighter, and grit to the last tissue; but he needed it all now—needed it all to stand the pain and fight the weakness that kept swirling over him in flashes.

On he went, on his hands and knees, slithering from tie to tie—and from one tie to the next was a great distance. The life and death, the dispatcher's call—he seemed to hear it yet—throbbing, throbbing on the wire.

On he went, up the track; and the green eye of the lamp, winking at him, drew nearer. And then suddenly, clear and mellow through the mountains, caught up and echoed far and near, came the notes of a chime whistle ringing down the gorge.

Fear came upon Toddles then, and a great sob shook him. That was the Limited coming now! Toddles' fingers dug into the ballast, and he hurried—that is, in bitter pain, he tried to crawl a little faster. And as he crawled, he kept his eyes strained up the track—she wasn't in sight yet around the curve—not yet, anyway.

Another foot, only another foot, and he would reach the siding switch—in time—in plenty of time. Again the sob—but now in a burst of relief that, for the moment, made him forget his hurts. He was in time!

He flung himself at the switch lever, tugged upon it and then, trembling, every ounce of remaining strength seeming to ooze from him, he covered his face with his hands. It was *locked*—padlocked.

Came a rumble now—a distant roar, growing louder and louder, reverberating down the cañon walls—louder and louder—nearer and nearer. "Hold second Number Two. Hold second Number Two"—the "seventeen," the life and death, pleading with him to hold Number Two. And she was coming now, coming—and—and—the switch was locked. The deadly nausea racked Toddles again; there was nothing to do now—nothing. He couldn't stop her—couldn't stop her. He'd—he'd tried—very hard—and—and he couldn't stop her now. He took his hands from his face, and stole a glance up the track, afraid almost, with the horror that was upon him, to look.

She hadn't swung the curve yet, but she would in a minute—and come pounding down the stretch at fifty miles an hour, shoot by him like a rocket to where, somewhere ahead, in some form, he did not know what, only knew that it was there, death and ruin and——

"*Use your head!*" snapped Donkin's voice to his consciousness.

Toddles' eyes were on the light above his head. It blinked *red* at him as he stood on the track facing it; the green rays were shooting up and down the line. He couldn't swing the switch—but the *lamp* was there—and there was the red side to show just by turning it. He remembered then that the lamp fitted into a socket at the top of the switch stand, and could be lifted off—if he could reach it!

It wasn't very high—for an ordinary-sized man—for an ordinary-sized man had to get at it to trim and fill it daily—only Toddles wasn't an ordinary-sized man. It was just nine or ten feet above the rails—just a standard siding switch.

Toddles gritted his teeth, and climbed upon the base of the switch—and nearly fainted as his ankle swung against the rod. A foot above the base was a footrest for a man to stand on and reach up for the lamp, and Toddles drew himself up and got his foot on it—and then at his full height the tips of his fingers only just touched the bottom of the lamp. Toddles cried aloud, and the tears streamed down his face now. Oh, if he weren't hurt—if he could only shin up another foot—but—but it was all he could do to hang there where he was.

What was that! He turned his head. Up the track, sweeping in a great circle as it swung the curve, a headlight's glare cut through the night—and Toddles "shinned" the foot. He tugged and tore at the lamp, tugged and tore at it, loosened it, lifted it from its socket, sprawled and wriggled with it to the ground—and turned the red side of the lamp against second Number Two.

The quick, short blasts of a whistle answered, then the crunch and grind and scream of biting brake-shoes—and the big mountain racer, the 1012, pulling the second section of the Limited that night, stopped with its pilot nosing a diminutive figure in a torn and silver-buttoned uniform, whose hair was clotted red, and whose face was covered with blood and dirt.

Masters, the engineer, and Pete Leroy, his fireman, swung from the gangways; Kelly, the conductor, came running up from the forward coach.

Kelly shoved his lamp into Toddles' face—and whistled low under his breath.

"Toddles!" he gasped; and then, quick as a steel trap: "What's wrong?"

"I don't know," said Toddles weakly. "There's—there's something wrong. Get into the clear—on the siding."

"Something wrong," repeated Kelly, "and you don't——"

But Masters cut the conductor short with a grab at the other's arm that was like the shutting of a vise—and then bolted for his engine like a gopher for its hole. From down the track came the heavy, grumbling roar of a freight. Everybody flew then, and there was quick work done in the next half minute—and none too quickly done—the Limited was no more than on the siding when the fast freight rolled her long string of flats, boxes and gondolas thundering by.

And while she passed, Toddles, on the platform, stammered out his story to Kelly.

Kelly didn't say anything—then. With the express messenger and a brakeman carrying Toddles, Kelly kicked in the station door, and set his lamp down on the operator's table.

"Hold me up," whispered Toddles—and, while they held him, he made the dispatcher's call.

Big Cloud answered him on the instant. Haltingly, Toddles reported the second section "in" and the freight "out"—only he did it very slowly, and he couldn't think very much more, for things were going black. He got an order for the Limited to run to Blind River and told Kelly, and got the "complete"—and then Big Cloud asked who was on the wire, and Toddles answered that in a mechanical sort of a way without quite knowing what he was doing—and went limp in Kelly's arms.

And as Toddles answered, back in Big Cloud, Regan, the sweat still standing out in great beads on his forehead, fierce now in the revulsion of relief, glared over Donkin's left shoulder, as Donkin's left hand scribbled on a pad what was coming over the wire.

Regan glared fiercely—then he spluttered:

"Who's Christopher Hyslop Hoogan—h'm?"

Donkin's lips had a queer smile on them.

"Toddles," he said.

Regan sat down heavily in his chair.

"*What?*" demanded the super.

"Toddles," said Donkin. "I've been trying to drum a little railroading into him—on the key."

Regan wiped his face. He looked helplessly from Donkin to the super, and then back again at Donkin.

"But—but what's he doing at Cassil's Siding? How'd he get there—h'm? H'm? How'd he get there?"

"I don't know," said Donkin, his fingers rattling the Cassil's Siding call again. "He doesn't answer any more. We'll have to wait for the story till they make Blind River, I guess."

And so they waited. And presently at Blind River, Kelly, dictating to the operator—not Beale, Beale's day man—told the story. It lost nothing in the telling—Kelly wasn't that kind of man—he told them what Toddles had done, and he left nothing out; and he added that they had Toddles on a mattress in the baggage car, with a doctor they had discovered amongst the passengers looking after him.

At the end, Carleton tamped down the dottle in the bowl of his pipe thoughtfully with his forefinger—and glanced at Donkin.

"Got along far enough to take a station key somewhere?" he inquired casually. "He's made a pretty good job of it as the night operator at Cassil's."

Donkin was smiling.

"Not yet," he said.

"No?" Carleton's eyebrows went up. "Well, let him come in here with you, then, till he has; and when you say he's ready, we'll see what we can do. I guess it's coming to him; and I guess"—he shifted his glance to the master mechanic—"I guess we'll go down and meet Number Two when she comes in, Tommy."

Regan grinned.

"With our hats in our hands," said the big-hearted master mechanic.

Donkin shook his head.

"Don't you do it," he said. "I don't want him to get a swelled head."

Carleton stared; and Regan's hand, reaching into his back pocket for his chewing, stopped midway.

Donkin was still smiling.

"I'm going to make a railroad man out of Toddles," he said.

XI.—CHRISTMAS EVE IN A LUMBER CAMP[11]

By Ralph Connor

IT was due to a mysterious dispensation of Providence and a good deal to Leslie Graeme that I found myself in the heart of the Selkirks for my Christmas eve as the year 1882 was dying. It had been my plan to spend my Christmas far away in Toronto, with such bohemian and boon companions as could be found in that cosmopolitan and kindly city. But Leslie Graeme changed all that, for, discovering me in the village of Black Rock, with my traps all packed, waiting for the stage to start for the Landing, thirty miles away, he bore down upon me with resistless force, and I found myself recovering from my surprise only after we had gone in his lumber sleigh some six miles on our way to his camp up in the mountains. I was surprised and much delighted, though I would not allow him to think so, to find that his old-time power over me was still there. He could always in the old varsity days—dear, wild days—make me do what he liked. He was so handsome and so reckless, brilliant in his class work, and the prince of half backs on the Rugby field, and with such power of fascination as would "extract the heart out of a wheelbarrow," as Barney Lundy used to say. And thus it was that I found myself just three weeks later—I was to have spent two or three days—on the afternoon of December 24, standing in Graeme's Lumber Camp No. 2, wondering at myself. But I did not regret my changed plans, for in those three weeks I had raided a cinnamon bear's den and had wakened up a grizzly—— But I shall let the grizzly finish the tale; he probably sees more humor in it than I.

The camp stood in a little clearing, and consisted of a group of three long, low shanties with smaller shacks near them, all built of heavy, unhewn logs, with door and window in each. The grub camp, with cook-shed attached, stood in the middle of the clearing; at a little distance was the sleeping camp with the office built against it, and about a hundred yards away on the other side of the clearing stood the stables, and near them the smiddy. The mountains rose grandly on every side, throwing up their great peaks into the sky. The clearing in which the camp stood was hewn out of a dense pine forest that filled the valley and climbed halfway up the mountain sides and then frayed out in scattered and stunted trees.

It was one of those wonderful Canadian winter days, bright, and with a touch of sharpness in the air that did not chill, but warmed the blood like drafts of wine. The men were up in the woods, and the shrill scream of the bluejay flashing across the open, the impudent chatter of the red squirrel from the top of the grub camp, and the pert chirp of the whisky-jack, hopping about on the rubbish-heap, with the long, lone cry of the wolf far down the valley, only made the silence felt the more.

As I stood drinking in with all my soul the glorious beauty and the silence of mountain and forest, with the Christmas feeling stealing into me, Graeme came out from his office, and catching sight of me, called out, "Glorious Christmas weather, old chap!" And then, coming nearer, "Must you go to-morrow?"

"I fear so," I replied, knowing well that the Christmas feeling was on him, too.

"I wish I were going with you," he said quietly.

I turned eagerly to persuade him, but at the look of suffering in his face the words died at my lips, for we both were thinking of the awful night of horror when all his bright, brilliant life crashed down about him in black ruin and shame. I could only throw my arm over his shoulder and stand silent beside him. A sudden jingle of bells roused him, and, giving himself a little shake, he exclaimed, "There are the boys coming home."

Soon the camp was filled with men talking, laughing, chaffing like light-hearted boys.

"They are a little wild to-night," said Graeme, "and to-morrow they'll paint Black Rock red."

Before many minutes had gone the last teamster was "washed up," and all were standing about waiting impatiently for the cook's signal—the supper to-night was to be "something of a feed"—when the sound of bells drew their attention to a light sleigh drawn by a buckskin broncho coming down the hillside at a great pace.

"The preacher, I'll bet, by his driving," said one of the men.

"Bedad, and it's him has the foine nose for turkey!" said Blaney, a good-natured, jovial Irishman.

"Yes, or for pay-day, more like," said Keefe, a black-browed, villainous fellow countryman of Blaney's and, strange to say, his great friend.

Big Sandy McNaughton, a Canadian Highlander from Glengarry, rose up in wrath.

"Bill Keefe," said he with deliberate emphasis, "you'll just keep your dirty tongue off the minister; and as for your pay, it's little he sees of it, or any one else except Mike Slavin, when you's too dry to wait for some one to treat you, or perhaps Father Ryan, when the fear of hell-fire is on you."

The men stood amazed at Sandy's sudden anger and length of speech.

"*Bon!* Dat's good for you, my bully boy," said Baptiste, a wiry little French-Canadian, Sandy's sworn ally and devoted admirer ever since the day when the big Scotchman, under great provocation, had knocked him clean off the dump into the river and then jumped in for him.

It was not till afterward I learned the cause of Sandy's sudden wrath which urged him to such unwonted length of speech. It was not simply that the Presbyterian blood carried with it reverence for the minister, but that he had a vivid remembrance of how, only a month ago, the minister had got him out of Mike Slavin's saloon and out of the clutches of Keefe and Slavin and their gang of bloodsuckers.

Keefe started up with a curse. Baptiste sprang to Sandy's side, slapped him on the back, and called out:

"You keel him, I'll hit [eat] him up, me."

It looked as if there might be a fight, when a harsh voice said in a low, savage tone:

"Stop your row, you fools; settle it, if you want to, somewhere else."

I turned, and was amazed to see old man Nelson, who was very seldom moved to speech.

There was a look of scorn on his hard iron-gray face, and of such settled fierceness as made me quite believe the tales I had heard of his deadly fights in the mines at the coast. Before any reply could be made the minister drove up and called out in a cheery voice:

"Merry Christmas, boys! Hello, Sandy! *Comment ça va,* Baptiste? How do you do, Mr. Graeme?"

"First rate. Let me introduce my friend, Mr. Connor, sometime medical student, now artist, hunter, and tramp at large, but not a bad sort."

"A man to be envied," said the minister, smiling. "I am glad to know any friend of Mr. Graeme's."

I liked Mr. Craig from the first. He had good eyes that looked straight out at you, a clean-cut, strong face well set on his shoulders, and altogether an upstanding, manly bearing. He insisted on going with Sandy to the stables to see Dandy, his broncho, put up.

"Decent fellow," said Graeme; "but though he is good enough to his broncho, it is Sandy that's in his mind now."

"Does he come out often? I mean, are you part of his parish, so to speak?"

"I have no doubt he thinks so; and I'm blowed if he doesn't make the Presbyterians of us think so too." And he added after a pause: "A dandy lot of parishioners we are for any man. There's Sandy, now, he would knock Keefe's head off as a kind of religious exercise; but to-morrow Keefe will be sober and Sandy will be drunk as a lord, and the drunker he is the better Presbyterian he'll be, to the preacher's disgust." Then after another pause he added bitterly: "But it is not for me to throw rocks at Sandy. I am not the same kind of fool, but I am a fool of several other sorts."

Then the cook came out and beat a tattoo on the bottom of a dishpan. Baptiste answered with a yell. But though keenly hungry, no man would demean himself to do other than walk with apparent reluctance to his place at the table. At the further end of the camp was a big fireplace, and from the door of the fireplace extended the long board tables, covered with platters of turkey not too scientifically carved, dishes of potatoes, bowls of apple sauce, plates of butter, pies, and smaller dishes distributed at regular intervals. Two lanterns hanging from the roof and a row of candles stuck into the wall on either side by means of slit sticks cast a dim, weird light over the scene.

There was a moment's silence, and at a nod from Graeme Mr. Craig rose and said:

"I don't know how you feel about it, men, but to me this looks good enough to be thankful for."

"Fire ahead, sir," called out a voice quite respectfully, and the minister bent his head and said:

"For Christ the Lord who came to save us, for all the love and goodness we have known, and for these Thy gifts to us this Christmas night, our Father, make us thankful. Amen."

"*Bon!* Dat's fuss rate," said Baptiste. "Seems lak dat's make me hit [eat] more better for sure." And then no word was spoken for a quarter of an hour. The occasion was far too solemn and moments too precious for anything so empty as words. But when the white piles of bread and the brown piles of turkey had for a second time vanished, and after the last pie had disappeared, there came a pause and a hush of expectancy, whereupon the cook and cookee, each bearing aloft a huge, blazing pudding, came forth.

"Hooray!" yelled Blaney; "up wid yez!" and grabbing the cook by the shoulders from behind, he faced him about.

Mr. Craig was the first to respond, and seizing the cookee in the same way, called out: "Squad, fall in! quick march!" In a moment every man was in the procession.

"Strike up, Batchees, ye little angel!" shouted Blaney, the appellation a concession to the minister's presence; and away went Baptiste in a rollicking French song with the English chorus—

Then blow, ye winds, in the morning,
Blow, ye winds, ay oh!
Blow, ye winds, in the morning,
Blow, blow, blow.

And at each "blow" every boot came down with a thump on the plank floor that shook the solid roof. After the second round Mr. Craig jumped upon the bench and called out:

"Three cheers for Billy the cook!"

In the silence following the cheers Baptiste was heard to say:

"*Bon!* Dat's mak me feel lak hit dat puddin' all hup meself, me."

"Hear till the little baste!" said Blaney in disgust.

"Batchees," remonstrated Sandy gravely, "ye've more stomach than manners."

"Fu sure! but de more stomach, dat's more better for dis puddin'," replied the little Frenchman cheerfully.

After a time the tables were cleared and pushed back to the wall and pipes were produced. In all attitudes suggestive of comfort the men disposed themselves in a wide circle about the fire, which now roared and crackled up the great wooden chimney hanging from the roof. The lumberman's hour of bliss had arrived. Even old man Nelson looked a shade less melancholy than usual as he sat alone, well away from the fire, smoking steadily and silently. When the second pipes were well a-going one of the men took down a violin from the wall and handed it to Lachlan Campbell. There were two brothers Campbell just out from Argyll, typical Highlanders: Lachlan, dark, silent, melancholy, with the face of a mystic, and Angus, red-haired, quick, impulsive, and devoted to his brother, a devotion he thought proper to cover under biting, sarcastic speech.

Lachlan, after much protestation, interposed with gibes from his brother, took the violin, and in response to the call from all sides struck up "Lord Macdonald's Reel."

In a moment the floor was filled with dancers, whooping and cracking their fingers in the wildest manner. Then Baptiste did the "Red River Jig," a most intricate and difficult series of steps, the men keeping time to the music with hands and feet.

When the jig was finished Sandy called for "Lochaber No More," but Campbell said:

"No! no! I cannot play that to-night. Mr. Craig will play."

Craig took the violin, and at the first note I knew he was no ordinary player. I did not recognize the music, but it was soft and thrilling, and got in by the heart till every one was thinking his tenderest and saddest thoughts.

After he had played two or three exquisite bits he gave Campbell his violin, saying, "Now, 'Lochaber,' Lachlan."

Without a word Lachlan began, not "Lochaber"—he was not ready for that yet—but "The Flowers o' the Forest," and from that wandered through "Auld Robin Gray" and "The Land o' the Leal," and so got at last to that most soul-subduing of Scottish laments, "Lochaber No More." At the first strain his brother, who had thrown himself on some blankets behind the fire, turned over on his face feigning sleep. Sandy McNaughton took his pipe out of his mouth and sat up straight and stiff, staring into vacancy, and Graeme, beyond the fire, drew a short, sharp breath. We had often sat, Graeme and I, in our student days, in the drawing-room at home, listening to his father wailing out "Lochaber" upon the pipes, and I well knew that the awful minor strains were now eating their way into his soul.

Over and over again the Highlander played his lament. He had long since forgotten us, and was seeing visions of the hills and lochs and glens of his far-away native land, and making us, too, see strange things out of the dim past. I glanced at old man Nelson, and was startled at the eager, almost piteous look in his eyes, and I wished Campbell would stop. Mr. Craig caught my eye, and stepping over to Campbell held out his hand for the violin. Lingeringly and lovingly the Highlander drew out the last strain and silently gave the minister his instrument.

Without a moment's pause, and while the spell of "Lochaber" was still upon us, the minister, with exquisite skill, fell into the refrain of that simple and beautiful camp-meeting hymn, "The Sweet By-and-By." After playing the verse through once he sang softly the refrain. After the first verse the men joined in the chorus; at first timidly, but by the time the third verse was reached they were shouting with throats full open, "We shall meet on that beautiful shore." When I looked at Nelson the eager light had gone out of his eyes, and in its place was a kind of determined hopelessness, as if in this new music he had no part.

After the voices had ceased Mr. Craig played again the refrain, more and more softly and slowly; then laying the violin on Campbell's knees, he drew from his pocket his little Bible and said:

"Men, with Mr. Graeme's permission I want to read you something this Christmas eve. You will all have heard it before, but you will like it none the less for that."

His voice was soft, but clear and penetrating, as he read the eternal story of the angels and the shepherds and the Babe. And as he read, a slight motion of the hand or a glance of an eye made us see, as he was seeing, that whole radiant drama. The wonder, the timid joy, the tenderness, the mystery of it all, were borne in upon us with overpowering effect. He closed the book, and in the same low, clear voice went on to tell us how, in his home years ago, he used to stand on Christmas eve listening in thrilling delight to his mother telling him the story, and how she used to make him see the shepherds and hear the sheep bleating near by, and how the sudden burst of glory used to make his heart jump.

"I used to be a little afraid of the angels, because a boy told me they were ghosts; but my mother told me better, and I didn't fear them any more. And the Baby, the dear little Baby—we all love a baby." There was a quick, dry sob; it was from Nelson. "I used to peek through under to see the little one in the straw, and wonder what things swaddling clothes were. Oh, it was so real and so beautiful!" He paused, and I could hear the men breathing.

"But one Christmas eve," he went on in a lower, sweeter tone, "there was no one to tell me the story, and I grew to forget it and went away to college, and learned to think that it was only a child's tale and was not for men. Then bad days came to me and worse, and I began to lose my grip of myself, of life, of hope, of goodness, till one black Christmas, in the slums of a far-away city, when I had given up all and the devil's arms were about me, I heard the story again. And as I listened, with a bitter ache in my heart—for I had put it all behind me—I suddenly found myself peeking under the shepherds' arms with a child's wonder at the Baby in the straw. Then it came over me like great waves that His name was Jesus, because it was He that should save men from their sins. Save!

Save! The waves kept beating upon my ears, and before I knew I had called out, 'Oh! can He save me?' It was in a little mission meeting on one of the side streets, and they seemed to be used to that sort of thing there, for no one was surprised; and a young fellow leaned across the aisle to me and said: 'Why, you just bet He can!' His surprise that I should doubt, his bright face and confident tone, gave me hope that perhaps it might be so. I held to that hope with all my soul, and"—stretching up his arms, and with a quick glow in his face and a little break in his voice—"He hasn't failed me yet; not once, not once!"

He stopped quite short, and I felt a good deal like making a fool of myself, for in those days I had not made up my mind about these things. Graeme, poor old chap, was gazing at him with a sad yearning in his dark eyes; big Sandy was sitting very stiff and staring harder than ever into the fire; Baptiste was trembling with excitement; Blaney was openly wiping the tears away, but the face that held my eyes was that of old man Nelson. It was white, fierce, hungry-looking, his sunken eyes burning, his lips parted as if to cry. The minister went on.

"I didn't mean to tell you this, men; it all came over me with a rush; but it is true, every word, and not a word will I take back. And, what's more, I can tell you this: what He did for me He can do for any man, and it doesn't make any difference what's behind him, and"—leaning slightly forward, and with a little thrill of pathos vibrating in his voice—"oh, boys, why don't you give Him a chance at you? Without Him you'll never be the men you want to be, and you'll never get the better of that that's keeping some of you now from going back home. You know you'll never go back till you're the men you want to be." Then, lifting up his face and throwing back his head, he said, as if to himself, "Jesus! He shall save His people from their sins," and then, "Let us pray."

Graeme leaned forward with his face in his hands; Baptiste and Blaney dropped on their knees; Sandy, the Campbells, and some others stood up. Old man Nelson held his eye steadily on the minister.

Only once before had I seen that look on a human face. A young fellow had broken through the ice on the river at home, and as the black water was dragging his fingers one by one from the slippery edges, there came over his face that same look. I used to wake up for many a night after in a sweat of horror, seeing the white face with its parting lips and its piteous, dumb appeal, and the black water slowly sucking it down.

Nelson's face brought it all back; but during the prayer the face changed and seemed to settle into resolve of some sort, stern, almost gloomy, as of a man with his last chance before him.

After the prayer Mr. Craig invited the men to a Christmas dinner next day in Black Rock. "And because you are an independent lot, we'll charge you half a dollar for dinner and the evening show." Then leaving a bundle of magazines and illustrated papers on the table—a godsend to the men—he said good-by and went out.

I was to go with the minister, so I jumped into the sleigh first and waited while he said good-by to Graeme, who had been hard hit by the whole service and seemed to want to say something. I heard Mr. Craig say cheerfully and confidently: "It's a true bill: try Him."

Sandy, who had been steadying Dandy while that interesting broncho was attempting with great success to balance himself on his hind legs, came to say good-by.

"Come and see me first thing, Sandy."

"Aye! I know; I'll see ye, Mr. Craig," said Sandy earnestly as Dandy dashed off at a full gallop across the clearing and over the bridge, steadying down when he reached the hill.

"Steady, you idiot!"

This was to Dandy, who had taken a sudden side spring into the deep snow, almost upsetting us. A man stepped out from the shadow. It was old man Nelson. He came straight to the sleigh and, ignoring my presence completely, said:

"Mr. Craig, are you dead sure of this? Will it work?"

"Do you mean," said Craig, taking him up promptly, "can Jesus Christ save you from your sins and make a man of you?"

The old man nodded, keeping his hungry eyes on the other's face.

"Well, here's His message to you: 'The Son of Man is come to seek and to save that which was lost.'"

"To me? To me?" said the old man eagerly.

"Listen; this, too, is His word: 'Him that cometh unto Me I will in no wise cast out.' That's for you, for here you are, coming."

"You don't know me, Mr. Craig. I left my baby fifteen years ago because——"

"Stop!" said the minister. "Don't tell me, at least not to-night; perhaps never. Tell Him who knows it all now and who never betrays a secret. Have it out with Him. Don't be afraid to trust Him."

Nelson looked at him, with his face quivering, and said in a husky voice:

"If this is no good, it's hell for me."

"If it is no good," replied Craig almost sternly, "it's hell for all of us."

The old man straightened himself up, looked up at the stars, then back at Mr. Craig, then at me, and drawing a deep breath said:

"I'll try Him." As he was turning away the minister touched him on the arm and said quietly:

"Keep an eye on Sandy to-morrow."

Nelson nodded and we went on; but before we took the next turn I looked back and saw what brought a lump into my throat. It was old man Nelson on his knees in the snow, with his hands spread upward to the stars, and I wondered if there was any One above the stars and nearer than the stars who could see. And then the trees hid him from my sight.

XII.—THE STORY THAT THE KEG TOLD ME

By Adirondack (W. H. H.) Murray

The author is "Adirondack Murray" because he, more than any other man, rediscovered for the past and present generation the wonderful Adirondack Woods. We are grateful to Mr. Archibald Rutledge for having shortened the story, and to Mr. Murray's publishers, De Wolfe and Fiske Company, for permission to print it in the abbreviated form.—THE EDITOR.

IT was near the close of a sultry day in midsummer, which I had spent in exploring a part of the shore line of the lake where I was camping, and wearied with the trip I had made, I was returning toward the camp.

The lake was a very secluded sheet of water hidden away between the mountains, not marked on the map, whose very existence was unsuspected by me until I had a few days before accidentally stumbled upon it. Indeed, in all the world there is hardly another sheet of water so likely to escape the eye, not only of the tourist and the sportsman, but also of the hunter and the trapper. Day by day as I paddled over the lake or explored its shores the conviction grew upon me that the place had never before been visited by any human being. The more I examined and explored, the more this belief grew upon me. The thought was ever with me. But on this afternoon as I was paddling leisurely along, my paddle struck some curious object in the water. I reached down and lifted it into the boat. It was a Keg!

Amazed, I sat looking at this proof that my lake was not so unknown as I had supposed it to be. Where had it come from? How did it get here? Who brought it, and for what purpose? These and similar questions I put to myself as I paddled onward toward my camp.

After having built my camp fire I seated myself with my back against a pine; it was then that my gaze again fell on the Keg, which I had brought up from the boat and had set on the ground across the fire from me. I sat wondering where it had come from, and what had become of him who must once have handled it. . . . It may be that I was awake; it may be that I was asleep; but as I was thus looking steadily and curiously at the Keg, it seemed to change its appearance. It was no longer a Keg: it was a man! A queer little man he was, with strange little legs, and the funniest little body, and the tiniest little face! Then, standing bold upright, and looking at me with eyes that glistened like black beads, the miraculous Keg-Man opened his mouth and began to talk!

"I desire to tell you my story," it said; "the story of the man who brought me here; why he did it, and what became of him; how he lived and died.

"The earliest remembrance I have of myself is of the cooper's shop where I was made. Although I look worn now, I can recall the time when all my staves were smooth and clean, so that the oak-grain showed clearly from the top to the bottom of me, and my steel hoops were strong and bright. The cooper made me on his honor and took a deal of honest pride in putting me together, as every workman should in doing his work. I remember that when I was finished and the cooper had sanded me off and oiled me, he set me up on a bench and said to his apprentice boy: 'There, that Keg will last till the Judgment Day, and well on toward night at that.' I wondered at that.

"One day a few weeks later a man came into the shop and said, 'Have you a good strong keg for sale?'

"He put the question in such a half-spiteful, half-suspicious way that I eyed him curiously. And a very peculiar man I saw. He was not more than forty years old, of good height and strongly built. He was a gentleman, evidently, although his face was darkly tanned and his clothes were old and threadbare. His mouth was small. His lips were thin, and had a look of being drawn tightly over his teeth. His chin was long, his jaws large and strong. His hair was thin and brown. But the remarkable feature of his face was his eyes. They were blue-gray in color, small, and deeply set under his arching eyebrows. How hard and steel-like they were, and restless as a rat's! And what an intense look of suspicion there was in them; a half-scared, defiant look, as if their owner felt every one to be his enemy. Ah, what eyes they were! I came to know them well afterward, and to know what the wild, strange light in them meant; but of that by and by.

"'Have you a good strong keg for sale?' he shouted to my master, who turned round and looked squarely at the questioner.

"'Yes, I have, Mr. Roberts. Do you want one?'

"'Yes!' returned the other; 'but I want a strong one—*strong*, do you hear?'

"'Here's a keg,' said my master, tapping me with his mallet, 'that I made with my own hands from the very best stuff. It will last as long as steel and white oak staves will last.'

"The price was paid with a muttered protest and Roberts hoisted me under his arm and bore me from the shop.

"As we hurried along, I noticed that my new master spoke to no one, and that people looked at him coldly or wonderingly. At last we came to a common-looking house set back from the road, with a very high fence built around it and a heavy padlock on the front gate. There were great strong wooden shutters at every window. My master entered the house and set me down on the floor, then went to the door and locked it, drawing two large iron bars across it. He went to every window to see if it was fastened.

Carrying a candle in one hand and a great bludgeon in the other, he examined every room, every closet, the attic, and the cellar. After this he came back to me, set me on a table, started one of my hoops, and took out one of my heads. From a cupboard he got a large sheepskin, and with a pair of shears fitted me with a lining of it. I must say that he did it with cleverness, and he seemed well pleased with his work.

"When he had done all this, he brought his bludgeon and laid it on the table beside me; also he laid there a large knife. Then he went to the chimney and brought the ash-pail, which was full of ashes; from the cupboard he brought an earthen jar; from under the bed he fetched a bag; from the cellar he returned with a sack, all damp and moldy. When he had all these side by side near the table, he sat down. Then out of the ash-pail he took a small pot, and having carefully blown the ashes off, he turned it bottom-upward on the table. And what do you think was in it?

"Gold coins! Some red and some yellow, but all gold!

"He emptied each of the other receptacles, and out there flowed heaps of gold coins almost without number! How they gleamed and glistened! How they clinked and jingled! And how the deep and narrow eyes of my master glittered, but how the lips drew apart in a wild smile!

"It was a fearful sight to see him playing with the gold and to hear him laugh over his treasure. It was dreadful to think that a human soul could love money so. And he did love it—madly, with all the strength of his nature.

"He would take up a coin and look at it as a father might look upon the face of a favorite child. Ah, me, 'twas dreadful! He would take up a piece and say to it, 'Thou art better to me than a wife'; and to another, 'Thou art dearer than father or mother!' Ah, such blasphemy as I heard that night! How the sweet and blessed things of human life were derided, and the things that are divine and holy sneered at!

"At length he fell to counting his gold; and for a long, long time he counted, until his hands shook, and his eyes gleamed as if he were mad. When he had counted all, he jumped from his seat, shouting like a maniac, 'Sixteen thousand, six hundred and sixty-six dollars!' Again and again he shouted this in wild triumph.

"After a while he sobered down, and inside of me he began to pack away his treasures—carefully, caressingly, as a mother might lay her children to sleep. When I was full to the brim with shining gold, he put my head on, fitted the upper hoop on snugly, and then put me in the bed. The great knife he slipped under the pillow. Then, blowing out the light, he lay down beside me with one arm thrown about me. So the miser, clasping me to his heart, fell asleep.

"Day after day, night after night, this selfsame performance was repeated. My master did little work; indeed, he did not seem eager to increase his store, but merely to hold it safely. But about this he was so anxious that he was in a fever of excitement all the time. For days he would not leave the house. Never was he free from the fear of losing his money. And this suspicion had poisoned his whole life, had made him hate his kind and lose all belief in the love and the goodness of God, that he had once professed.

"One day in summer he left the front door open. I was drowsing, when suddenly I heard him give a frightened yell. In the doorway stood a man and a woman. The man was the village pastor, and the woman, I soon learned, was my master's wife. For a moment my master stood looking angrily at them. Then he said abruptly, 'Why did you come here?'

"'John,' said the woman, 'your child Mary is dying; and I thought that you, her father, would want to see her before she passed away.' Her voice choked, and her breast heaved with sobs.

"'Dying, is she?' said my master brutally. 'I don't believe it. You are simply after my gold. You might as well get away from here,' he added with a threatening look.

"'John,' returned the woman, great tears coming to her eyes, 'I never in my life lied to you. Mary is dying, and I could not let her go without giving you a chance to see her. Last night in her delirium she begged for you. She wants you, John; she wants to say good-by to you!'

"But my master remained unmoved. The sinister look in the eyes, the doggedness of the face did not change. He stared at them; then he shouted in frenzy: 'You lie! You want my money! Everybody wants it! Everybody loves it! There isn't an honest man in the world! All are thieves! All are lovers of gold! I know by your looks that you love it,' he went on; 'and you can't fool me by your tears and your preaching. You get out of this house!' he suddenly shrieked, 'or I will kill you,—both of you!' He swore a terrible oath and stepped back to seize the heavy bludgeon on the table. The woman cried out in fear and turned away weeping. But the parson stood his ground.

"'John Roberts,' he said, 'thou art a doomed man. The lust of gold that destroys so many is in thee strong and mighty, and only God can save thee, nor He against thy will. Repent, or thou shalt perish in a lonely place, on a dark night, with none to help thee or hear thy cries; and all thy gold shall perish with thee.' So saying, he turned and slowly left the house.

"For a moment my master stood glaring at the retreating forms of those who had come to him as friends, but whom he had treated as enemies; then he rushed for the door and locked it. After that he lifted me tenderly upon the table, laughed softly, patted me with his hands, and stroked me caressingly. 'My gold,' he kept repeating, 'my precious, precious gold!' And as night came on, he poured out the gold and counted the glittering pieces. Again and again he counted his treasure until deep midnight had settled over all.

"But when he awoke in the morning he was very nervous. All day long he neither opened the door nor unbarred the shutters. All the while he kept muttering to himself as if planning some crafty plot. I could not know what all this might mean, but I caught enough of his talk to understand that he was more than ever suspicious of losing his money, was fearing all man-kind more and more, and was trying to devise some scheme whereby he could find a place where no one could molest him or try to steal his gold. 'They will get it yet,' he kept saying, 'unless I can go where no one can find me.' Then he would curse his kind.

"At last, after hours of muttering and tramping back and forth in the darkened house, he suddenly seemed to find his decision. I shall never forget the terrible expression of evil triumph on his face as he paused before me and shouted:

"'I'll go! Go where they can never find me! I want to be alone with my money, where I can spread it out and see it shine! I will go where there is not a man!'

"After my master had said that, he made no further remarks; but he began with eager haste to pack a few things for his journey. He put me in a sack in which I could neither see nor hear what was happening; and that was all I knew for many a day. But all the while I felt myself being *carried, carried, carried!* One day I realized that I had been put in a boat; then we went on and on, day after day. Finally the boat was stopped and I was carried ashore. Then for the first time in many a long day I was taken from the bag. Again I saw the world about me. But how different were my surroundings from those of my old home! Where was I? I was on the very point of land off which you found me this evening.

"For the first few weeks of our stay on the shores of this lonely lake, things continued almost as they had been at home. The gold was my master's single thought. He seemed happy, almost joyous, in the thought that he and I were at last out of the reach of men. Most of his time was spent looking at his gold. Every morning and every evening he would take me down to that point yonder where the sun shines clearly, and there would pour the treasure out in a great pile. He always did this exultingly. And his greatest pleasure was to play with the yellow coins, to count them over and over, and to laugh to himself in a satisfied way.

"But after a time I could see that a change was coming over my master. He grew grave and quiet. No, more, as he poured out his gold, did he chuckle and laugh to himself. All his movements seemed listless. He counted his money less frequently, and when he did so it was in a half-hearted manner. One day I even saw him go away and leave the yellow heap lying on the sands. At last one day he came, packed the gold in me, and put in my head with the greatest care. Moreover, when he went back to the camp, he left me there on the beach! I felt very strange and lonely, and the night seemed long indeed.

"At last the daybreak came, and glad I was to see it. But it was not until near sunset that my master came down to the point where I was. His face was as I had never seen it before. It was the countenance of a man who had suffered much, and who was still suffering. He came to me, paused before me, and said: 'For thee, thou cursed gold, I have wasted my life and ruined my soul!'

"For some time he stood thus looking at me; then he began to walk up and down the strip of beach, wringing his hands and beating his breast. 'Oh, if I could only do it!' he kept saying; 'if I could only do it! If I could, there might be hope, even for me. Lord, help me to do it! Lord, help me!'

"After many hours of this, which I knew to be mental torment for my poor wretched master, when he was exhausted in body and in mind, he came back along the sands toward me. To my astonishment he knelt down beside me, he placed his hands together, he lifted his face skyward. My master prayed!

"'Lord of the great world,' he said, 'come to my aid or I am lost. In Thy great mercy, save me! Hear where no man may hear, hear Thou my cry; Thou Lord of heavenly mercy, lend me thine aid!'

"He paused, and over his face I seemed to see the dawning of a deep peace. He rose to his feet, lifted me, and bore me down to the boat. Then he slowly paddled away toward the center of the lake, repeating his prayer. At last he checked the boat; then, having looked toward the sky, he said in a low, sweet voice, 'Lord, Thou hast given me grace and strength.' At that he lifted me high above his head——"

There was a crash as if pieces of wood were falling together and my eyes opened with a snap. My fire had smoldered down. The Keg, heated by the fire, had tumbled inward, and lay there in a confused heap.

"What a queer dream," I said to myself. I was really beginning to believe that these things had happened. I rose to my feet and stepped down to the edge of the lonely water. I am not ashamed to say that my blood was chilled at what I saw. As I looked across the lake, within twenty feet of where I had found the Keg, there was a boat with a man sitting motionless in it!

When that mysterious canoe appeared on the bosom of the lonely lake, I thought that I was looking upon a vision of a spectral nature. In spite of all my belief that I was alone on this remote beach, there sat the man in the boat, only a few rods off shore. He was as a mirage, as silent as the very lake itself. A few eerie moments passed; then the boat began to move slowly toward me, gently propelled by a skillful paddle. As it approached, the light of the full moon streaming upon it made it easy for me to study its occupants. Near the bow I could discern a hound crouching. In the stern sat the paddler, his rifle across his knees.

"Hello, the camp there!" shouted the man in the boat.

"Hello!" I called, glad enough to find that my strange visitor was no apparition.

The canoe came ashore, I greeted the boatman, and together we walked up toward the camp, the hound following us in a leisurely fashion. There I replenished the fire. Then for a moment the stranger and I stood and looked at each other. He was over six feet in height, but so symmetrically proportioned in his physical stature that, great as it was, he was neither awkward nor ungainly. But for the fact that his eye had lost its earlier brightness and that his hair was sprinkled with threads of gray, it would have been impossible to believe that he had reached three-score years and ten, for his form was still erect, his step elastic, and his voice clear and strong. His features were regular and strong, giving proof of the man's self-reliant and indomitable character. Years, perhaps a lifetime of activity in the woods and on the lakes, had bronzed the man. From beneath heavy eyebrows looked eyes gray in color and baffling in depth. The man's whole appearance attracted me singularly.

"Thank ye for your welcome, mister," he began. "I shouldn't have dropped in on ye at this onseemly hour, but the line of your smoke caught my eye as I was turning the point yonder. I didn't expect to find a human being on these shores. I ax your pardon for comin' in on ye, but I have memories of this spot that made me think strange things when I saw your camp. I am John Norton, the trapper. And who might you be, young man?"

"I am Henry Herbert," I replied; "but just call me plain Henry."

"Well, Henry," began the old trapper, "I am going to call you that. When men meet in the woods they don't put on any airs. I have been in these woods sixty-two years, and they have been a home for me, for my father and mother are gone, and I have never had wife nor child of my own. And I have heard of you, Henry. Ye be no stranger to me. For ten years back I have heard how you like to travel the woods and the waters by yourself, larning things that Nature does not tell about in crowds. I have heard, too, that you be a good shot, and that you know the ways of outwitting the trout and the pickerel. Hearing about you this way, I knew some day that I would come across your trail; but I never thought to run agin you to-night, for I'd no idee that mortal man knowed this lake, save me—save me and that other. . . ."

The old man paused, seated himself on the end of a log, and gazed into the fire with a solemn look on his face.

I did not feel like breaking in on his meditations, whatever they might be. I was silent out of deference to his memories.

"This lake," John Norton said at length, "this lake is a strange place. I have been here for eleven years. No other place in all this wide country makes me feel as this place does."

Again he fell into a reverie. I, meanwhile, busied myself with supper; and as soon as this was prepared, the two of us enjoyed it as only woodmen can.

"If you know me," I said, "we are no strangers to each other, for I know you. Who draws the steadiest bead with a rifle; who is the best boatman who ever feathered paddle, and who is as honest a man as ever drew breath?—who, but John Norton, whom I have always been wanting to meet. No man could be as welcome to my camp."

"Well, well," laughed the old man, "when you're at home you must be one of them detective fellows. I see we aren't no strangers to each other. And if while in these woods old John Norton can teach you any trick of huntin' or of fishin' or of trappin', be sure he will do so for the welcome you have give him."

So we sat on either side of the fire, silent for a few moments. Then the old trapper said:

"I am thinking of the things that happened here long years agone. Strange things have come to pass on this very point. It is eleven year this very night that me and the hound slept here, and a solemn night it was, too. . . . God of heaven, man, what is that?"

The old man's startled ejaculation brought me to my feet as if a panther were upon me. Glancing at the spot he had indicated by look and gesture, I beheld only the shattered portion of the Keg. Not knowing what to make of the trapper's excited action, I said: "That? That is only a Keg I picked up in the lake this evening."

John Norton rose in silence to his feet and went over to where the staves lay. One of these he picked up and held contemplatively in his hand.

"The ways of the Lord are past the knowing of mortals," he said. "But perhaps in the long run He brings the wrong to the right, and so makes the evil in the world to praise him. Henry," said the Old Trapper, looking keenly at me, "I have a mind to tell you the story of the man who owned that Keg. A strange tale it be, but a true one, and the teachings of it be solemn."

Eagerly I urged him to give me the story, a part of which, at least, I felt that I already knew.

"It was eleven year agone, in this very month, that I came down the inlet yonder into the lake. The moon was nigh her full, and everything looked solemn and white just as it do now. Lord knows I little thought to meet a man in these solitudes when I run agin what I am telling ye of.

"I was paddling down this side of the lake when I heard the strangest sounds I ever heard coming out of a bird or beast. Ye better believe, Henry, that I sot and listened until I was nothing but ears. But nary a thing could I make out of it. After awhile I said I would try to ambush the creetur and find out what mouth had a language that old John Norton couldn't understand. As I got nearer the shore, my boat just drifting in the moonlight, I heerd a kind of crawling sound as if the brute was a-trailing himself on the ground. The shake of a bush give me the line on him, and I felt sure that in a minute I could let the lead drive where it ought to go. I had my rifle to my face, when by the Lord of marcy, Henry, I diskivered I had ambushed a man!

"And, Henry," he continued, "the words of the man was words of prayer. Never in my life was I taken so unawares or was so unbalanced as when I heard the voice of that man I had mistook for an animal break out in prayer. For a minute the blood stopped in my heart and my hair moved in my scalp; then I shook like a man with the chills. I had come that nigh being a murderer, Henry!

"How that man prayed! He prayed for help as one calls to a comrade when his boat has gone down under him in the rapids, and he knows he must have help or die. This man's soul was struggling hard, I tell ye. The words of his cry come out of his mouth like the words of one who is surely lost unless somebody saves him. It's dreadful for a man to live in such a way that he has to pray in that fashion; for we ought to live, Henry, so that it is cheerful-like to meet the Lord, and pleasant to hold converse with Him.

"I sot in my boat till his praying was done; then I hugged myself close in under the bushes, for I heard him coming down toward the shore. And he did come, and come close to me; and in his arms he carried something very heavy. In a moment I heard him shove a boat out from the bushes; then, getting in, he pushed off into the lake. He held for the center of it; and when he had come nigh to the middle of it, he laid his paddle down, and lifted something into the air. This he turned upside down, and out streamed into the water something that glinted in the moonlight. After that, he come paddling back for the shore. Myself—I kept shy of the man that night, but the next morning I went to the stranger's camp.

"There was nothing in sight but an old ragged tent, sagging at every seam. I called aloud so that mayhap the man would answer me. But no answer came. I walked up to the tent and drew aside the rotten flap. And, Henry, there lay the man senseless before me! I thought he was dead, and I onkivered my head. But the hound here knowed better, for he began to wag his tail. I went in, and found that the man was still breathing. I lifted him in my arms, Henry, and bore him out of the foul air of that tent, taking him down to the warm sunshine on the point.

"For a long while I thought he was going to die in my arms. He just lay there lifeless-like, a-looking across the lake with eyes half-shut. But the sun and air revived him; and after a long while he stirs and says:

"'Old man, who are you who are so kind to me?'

"I tells him I was John Norton, the trapper.

"'I am John Roberts,' he says, 'and I haven't a friend on the earth, nor do I deserve one. Old man, you cannot understand, because you have lived an innocent life, but I am a sinner—a wretched sinner. And my moments here are numbered. I will tell you of my crimes; I will confess them, for they lie heavy on my heart.

"'John Norton, I was a miser; I had a heart with a passion for gold. For the evil love of money I turned my face away from my kind. My wife I deserted. My only child I refused, with curses, to see, even when she sent for me as she lay dying. John Norton, I gave all for gold. And the more I loved it, the more I hated man. With my dreadful lust there grew suspicion of every one. All ties of affection were severed. I lived alone, hoarding my gold and gloating over it.

"'At last I fled from the habitations of men, bringing my gold, my god, with me in a Keg. Here on this lonely shore I thought to be happy, far from my own kind, far from any danger that my precious treasure be stolen. But, John Norton—and a dying man is speaking—for all my counting of the bright gold on the sands here, and my dancing about it as a devil might, laughing and singing—I was unhappy. I knew that God was watching me and was disapproving. I could not but think of my wife and child. The thought of them began to make the gold hateful to me. Ah, then, old man, I began to pray the Lord to deliver me! It was a bitter struggle I fought, but at length He rescued me. He gave me strength, John Norton, to overcome the Wicked One; He gave me strength to break away from my sin; He gave me strength last night to pour every piece of gold that had been for me both love and life, into the lake there. I shall never see it more, and I am happy.'

"After that, he lay silent-like, looking up at the blue sky. Then his eyes closed, and I thought him sleeping. But suddenly he started up, 'A light, a light! I see a light!' Then, Henry, he sank back into my arms and spoke no more. I hope my passing may be as peaceful as his, and my face as calm as was his after his battle of life was over.

"The next day I buried him up yonder under them hemlocks—having no one to help me, but doing it respectful-like, as all such should be done. There he lies, Henry, the man who was the owner of that Keg—John Roberts—the miser who repented before it was too late. Nor do I doubt," he added, in his kindly tone, "but he's been forgiven by those he wronged."

THE END

Printed in Dunstable, United Kingdom

73499528R00102